THE
IMPOSSIBLE
PRINCESS

—·—

KEIRA DOMINGUEZ

KLICKITAT CANYON

Contents

		V
1.	Royal Crush	1
2.	Dragonslayer	9
3.	Laser Eyes	17
4.	Body Language	23
5.	Slay, Queen	29
6.	Ripe Berries	39
7.	Hello, Peasant	47
8.	There Be Dragons	55
9.	Supposing Things	63
10.	Nothing Serious	73
11.	Chocolate Cake	79
12.	Her Company	89
13.	Blurry Abs	93
14.	Lutheran Babies	99
15.	Junior Associate	109
16.	Hot Skillet	117
17.	Historically Speaking	125

18.	Open Access	133
19.	About Butter	141
20.	Sexy Pirate	147
21.	Disputed Territories	153
22.	Act of War	159
23.	Clash Horribly	167
24.	Resistance Fighter	177
25.	Still Friends	182
26.	Strategic Importance	193
27.	Battered Tiaras	201
28.	Queen's Standard	209
29.	Relationship Wrecker	219
30.	Life Raft	229
31.	Enough Scandal	237
32.	Damage Control	249
33.	His Personal Space	257
34.	Welcome Home	265
35.	Chain Link	268
36.	Epilogue	273
Also By Keira Dominguez		276
Acknowledgments		277
About Author		279

For the Murder Circle

1

ROYAL CRUSH

CLARA

The shoes are a mistake.

I rush down the marble stairs of the Summer Palace, skidding to a stop on the black and white tiles with seconds to spare. My heart is racing in my chest as low chimes sound from a massive clock, carrying across the grounds and filling the Grand Hall.

Bong, bong, bong.

"That was cutting it close," Ella whispers, leaning around Freja and sliding me a look. Her eyes widen at my ensemble and she lets out a whistle. "Who did you get dressed up for, little sister?" There's a wicked glint in her expression, and if I didn't think it would disarrange my outfit, I would kick her in the shins.

I know what the rules are, and I know I've followed them. I'm wearing a nicely tailored coat dress that will photograph well, and I've had weights sewn into the hem of the skirt so that the frisky wind gusting off the North Sea won't send it flying over my head. The cut of the dress is conservative. It won't draw more attention to me than to the job at hand. I'm wearing stockings, tasteful make-up, and an unfussy hat.

But within these narrow, unyielding confines, I know I've never looked better.

Bong, bong.

Ella's twin, Freja, glances sideways, giving me a cursory perusal. "She looks fine," she tells Ella, her words perfunctory but welcome.

Bong.

"It's her shoes," my oldest sister Alma diagnoses from further up the line, not stepping a millimeter out of place. Her hands are folded neatly in front and her eyes are fastened straight ahead. I mimic her pose and see our images reflected in one of the massive antique mirrors lining the Great Hall–the four princesses of Sondmark lined up according to rank, our brother Noah towering above us at the head, looking faintly bored.

"They're *really* sexy shoes," Ella points out, as the last of the chimes dies away.

I wonder if she knows how much dithering I did about my footwear this morning. I must have spent the last hour balancing on a basic brown leather pump and then switching feet to balance on a brushed velvet shoe in a shade somewhere between blue and violet, the heel curving down to a tight stiletto. I finally made the decision to choose something that looked like it belonged on the feet of a 24-year-old princess with a shoe obsession instead of the footwear that looked like it belonged on her mother.

Freja tilts her head. "They're close-toed and not outrageously high. Those are the only rules. Anyway, they match her hat. Clara's shoes are fine."

Freja is as wise as she is beautiful.

"Fine?" Ella laughs. "Mama's sure to find them inappropriate or immodest."

I shake my head. "There's no such thing as an immodest shoe."

My tone is decisive, but even as I straighten my posture, my throat tightens when I hear the steady clip of footsteps heralding Mama's arrival. Too late to change now. I am perfectly still, but my eyes dart around, looking for anything to calm my nervous energy. The Great Hall was constructed during the 17th century when Sondish cloth merchants robed every monarch in northern Europe, and my gaze fixes on the exquisite painted ceiling. Then I remember that the riot of angels and apostles was rumored to have driven Oppeger the Elder insane in its creation.

So much for calm.

Her Majesty enters, trailed by her private secretary, and I dip into a curtsey along with my sisters, my shoes performing the function with as much elegance as a basic pump. Noah bows. On some level, I know it's ridiculous to curtsey to one's mother, but she is also the Queen, and when we are inspected under her exacting eye, we all feel the tension.

She gives Noah a brief, official nod and moves to Alma. A twinge of envy tightens my stomach as I anticipate Mama's smile of approval. Sometimes I think that if I could look as perfect as my sister, *be* as perfect, then I might finally feel like I belong in this family of bracingly smart, modern royals.

I frown at the thought, my wish just another kind of mirror to check my likeness against. Being the spitting image of Mama tells me I'm no changeling. I do belong here. I only need a chance to prove it.

Freja gets another cursory check. Though her ensembles aren't as conventional as the rest of ours are, a history of childhood illness means that Mama allows Freja a long leash.

"Is that one of my dresses?" Mama asks.

"Yes. You wore it to a rose show in 1983."

As ever, I am impressed at what Freja manages to make look chic—this time, lace insets and unnecessary flounces.

Mama glances at Ella. "Pinch," she says and Ella bends, plucking the thinnest, most-invisible nylons between her thumb and forefinger, proof that she's actually wearing the hated stockings.

"Satisfied?" Ella asks.

But Mama has moved on, turning her attention to me. Her critical gaze travels a path down my outfit. She seems to check items off a list, and for all I know, her efficient secretary is doing exactly that. Hat, hair, hem. Check, check, check.

The Violet Presentation will be the rare royal event where I am front and center, and I can detect the unease in Mama's eyes and feel how unsettled she is this year. I am currently the favorite chew toy of the tabloid press, and I have no doubt that, were it the 15th century, she would have already packed me off to a nunnery to save her peace of mind.

I feel the moment she sees my heels, watching as she lifts her brow and opens her mouth. There are rules about what a princess of Sondmark may wear, and these shoes are dancing right on the line. They are a mistake and I wait for her to tell me so.

But then Père breezes into the hall, nodding vaguely to everyone and heading directly to the doors. "Are we going?"

Mama's expression sets as soon as her royal consort appears, and without a word, she holds out her hand. Her secretary places her gloves in her palm and Mama turns. I breathe a sigh of relief. Père waits for her to pass, follows neatly two paces behind her, and the rest of us trail after them like ducklings in a row.

The ride to the Royal Mews is short, little more than five minutes from one end of the grounds of the Summer Palace to the other, but I try to calm my nerves by reminding myself I've been performing this ritual since I was sixteen. That makes eight scandal-free years. Eight is a nice, big number. It's a cheering thought until I remember that it's impossible to do anything ruinous at such a simple event.

A thousand internet posts dredging up the midriff tops I wore to college football games won't change my perfect record. Dozens of style retrospectives featuring covert photos of me crossing the Stanford campus or locked in an upperclassman's embrace after sneaking off to Full Moon on the Quad, or dancing at dive bars can't undo eight years of Violet Presentation competence. I want to point out that the press has gone absolutely insane since I graduated and returned home, dissecting every aspect of my life in gossip columns and online tabloids.

I tell myself these things but glance at Mama and mirror her ramrod posture. "Never dwell, never tell" is the unofficial family motto, and she would say that trotting out explanations and excuses for the bad press is unwise and, worse, unhelpful.

We drive into the massive interior courtyard of the mews and disembark to the sounds of the military band warming up. The carriages are polished, and the massive Friesian horses are standing stock-still in their traces, rigorously trained to disregard the commotion of such things. Navy men fill the rest of the space, milling about and comparing dress uniforms, laughing at the stiff forage cap arranged on each head. In years past, I have loved Queen's Day, sailing through my part in it so comfortably I might as well be wearing an old pair of sweats. But this year I have more than Mama's watchful eyes tearing my nerves to shreds.

My gaze arcs over the knot of men, horses, and brass instruments, and it astonishes me how easy it is to pick him out of the crowd. In about half a second, I've located Lieutenant Commander Max Andersen of Her Majesty's Royal Navy. The entire point of a uniform is to turn the crew into an intimidating, faceless mass, but there he is, looking as fine as a new *fennig* in his crisp blues and brass buttons. My pulse kicks up, and it becomes difficult to recall the exact mechanics of breathing in and out. A blush swirls up my cheeks.

Panicking, I glance quickly away, looking for something to smooth or straighten. Instead, I encounter Ella's bland, wide-eyed smile and she joins my side, sliding an arm through mine. We look friendly, but if I had an ax, Ella would be in serious danger.

"Isn't it an absolutely gorgeous day? The scenery is"—she glances over my shoulder at the knot of military men—"exceptionally good."

"You're dead to me," I say through a brilliant smile, vowing never to let Ella near my computer ever again. "Dead-dead. Like, 'sweep aside the bones in the family crypt because we are going to need the room' dead."

A smirk tucks Ella's cheek, and she raises a hand, shielding her eyes from the sun. "I don't know why you're upset. *I'm* not a cyberstalker."

I will kill her for toying with me. I hiss from between my clenched teeth, "The graduation records of Knutsen Naval Academy are public information, and his mother has nonexistent social media security protocols."

She snorts, putting a gloved hand to her nose to cover the sound. Mama looks up, and finding no easily identifiable lapse of decorum, only narrows her eyes at us before her glance slides away again.

"If it looks like a lovesick princess and quacks like a lovesick princess," Ella chants under her breath.

Decapitation is too good for my sister, but the mass of evidence is on her side. Last year was sweltering, and when a sailor fainted right on the parade ground, Lieutenant Commander Andersen stepped forward in a brisk, sensible manner to sort the entire thing out, almost before the photographers noticed. I was impressed. That his shoulders are so broad you could park a truck on them has nothing whatsoever to do with my internet habits, but one princess's citizen outreach hobby is another princess's cyberstalking. Po-tay-to, po-tah-to, as the Americans say.

I have uncovered the following facts:

Max Andersen graduated first in his class from the naval academy seven years ago. He has an older brother and a younger sister along with a small niece who likes to ride on his shoulders. His family spends every August in a tiny cottage somewhere on a lake.

For a while, there was an icy blonde in family pictures who didn't look more than mildly pleased to have his hand resting on her waist, but I haven't seen her in ages, and I assume her soul was sucked into the black abyss from whence it came.

I tug at the cuffs of my coat-dress, uncomfortably aware of why I chose my wardrobe with painstaking care for this year's event. It wasn't only because I have to nail my engagements in front of Mama. No, I've got a crush on someone who doesn't know I exist. My brow wrinkles, and I hastily smooth it. He surely knows I exist. Anyone passing the tabloids at the grocery store knows I exist. He doesn't know that I know *he* exists.

A call to form up rings out, and I observe the flurry of activity as Max brings his sailors into formation with one clear command. In a heartbeat, the blurry assembly snaps into focus, a sharp contrast to the milling about of only moments before.

No one would blame me for having a crush on a man like this. He's handsome, competent, and...safe. It is a plain, depressing fact that nothing could ever happen between us because our lives are too different, intersecting only once a year. I know how foolish it would be to form an attachment to one of my mother's subjects, a commoner, but infatuation is a victimless crime, and nobody—nobody but Ella—ever has to know.

While his face is hard and his eyes stare into some military middle-distance, I allow myself to look my fill. Is it so weird to feel this way about a stranger? Is it any different than having a crush on a Hemsworth brother? A sigh escapes me. The press would have a field day if they knew.

I take in his light brown hair, cropped short, and the uniform which accentuates his broad shoulders and long legs. I know that the top of my head comes up to his lower lip when I'm in heels. A very agreeable thing that has me imagining going up on my toes ever so slightly. My own eyes must have wandered into some princess-y middle-distance because Freja emits a tiny cough as we mount the carriage steps. I offer to sit facing backward and she casts a look at the wall of uniformed officers behind us with a notch of her brow.

"Ew," I say, outraged. "I'm not going to ogle them."

Not all of them.

Just one.

Really well.

2

DRAGONSLAYER

MAX

My uniform is like a second skin. As I move through
the ship's company, I hardly notice the tight collar, white
gloves, or peaked cap, which settles precisely on my head
like I'm one of the plastic figurines my niece uses to stage
her dioramas.

I move quickly to break up a knot of roughhousing,
unsurprised that the sailors are in high spirits. Of course
they are. Most of them are a few hours away from having
the run of Handsel for Queen's Day celebrations–a time
of year during which a non-negligible number of Sondish
women feel it's their patriotic duty to fling themselves at
anything in a uniform.

I shake my head and squint against the bright sunshine
as a line of cars enters the courtyard. Assorted royals
disembark and I look for Her Royal Highness, Princess
Clara, Duchess of Reike and Felsland. I see a flash of
purple that might be her. I'm jostled from behind and
turn, reminding myself that I'm here to do a job.

Though Queen Helena was born in January, the entire
nation of Sondmark spills into the streets on June 15th
to kick off a week of drinking, parades, and concerts
to celebrate her official birthday. It begins with a quiet
ceremony on the parade grounds of the Summer Palace.
There, as tradition dictates, the youngest princess of The
House of Wolffe hands out bunches of violets for each

sailor in the Handsel Company of Her Majesty's Navy to tuck into the band of their uniform hat.

The tradition goes back to the days of King Harald Dragonslayer and is a far cry from my usual duties as the executive officer aboard the *HMS Thetis*, one of Her Majesty's frigates.

I glance again at the royal party from the corner of my eye and catch my commanding officer, Captain Dusstock, making the rounds, the gold stripes on his cuff signaling to even the most ignorant midshipman that this is someone they can't afford to cross. He growls, tugging an ensign's uniform into orderliness, moving through the crowd like a feral tiger.

"The only kind of words your subordinates will recognize are loud and clear," he likes to bark, holding two fingers in front of my nose. I could add "profanity-laced." Those are the kind of words the captain likes, too.

The final call to assemble rings out and I hear him inhale, ready to bellow. My crew looks to me.

I nod, my voice hardly raised. "Attention."

They snap into position. Captain Dusstock sends me a dark glance, and I set my jaw. Here is the man who holds my rank advancement in his hands. My future—of being in command of my own vessel—is subject to his whims.

We march in formation through the heart of the old city, a crisp contrast to the crowds lining the route, already drinking and waving the flag of Sondmark. Three royal carriages precede us up the tree-lined avenue and through the turns. I can see glimpses of Queen Helena and Prince Consort Matteo, behind them Crown Prince Noah escorting his sisters Princesses Alma and Ella, and, last of all, a carriage carrying Princess Freja and the youngest, Princess Clara.

After all these years, the marching is automatic, and my focus keeps shifting to Princess Clara. I catch glimpses of reddish-blonde hair and bright green eyes.

By the time we march onto the parade grounds under the steady gaze of Queen Helena, I'm thankful the Navy band is playing our national anthem, flags snapping in the light wind.

Sons of Sondmark
slide your blades
beneath the fleshy chin
of Vorburg.
Spill his cowardly blood,
Upon his breast.
None will bridle the dragon of Sondmark.

It's the best anthem in northern Europe and stirs the usual feelings—national pride and the wish to lead a raiding party against our nearest neighbor, slaughtering as we go.

But then a bugle sounds, and Princess Clara separates herself from her family, descending from the podium and crossing the expanse of paving stones. Though I remain at attention, my mental discipline deserts me. Hot damn. The woman has legs for days, and she hasn't entirely covered her knees. Seeing her knees is like seeing rain on Saint Wyten's Day, an omen of a good year to come.

She greets our commanding officer and the company mascot, a wolfhound named Ollie, bending over to tuck a posy into Ollie's collar with a ruffle of his fur. His tongue lolls out of his mouth as he stares up in canine adoration. I release a derisive snort. Get it together, Ollie.

But I'm hardly better than the wolfhound and only the familiar routine of this event is keeping me grounded. When I was a kid, my mother used to herd us in front of the television to watch the ceremony, sticking tiny flags in our hands. When I began to take part as a young ensign, she started saving newspaper clippings even though I was hardly a blurry dot in the back row of the group picture invariably printed on the front page of *The Holy Pelican* with one of their dull headlines. "Princess Clara Commemorates Queen's Day Celebrations".

Despite her deluge of press—the tabloid headlines that hint at wildness and youthful excess—I've been watching long enough to know how good the princess is at her job. She has a way of accepting the flowers from a courtier, presenting them to a waiting officer, and bantering for ten seconds with the addled man before sending him back in line. It must be the executive officer in me that likes the way she keeps things moving without appearing to hustle anyone along.

As the most junior lieutenant commander, I am the last officer to receive her tribute, and I know my role, stepping

forward to give a short bow. I take off my hat and the wind ruffles my hair. I reach for the posy in her outstretched hands, careful not to brush her fingers. Once accomplished, I congratulate myself on managing these simple mechanics, even as my heart charges in my chest.

After some fumbling, I jam the flowers into the hatband, half the petals scattering at our feet. Now we are supposed to chat for a few moments.

"Welcome home, lieutenant commander," she says in a husky voice the public hardly ever hears. The richness was a surprise to me last year. Everything was a surprise last year, not least my reaction to her.

"Thank you, Your Royal Highness," I answer, feeling for the first time how snug my collar is around my neck. "The thought of returning to Handsel in time for Queen's Day gave the entire crew something to look forward to."

I'm almost finished, and just in time. My nerves are tighter than if I were piloting a ship through forty-foot swells. It has never been like this with anyone else, I think, in a kind of desperate need to justify my reaction. When I dated Liva, I used a spreadsheet to sort out my feelings. A spreadsheet. I do not need a spreadsheet now. Clara smiles. I hear the harsh klaxon of a distress signal ringing between my ears. This girl is dangerous.

"I'm happy you're home safe," she says.

The remark sounds as if she knows the details of the voyage. For all I know, she might. Her mother receives regular updates from the Prime Minister. I drag my gaze away from hers, reminding myself that my mother receives regular updates from NewsNook. Reverse course, Andersen. This girl isn't even real. She's some projection I have of what the perfect woman would be. We have nothing in common.

I bow again. My time is up. I admit to myself that I'm no better than last year. Judging by the pulse pounding in my ears, I might be worse. *Stultes es.* Princess Clara signals the courtiers to carry the baskets of flowers to the enlisted men. They depart and she shifts her weight.

I'm half turned from her when she catches my arm, her fingers curling around the muscle and her eyes widening in alarm.

"Max—" she gasps.

Shock freezes me in place. I heard wrong. It wasn't my name she said. It was just the kind of noise you make when you're surprised.

"What is it?" I feel the collective weight of the TV crew and bank of photographers; can hear how the steady click of shutters has picked up. My mother is likely shouting for Dad to come in out of the garden because her baby is on the telly.

Clara's princess smile sets into rigid lines, and I see a flash of panic in her eyes. "*Vede.* My shoe is stuck."

I can't help it. My gaze flicks down to those world-famous legs, encased in transparent stockings. Handsel Guards are about honor, integrity, and discipline, I remind myself, forcing my gaze to continue past the inviting sight. The thin heel of her shoe is wedged between two hand-cut 18th-century paving stones.

"Maybe just slip your foot out and—"

She inhales sharply. "These stones will shred my stockings."

Under the glare of the international media, the pride of Sondmark is at stake. I could call for a courtier and return to my company, but a Handsel Guard would never abandon his nation. That charge must explain the sudden fire that lights in my stomach.

"I'm going to kneel," I say, taking command of a delicate situation in a way that my job often requires. "You hold onto my shoulders and I'll ease the heel—"

She swallows hard. "That's a terrible idea."

"I could leave you here while I get a block and tackle, maybe rig up a pulley system..." I coax.

An unexpected gleam of amusement comes into her eyes. "Fine. We'll do it your way, Lieutenant Commander."

The phrase curls in my belly, and it's hard work to keep my face expressionless. The sharp lines of my uniform crease as I kneel on one knee at her feet. A further uptick of noise greets my ears, but I tune it out to wrap one hand around a shapely calf and another under the arch of her foot. I refuse to enjoy this. It's just one of the demands of the job. I repeat these phrases again and again until I feel her hands settle on my shoulders. Then I tell myself to shut up.

"Ready?" I ask.

"Try not to knock me off my feet," she says.

A quick tug and the shoe is free, but when I release her, she wobbles and makes a sharp cry of surprise. She tips forward and falls across my back. Her shoes lift off the ground and I quickly wrap my arm around the backs of her knees, the other hand securing her hemline. I have my arms full of princess and only have to stand to look like we're in one of those wife-carrying competitions where the prize is free beer for a year.

She scrambles blindly, tugging at the bottom of my coat as she struggles to get upright. I'm about to be knocked on my backside.

"Stop," I command, and to her credit she does. I angle my shoulder forward and reach back, my hands spanning her waist. I lift her up and away, standing her neatly on her feet.

"You're good?" I ask, slightly out of breath. She nods, shaken, and places a hand over mine, where it still rests on her waist. Oh.

I let her go and I kneel back on my heel, looking up into her face. She steps slightly away but reaches a hand to lift me. I don't need the help but won't turn down another opportunity to touch her.

"Regret, regret, regret," she chants, pain tightening the edges of her smile.

I grunt. I am not filled with regret. It's going to be another long, lonely year, I think, as we hold onto one another for that brief second.

I never hear the click of the camera that takes the picture seen around the world.

3

Laser Eyes

CLARA

When we return to the palace, lasers are shooting from Mama's eyes. Not actual lasers, just metaphorical ones with crawling text that reads, "No one in the 800-year tradition of Sondmark Violet Presentations has ever managed to turn it into such a thorough-going cock-up as you have."

Pew goes the Sèvres vase. *Blast* goes the heraldic crest. *Pop, pop, pop* go the marble treads on the staircase.

My head is high and I look calm, but I'm gripping my handbag like it's the last life preserver on a sinking ship. It was Max Andersen, I decide. I got cocky thinking how easy it would be to run the presentation with most of my thoughts centered around a certain officer. Eight years of perfection and I practically dared hubris to knock me down. Eight years, all gone in a single moment.

Even though this is one of the least important royal responsibilities, my mother treats it with all the gravity of welcoming foreign dignitaries or signing peace treaties. She's always held the belief that following protocol is more important than personal comfort or creative expression. This is fine. She's the queen. But my thoughts slip away from this line of filial duty. *If Lieutenant Commander Andersen and his slow smile hadn't distracted me— Vede, why does it have to be such a tightrope? I'm trying.* A mountain of defeat landslides onto my lungs. I can't breathe, and I want to cry. *Clara, you've messed up again.*

Before I can stop it, my mind drags out the events of last year, replaying them like a hard-nosed prosecutor with a quota to meet. The images are bright. Graduation from Stanford with my parents in the crowd, the decorous dinner party they hosted before travelling on to Ottawa, celebrating grad night in the tiniest, shiniest dress I own, the race to the airport in the morning to hop on the family jet, and sleeping almost the entire flight. Then, high above the skies of Handsel, discovering that my sorority sisters had replaced every stitch of my luggage with decorative pillows and that the cabin attendant, a man, was not my size. I remember the panic. So much panic.

There is nothing quite like returning to one's country and being greeted by press photographers, a brass band, and local officials while wearing a sequined, thigh-skimming dress.

A shudder rolls across my shoulders, and the palace doors click shut. Père waves off the butler and it's only family for once. Mama takes a deep breath, then another, and when she blinks, her expression is tight with conspicuous patience. It is an expression I have grown familiar with this year but never imagined I would encounter today. The Violet Presentation is the first official duty given to a young princess precisely because it is impossible to ruin.

Or it was.

Though it looks like she wishes she could resurrect some of the grislier punishments of Frederick IV, her words are even.

"I am aware these things happen," Mama says. But there is a tone in her voice that suggests she is aware in the same way that equatorial societies know that some people, somewhere, spend their winters surrounded by snow and darkness. She is aware but unfamiliar with these things that happen.

She doesn't even need to finish her thoughts. I can read them clearly. *What has happened today will not ever happen again.* The words are chiseled into my brain.

Mama wheels to the left, and Ella tugs my arm, peeling me away from the Great Hall. "What in the name of Erasmus's cap was that?"

I thrust my handbag at her and begin fanning my underarms, my face, tugging at my neckline. "It was nothing," I huff, galloping up the stairs.

It was *not* nothing.

I can't exactly be fired from the family business, but Mama's banked fury feels like the unpaid intern got a scathing performance review from the CEO in an office-wide email. Fifteen years ago, Alma performed the same presentation, accidentally calling the captain "Père" and we've only recently started laughing about it. I figure my faux pas will be spoken of in hushed tones twenty years from now, and I'm sweating so much this dress is probably ruined forever. "It's not the end of the world. I know she'll calm down. Tomorrow—"

"She? No, Clara, what was that with your Navy officer?" Ella, who never seems to take any of Mama's disapproval to heart, is grinning.

I halt outside my door. I'm not ready for that talk. "Can I give you the postmortem tomorrow?" I plead. Today is a day for catastrophizing and histrionics.

She gives me a penetrating look. Finally, she lifts her shoulder. "Okay," she answers, tugging on my hair.

I push through the door, very deliberately do not slam it, kick off my really sexy heels, and flop backward onto the bed. This is not how today was supposed to go.

My plan was to spend the rest of my day looking for internet footage of the entire Queen's Day ceremony and replaying my common, ordinary exchange with a certain lieutenant commander. I hadn't expected to almost fall on my face on national television.

I pull up a video and see myself handing him a posy of flowers, trapped like a mouse in the high-walled maze of official protocol. His eyes hardly meet my face and he seems to have some difficulty placing his bunch of violets into his hatband. "Goodbye for another year," I thought as Lieutenant Commander Andersen wheeled from me.

I was careful not to show my disappointment. I resolved to accept the next date I was asked on, or to say yes to one of Mama's arranged introductions, and to turn off notifications for *Vrouw* Andersen's occasional social media posts. I thought that it had been a ridiculous year, and it was time to move on.

And then disaster. I watch as, alone in the center of the parade ground, Max caught me as though, alongside rescue diving and navigation, he had trained for this too.

"Regret, regret, regret," I said when we untangled and he set me on my feet, rising to his own. I knew the faux pas would reinforce my public image of being an inconsequential lightweight, but I smiled anyway. The press had to see that I could take setbacks with good humor. My mother had to see that I could handle this. "I hope I haven't scuffed your uniform. It would be a shame to disarrange such perfection."

Such a narrow, impossible line I am being asked to walk. The weight of my role—a role I want and am anxious to show I'm capable of—settles on my shoulders as my mind replays the event over and over. I mean to dissect what went wrong—what I did wrong—but I keep halting at the smile he gave me after I fell all over him.

I wasn't prepared for what it did to me in the flesh. At that moment, I wanted to forget that I was a grown woman in a position of responsibility under the glare of the watchful press. I very much wanted to disarrange his uniform.

Impossible to do that when he called me ma'am. Yes. He did.

"Executive officers are trained to take initiative, ma'am." His exact words.

Ma'am. Even now the memory makes me want to sink through the floor. It's perfectly correct to switch from the ponderous *Your Royal Highness* after the first greeting. And in all fairness, the correct form of address is ma'-am, but it never before conjured orthopedic shoes and polyester stretch pants as it did then. *Would you like your prune juice, ma'am? Can I help you cross the street, ma'am?*

"May I escort you back to your family?" he asked, offering his elbow.

I let out a silent sigh, recalling myself to the gilded walls of the Summer Palace. I expect an addendum to the House of Wolffe Dress Code any minute now. I expect to have my history of ill-advised crop tops and late-night clubbing dredged up for minute reexamination, but I cannot regret the part where I got to meet my crush. The man had smelled like ripe tangerines, warm puppies, dusky sandalwood, and world peace.

My wayward thoughts call forth the memory of Lieutenant Commander Andersen bowing to my mother and then to myself. When he turned and began the long walk back to his company, I got to check out his backside.

Honestly, the man is a national treasure.

Before I can spend more than a moment considering the fact, my phone pings—Mama's secretary with a link to Prada's latest season, which features a positive deluge of sensible block heels. She titles the email "Queen's Day Footwear".

4

BODY LANGUAGE

MAX

I start the morning with ten miles on the treadmill tucked into a corner of the helicopter hanger, the massive bay doors open to the rising sun. I finish with a cool down and pull up the hem of my Navy t-shirt, wiping the sweat from my face. Turning, I reach for my duffel bag, and my hand freezes.

There's a flutter of newsprint taped to the wall like a paper explosion. The crew was suspiciously tactful yesterday. Though I expected some *probish* from them about the princess, they were, to a man, silent, and now I know why. Probably busy sourcing every print outlet in Handsel. I lift a corner of one article and feel the telltale softness of newsprint. These are real.

From *The Daily Missive*, a Sondmark tabloid, the tone is gushing. The headline reads "The Siren and the Sailor" followed by no less than fifteen full-color pictures—me in my dress blues, me accepting the posy, Clara holding her head up as she returns to her family on my arm, me walking away. I grunt away a laugh. The photographer used a clever angle, and they've made it look like she's eyeing my backside approvingly.

I flatten a dingy grey page from the left-wing *Sondish Worker* with my palm. "Coup! Navy Topples Monarchy." The picture they've chosen to highlight is one showing both of my hands wrapped around her silk-clad leg. She's gripping my jacket, with a shocked smile on her face, and looks like a stone goddess I'm about to knock off her plinth and toss over my shoulder.

Even the stodgy *Holy Pelican* has gotten into the act with bold type shouting "The Little Princess Goes Fishing," dryly captioning their picture, "Princess Clara makes a close inspection of the Handsel Company on Queen's Day".

I lift my brows when I see that several overseas publications from New York, San Francisco, London, Hong Kong, Berlin, and Vorburg have picked up the story, each selecting the damning image of me kneeling at Clara's feet, holding her hand. It looks like they've caught me mid-proposal and that she can't wait for me to finish before jumping into my arms. I look like I'm about to pull her into them.

From the hanger behind me, I hear the whistled strains of a wedding march and the sound of laughter. It cuts off when I spin around and fold my arms over my chest, bracing my feet in a deliberately imposing stance.

"Moller," I snap, and the lieutenant presents himself before me, his expression almost innocent.

"Want me to clean it up, sir?" he asks, a laugh ghosting his voice.

Command is a delicate line to walk. These men and women, shuffling awkwardly in the cavernous space, are my closest compatriots. I live with them and work with them, but there are times when I can't be one of them.

I could let that go to my head, mustering a line of sailors to shout at, making a subordinate sweep away the mess, demanding a detail to clean the hanger top to bottom and perform a meticulous foreign object walk. Heaven knows that's what the captain would do in my shoes.

In my hesitation, I see Moller swallowing thickly. He knows I could make his life hell, knows I could keep him from his family and fiancée tonight, forcing him to use a toothbrush to scrub the deck. And he's coming to see what a stupid move this was. I let him balance on the sharp edge of that painful realization for a long, silent moment.

A flush mottles his neck, and his ears turn scarlet. Only a monster would force an extra shift on men and women who have been aboard a ship for the better part of three months.

"We're done with this." My tone is crisp, but there is no heat in it. I can't afford to let the sailors think I'll lose my cool over a simple prank, but I can't let them think I'll allow it to happen again either.

Moller exhales and salutes, and I turn back to the newspapers. When I'm certain that no one can see me, I grin.

I make a great show of stripping the articles from the wall, careful to hide the fact that I fold the tape over so the pictures don't stick together before shoving them into a bag. I'm not going to make a scrapbook or anything, but it seems a shame to see them swept into the trash.

I spend the rest of the morning filling out reports, and that's what I'm doing when my captain strolls into my small workspace and drops into a chair, indicating a less formal interview. "Twenty-five years I've been in the Navy. Enlisted ten, another fifteen as an officer busting my hump past you Academy boys," he growls, a litany I have heard again and again. He's not like me, the story goes. He came up the hard way. "That flower ceremony was never a disaster until you got involved. I wouldn't have chosen to knock over one of the royal family, Andersen, but what do I know?"

I do not move. I do not blink. This is the detour my life has taken, landing me under the command of a captain who could turn my once-promising Navy career into a dead end.

"Not once has the blasted thing ever excited any comment from my wife."

I try to imagine the kind of woman who would be married to Captain Dusstock. Someone dressed in a tracksuit with a strong discus throwing arm, I guess.

"She said we ought to put you in recruitment ads."

I'm not sure how to respond, so I follow his example, crossing my arms over my chest, and look grim.

He picks up a pen from the desk and rolls it between his hands. "We've been invited to a reception at the Vorburg ambassador's residence tonight. Ball gowns, tiaras, that nasty pickled herring they can't get enough of in that cursed country. I have to attend. My wife wants to meet you. You'll be our guest," he orders, no consideration for a waiting fiancée, if I had one. "Dress whites. You live off base?"

"Yes, sir."

He nods, tossing the pen back to the desk and standing. "Drive over with us. Ring my doorbell at nineteen hundred hours."

I should be furious. Deployed for three months and I haven't even stepped across the threshold of my own house yet. Now I have to go to a party. One word, however, changes my attitude.

Tiaras.

How many people wear tiaras in Sondmark? This is not the kind of thing I pay attention to, but there can't be more than a handful. The queen, a couple of ladies-in-waiting, and a few princesses. The odds of seeing Clara again have gone way up.

At thirteen hundred hours I've released my men and been released from duty myself. I fight through Handsel traffic, shooting twenty minutes up the coast to a small stone cottage. Situated on a lonely spit of land, it's on the edge of a nature reserve and there isn't another house in sight, only the soft water of the lake rippling twenty meters from the back door. If the cottage, down-at-heel and peeling, still needs plenty of work, at least it's snug and tidy. I hire a caretaker to look after it when I'm at sea, so the weeds are manageable and the rooms are well aired. I push open the door, hating this part of the job.

As I've found over the last few years, not many women are willing to put up with the Navy—the long absences, the regimented hours. Leaving is the easy part. I text the caretaker, flip the light switch, and bolt the door. I can focus all my attention on my job because I haven't left anybody behind, and there's no one to miss me when I'm gone.

It's hard when I walk into an empty house.

I hang the key up on the hook and take off my jacket, slipping it onto a hanger and placing it in the closet. The tie comes off next, slotted in position on a tie rack. I know there will be groceries in the fridge to get me going (a couple of steaks, eggs, milk, bread, a bunch of grapes, and Sondmark chocolate spread—all the basic food groups covered) and I flip on the television, leaning against the counter to sort the mail.

"Watch her lips," comes the clinical voice of a guest on the 24-hour news channel. "She's biting them."

"I don't see any teeth. How can you tell?" asks the host.

"A tightness here and here in this cheek. I have no doubt she's nervous."

I'm lending the show half an ear, but if I had to guess, I would have said they have body language experts in to dissect the latest G10 summit, parsing out every bit of information, betting fortunes on the quivering, hairy chin of a Himmelsteinian dignitary and wondering what it might mean for cattle tariffs. As ever, it is difficult to fill 24 hours with news in Sondmark.

"She's much harder to read than he is," the speaker goes on. "Well, I would imagine with the training she's received, she would be. But the princess is definitely nervous."

My head snaps up from my task and I fumble for the remote, turning the television up and leaping over my sofa in one smooth motion.

The host is laughing. "Nervous? Oh honey, make way for a woman of experience."

"Yes," the body language expert continues, missing her joke. "She's perfectly relaxed giving out violets until he steps close and..."

The video slows down like an instant replay of a goal in a football match. I can almost see the crowd rise and hear the announcer begin to shout. The guest is using a stylus and tablet. Circles appear on the larger screen, superimposed on Clara's face.

"There's the telltale breath, the dilating pupils, and the tuck in her cheek. Mind you, all this comes before she realizes her heel is stuck." Bright orange arrows materialize, pointing at a pulse beating in her neck. "She's practically hyperventilating, and it has nothing to do with the catastrophe that's about to unfold. I would bet my career on it."

My mouth dries and I'm sitting on the edge of my seat, waiting for more. But the host touches her ear. "My producer is telling me our time is up. Thank you, Dr. Broust, for a fascinating look into the human mind. Your book *Body Talk* is available at retail outlets everywhere, I understand?"

The man laughs. "And if you like it, leave a review! If you hate it, stuff that feeling deep inside and never let it out."

The host smiles. "I only wish we had a few more minutes to talk about the officer."

The man was supposed to say, "Thank you for having me on. It was a pleasure." But his parting words are, "That one? He's a mess."

5

SLAY, QUEEN

CLARA

I spend the night dreaming about shoes—stuck shoes, shoes that fly off, shoes that fall apart with every step I take. I am exhausted when I wake and stagger downstairs to a breakfast with my sisters of strong chocolate, hot rolls, and soft cheese. Alma and Freja are quick to offer their commiseration for my public humiliation.

"It could have happened to any of us," Freja says. "It was just bad luck."

"And gravity," adds Alma. "Mama can't be upset about physics."

I smile as though I agree, but I know better. Nothing less than the perfect balance on this narrow road of royal protocol will satisfy Mama, and neither Freja nor Alma would understand. Freja has constructed her own bridge from point A to point B, and Alma manages to walk Mama's line, all the while appearing to juggle flaming chainsaws without breaking a sweat.

If I keep trying, there's no reason to think I can't become that good at it.

The newspapers are spread across the table, each one more inventive than the last, and my stomach sours when I see how many there are. This is why what happened on the parade ground was consequential. Mama has a full agenda planned this week, and it's been relegated to page three while my drama has claimed the spotlight.

My sisters finish their meal, but Ella hangs back, pauses for a few beats, and turns a smile on me, positively triumphant.

"You're a GIF," she squeals.

I growl. Alma is already a wildly popular GIF. Whenever people search the internet for a short, looping video of *disdain*, *Slay Queen*, *die peasant*, or *Thanks, I hate it* to attach to their social media posts, the first choice to pop up is usually my oldest sister arrogantly lifting her brow.

Never mind that she is hilarious and sweet. Never mind that she was scared out of her mind. The GIF shows two scant seconds of video captured from an hour-long event highlighting endangered animals. It was the moment right when the giant Hispaniolan galliwasp escaped its handler and slithered up her leg. Alma has a special terror of lizards, but as she explained to us later, giant Hispaniolan galliwasps look like scuttling thumbs and have an uncanny necklessness, which made it a billion percent worse. That she didn't run screaming or kick it, sending the species one step closer to extinction, was an act of heroism. But two seconds is enough to make her live on in perpetuity as a two-dimensional cartoon, the first image most foreigners ever see of our country.

We all received two months of intensive comportment training for that. A shudder dances down my spine, and I grip my mug tightly. I do not want to be a GIF.

Like a doomed queen marching up the steps to the guillotine, I say in a tone of deep resolve, "Show me."

Ella hands me her phone. A member of the press has caught the two seconds I've been reliving since the moment they happened. Lieutenant Commander Max Andersen is kneeling with the most heart-stopping expression. Then he stands, his eyes tracking my face as he rises to his feet. It's a simple image, but it looks as though he's about to drag me into a dark closet somewhere and—

I blink back the thought. Yesterday was a calamity for my public image, and here's why. Over thirty years ago, after the birth of a new baby, a European princess slipped on a bit of wet pavement as she went to greet the public. A tiny slip. She didn't even fall. That clip resurfaces again and again on biographical programs, visual shorthand for why she became an ex-princess, got caught in an influence-peddling scandal, and gained all that weight. It lets people think that the seeds of it were there all along.

But as I watch my GIF play and replay, my feelings of embarrassment and frustration are nudged gently aside by the secret pleasure of remembering what it felt like to have Max Andersen look at me like that.

"What are the search terms?" I ask, tracking Lieutenant Commander Andersen's eyes tracking mine.

"*Princess, true love, say yes, proposal, Navy stan, do it...*"

I groan.

"*...royal wedding, hot man, shipping, yes sir...* Shall I continue?"

"No, no. I've got it." I drop my head in my hands, plunging my fingers into my hair. "Curse my heel."

"Curse all heels."

I grumble, "Curse the stone-cutter who bungled that paving stone—"

"Don't you think he's dead?" Ella giggles, entering into the game, firing off responses as quickly as I make complaints.

"I wish long-range camera lenses had never been created."

"To hell with deep-space telescopes," she rejoins.

"I'd like to uninvent the Navy."

Ella nods sagely. "Our national sovereignty is a small price to pay for your feelings."

"Curse hot sailors."

She laughs. "Alas, you've lost me."

I glance up and whack Ella on the arm. She laughs at me, rubbing the spot. "You're not really upset, are you? You basically got to meet the God of Thunder in the actual, sun-kissed flesh," she says, raising her eyebrow like I may have something new to impart that the world's press didn't manage to capture.

I fight back a yawn, shaking my head at her incorrigibility. Tonight, I vow to think less of footwear and get some sleep.

"I am upset," I say, pointing at the newspapers, dragging over one with the pad of my finger. "This isn't great for me."

Every other member of the Wolffe household has a full slate of established patronages and charities, offering us a real chance to do good and highlight causes that will mean so much for Sondmark's future. I'm supposed to have these duties too, but I'm often relegated to being a placeholder or seat filler, dedicating the mass transit car parks no one else has any time for.

For months I've ascribed this lack of designated responsibilities to the fact that I've only been out of college for a year and my position isn't nearly so well established as everyone else's. But I'm coming to the conclusion that it's more that my mother doesn't trust me, and this latest debacle doesn't help my case.

I thought I was supposed to actually enjoy college. For four years (and the gap year in South America), I operated under the assumption that the rigid rules of royal protocol might relax from a distance of nearly 9 thousand miles—allowing me to go to clubs, host sorority parties, and tailgate. It was all pretty harmless, but the pictures bubbling up every day since graduation make it look like I was in a sustained, years-long bacchanal. It doesn't help that the press discovered that my name makes a fun rhyme in Sondish.

"Alma could have sailed through yesterday and it would hardly have been a footnote. But I'm Princess Party."

Ella groans. "Not that again. It'll go away if you ignore it."

I can't ignore it. I know the consequence of slipping into a life of insignificant duties, my workload limited to showing up to galas and wearing expensive clothes. I would still live in a palace and be a princess, but over time, my life would be leached of meaning. I've seen it happen to cousins, aunts, and uncles as they become frothier and frothier versions of themselves, appearing on the cocktail circuit, honored guests of some corrupt official looking for legitimacy and finding it with ancient titles.

I don't want my life to look like that.

"Princess Party won't go away if I'm never allowed to do anything of substance," I insist, lifting the corner of a newspaper and letting it fall. "Until I do, I can't afford to mess up my future by presenting anything less than perfection."

Ella shakes her head and I see some of her banked frustration. Unlike my other sisters, Ella isn't trying to walk Mama's road in a roundabout way or do it while juggling flaming chainsaws or anything. It's like she was handed a map and proceeded to rip it up, preferring to hack her way through the wilderness with a machete. She cannot stand anything that smacks of cheerleading for Team Royal.

"And here I was hoping you were going to ask me to disable the palace security system so you could sneak out for a night of semi-illicit man-snogging."

"You could do that?" I try to look skeptical and disapproving, but there my imagination goes, pulling me after it, and I'm distracted by the idea all day.

It's not a good day to lose my focus. Tonight's event is a tiara occasion—one of only a few we'll have all year—and there is much to be done before I arrive at the Ambassador's residence looking like I spend every waking moment in full court dress.

There's the manicure, pedicure, final dress fittings, a session with a hairdresser knowledgeable about the kind of invisible anchors which will need to be braided into my hair to support the tiara, and a tense visit with Mama's dresser, who will make me promise on the lives of my children and my children's children that I will not lose or remove the sapphire necklace and chandelier earrings I am being lent from the royal vault.

During it all, I bone up on obscure Vorburgian history. Ella has developed a computer program that creates randomized digital flashcard decks of anyone remotely noteworthy or powerful, and I sit in the hairdresser's chair, the filter picking out only those from Vorburg, quizzing myself.

That night, I'm keyed up, aware that every stumble I make puts more pressure on the events which come after. We arrive in vintage Rolls Royce limousines maintained in pristine condition by the royal mews, the fleet of automobiles fitted with large windows and seats wide enough to accommodate our gowns without the risk of them being crushed.

When I see the number of press gathered outside the embassy, I grip my hands together. Mama glances at me, her expression implacable. "Give it no fuel and even the most raging fire will die down."

Her brow lifts. Give it no fuel. It is a directive.

When the door opens, I press my knees together, unconsciously swinging my heels onto the pavement in a maneuver I was probably taught at the same time I learned to walk. My man from the security detail shuts the door behind me and I follow behind my parents, brother, and three sisters. I pause at the entrance to allow my picture to be taken and make no response but to pin my smile in place when photographers shout, "Where's the lieutenant commander? Are you seeing him?"

Mama's face is as frozen as a Nordic pond in the depths of winter. Since she gives away nothing, I give away nothing, merely nodding when I turn to the arched doors.

In the vaulted entrance hall, our family is greeted in Vorburgian fashion (a heel click and an inexplicable scowl) and I am offered a cocktail as we merge into the party—ceremonial swords and orders bristling from our menfolk, tiaras, and heirloom jewels dripping from our womenfolk. We are an attractive family, and Mama enjoys making the most of such an asset. I'm wearing a sparkling midnight blue dress with an insane amount of tulle, and the color matches the rather difficult sapphire tiara habitually relegated to me. It consists of two simple bands widening at the brow with a massive gem plonked in the middle. Among the sisters, we call it The Cyclops.

The party looks like the kind of place where an international spy would meet his contact, but the truth is that I'm not a fairytale princess, and I'm not going to encounter a spy. I'm a mid-level public servant in a fancy dress.

A footman glides by holding a silver platter full of the pickled herring canapes these barbarians love serving and I swallow back a gag when the scent assaults my nose. I make my way into the crowd, pleased to find that Ella's program has taught me the faces of the Vorburg Minister of Climate and Utilities and the Undersecretary of Defense. Still, ten minutes before we are to be seated for dinner, I have to excuse myself into the garden for some fresh air or risk more headlines by tossing my crackers on the hand-woven carpets of Vorburg House.

I step through the narrow doors and into the inner courtyard, pulling a draught of air through my lungs. The night is warm, the air is soft, and distant thrumming echoes from an open-air concert on the waterfront being thrown in my mother's honor. I tip my head back, unworried that The Cyclops will tumble off my head. The tiara has been sewn into a ring of tiny braids and is more secure than the locks on the national mint.

A small movement signals that I am not alone. Damn. I close my eyes, briefly recomposing my official mask, and turn to see a figure in white giving me a brief bow from the end of the terrace. White. This is a man in uniform. As he straightens, I draw in a sharp, silent breath. I would know the set of those shoulders anywhere. Hadn't my hands been gripping them only yesterday?

My pulse leaps into my throat and my palms go clammy. It's Max and this is the first time I'm meeting him without a royal pavilion at my back or an entire phalanx of sailors at his. There are no violets. There is no script. But the image of our GIF flashes in my brain, and I am freaking out.

I take a drag of fresh air and pace forward.

"Your Royal Highness," he says, his voice matching the atmosphere of the garden, dark and soft. My fingers tighten around my drink. I stop a few steps from him and set my glass on the stone balustrade before it tumbles from my unsteady fingers.

"Lieutenant Commander." I nod my head. "Are you enjoying your Queen's Week festivities?"

What are you doing, Clara? I could kick myself as the words launch themselves prepackaged from my mouth like a bag of pretzels. I'm not on camera now. This isn't some ceremony.

I exhale gustily and say with a tight laugh, "I'm sorry. Force of habit. Let me start over. I'm Clara, of course, and you are—"

"Max," he supplies, and that's nice because now I don't have to pretend I don't know.

I spare an anxious glance over my shoulder. I can't see anyone else. No press. No Queen of Sondmark and the Sonderlands to tell me how to do this—to tell me *not* to do this.

"I'm glad I ran into you," I begin, hoping the right amount of *this is no big deal and I don't even know you* is showing. "It gives me the chance to apologize in person. I'm sure you had no idea when you woke up yesterday that my heel would drag you into an international news story. Have you seen the papers?"

Lieutenant Commander Andersen's mouth curls into a smile half-revealed in the light spilling from the reception room. He seems to have a different smile for every occasion, and this is a very good one.

"I've got a better source of news than papers." He reaches into his pocket and pulls his phone out, tapping it several times, tilting the screen towards me and scrolling through numberless text messages. "My mother, keeping her finger on the pulse of the nation."

I laugh.

6

RIPE BERRIES

MAX

She laughs.

I lean back against the railing and brace my hands against the cool stone, eyes skimming the curving line of her collarbones, the heavy jewels lying against her neck. Outside of the military, I'm not sure I've ever met anyone with better posture.

"I hope you don't find it too awkward," she gestures to my phone. "Most people don't understand that the tabloid press doesn't need any help making up stories out of thin air. They'll have us engaged by the end of the week and married by next year."

I swallow hard at the thought, a flare of want lighting in my chest. She's not wrong. The stories printed in newspapers and on internet sites all over the world bear little resemblance to what happened—the bare facts of a gap in the paving stones and simple extraction. But their "facts" didn't come out of thin air either. I did look (How did the *Vorburg Trumpet* put it?) like "a hungry bear sighting a patch of sweet, ripe berries."

I lift my phone, my brain receiving so many signals as it takes in every detail of her that it's an effort to slow it down enough to speak. "It's not too bad. My family's giving me a bit of a hard time—asking how I hid you away for so long and if they should start bowing now or later. My superior officer had a few words. You?"

She looks back to the open doors of the banquet, the sounds of the party carrying to us. She gives a graceful lift of her shoulder, and it creates a deep shadow below her neck. I'm only a step away from her, but it may as well be a thousand miles.

"My superior, too."

Her Majesty. I look up past the garden to the banquet hall. I can't conceive of rating a mention by my commander-in-chief and head of state. The realization of how insane it is to be standing here is almost enough to propel me back inside where there are bright lights and noisy guests. But a breeze kicks up, and I catch the scent of her perfume, something warm and flowery. I inhale, and while I can, I want to lean in closer, recording every detail of her as carefully as newspaper clippings, the tape folded over just so.

She tilts her head, and the tiara moves with her. "I hope the publicity hasn't upset your girlfriend or..."

Her fingers wind through the air, spooling out the question, like Sleeping Beauty coaxing a forest creature to perch on her hand. For a second, I think I sense tension beneath her easy manners.

I know what a similar statement would mean from a girl I might meet at a cafe table or in a bookstore. It would mean, "Hello, sir. I am here to scout the lie of the land in an undemanding but determined way. If uninhabited, expect further incursions on your personal space."

But what does it mean when a princess asks?

"No girlfriend. Nobody," I answer, voice rough.

She nods, eyes shifting towards the fairy lights in the garden. "Next year, when we're making our small talk at the Violet Presentation, all this will be something to laugh about."

That's a dismissal if I've ever heard one. I should say something about finding my captain, tell her how she's been generous with her time. Another bow and back to the party. But even though I'm in my uniform, I'm not under orders. I bump my chin towards the banquet hall.

"We'll be too busy talking about pickled herring next year. Do you think the entire menu has it?"

A smile, different than any I've ever seen in the press, tucks her cheek. "You think they've made pickled herring sorbet...?"

"Pickled herring medallions of beef," I murmur.

"Pickled herring vichyssoise."

"Pickled herring jacket potatoes."

"Pickled herring tiramisu."

I make a face, and she laughs again.

It's the laugh that loosens my tongue and makes me forget for a fraction of a second whom I'm standing next to. "We don't have to wait a year for small talk."

She stills, her hand resting lightly on the stone, and my common sense catches up to me, telling me not to be such a *flamen* fool. In my mind, I can already see myself holding a grandson on my knee one day, telling him about this moment; how I was possessed by a spirit of idiocy and made a pass at a princess. And then I imagine telling him about how I retreated.

"Discretion is the better part of valor," I will remind him.

In the darkness, my lips twist in a grimace almost worthy of pickled herring. Discretion is overrated. When I tell this story someday, I want to say that I saw my chance and took it. I want that grandson to give me finger guns and a high five.

"I don't always wear a uniform," I continue.

"You don't say." Her low laugh makes me want to hear it forever.

"Sometimes I don't even put a crease in my dress shirts."

"Shocking, lieutenant commander."

I grin and shake my head. "We should get together sometime. Unless it would upset your boyfriend or..."

My fingers sketch out the question, but it's a direct flick, the sharp cast of a fishing line.

Her delicate chin lifts, and she darts a tongue across her lip. The massive sapphire on her tiara catches the moonlight. "No boyfriend. No one to mind. I—"

This is the first time I've ever seen her in less than perfect command. Even tangled up with me in front of fifty cameras, she was more poised. Then she nods quickly and unclips the clasp on her purse, giving me a peek behind the curtain.

"What do you think those handbags hold?" my mother always asks. And now I know. A cell phone. Lip balm. An actual cloth handkerchief.

She hands me the phone and beckons for mine. I'm almost stunned, and she has to tug it from my grasp, our skin brushing for a brief moment. I stand there like the statue in the harbor of Horst the Invader, waves crashing up my legs, but she's already tapping her contact info into my device.

Holy hell, I can't believe it worked. I jerk from my stupor and navigate to her contacts, checking my number three times before I'm certain it's correct. Then I type "Max". That's all. Max. Like I'm Morrissey or Beyoncé or something. Maybe she knows dozens of Maxes. I want to elaborate so she won't forget: Lieutenant Commander Max Andersen From That Time I Touched Your Legs on National TV.

But before I can do anything more, the chime of the dinner bell echoes in the night and she plucks her phone back, trading it with mine as her escort—a chinless, inbred Lanagasquen if I had to guess—dashes out of the garden doors and waves.

"Coming." She gives me another smile and moves off without another look back. I glance down at the phone.

C.

I follow them, grinning, and I'm quickly relegated into a seat at the back of the banquet hall, so insignificant that a palm frond keeps brushing against my shoulder. The food is not as bad as I thought it would be. Only the soup course contains the dreaded fish, and as it is brought to each table, I glance at Clara, who is conversing with the chinless princeling. She wears the same look of interested pleasantness that I've seen a thousand times, and then, sniffing the soup, her nose twitches.

She's biting her lip and her eyes lift, flicking from their official line for a single heartbeat. Her green gaze lands squarely on me and I lift my brow. She gives the tiniest shake of her head, and though her mouth returns to its ordinary shape, I can tell she's laughing. I wink. *Vede*, how could I not? I have the satisfaction of watching her cheeks turn pink before she looks away.

After the final entree is cleared, the Vorburg ambassador raises his glass to toast the royal family of Sondmark. He praises the trade talks recently begun, vows decades of peace and prosperity, etc. The captain and his wife leave early, and I join them, satisfied at the thought of Clara's number on my phone. *Vrouw* Dusstock, who is nothing like the discus thrower of my imagination, fills the quiet car with her bright chatter.

"I hoped you would have a chance to speak to Her Royal Highness, lieutenant commander," she says. "Ah well. I had fun 'shipping' you two. Is that what the kids say?" she asks.

The captain grunts. "The lieutenant commander has too much sense to go chasing after trouble, Bette."

Captain Dusstock's wife might look tiny and fragile, but she is uncowed by her husband's gruffness. "Trouble, Art? She's a girl, not a bomb."

Captain Dusstock grunts again. "She's not a girl. She's a princess, and any link with her is trouble. A Navy man doesn't get himself in the newspapers."

"Unless it's his obituary, I suppose," she mutters.

Ten points for *Vrouw* Dusstock.

But the captain isn't finished. "Andersen wants to be a commander in a few years and captain after that. You want to know what the promotion board is looking for? Someone smart enough to keep his name out of the *flamen* papers."

"Language, Art." His wife shoots him a glare, and he offers her a conciliatory, apologetic murmur his crew would not recognize. "Well, anyway," she rattles on, "I did not favor her dinner companion in the least. Now, Princess Alma's escort was impressive. Pity she's already engaged..."

I drive back to the cottage in the dark, and when I arrive, I turn off my car and sit there on the gravel driveway. I swipe my phone from the seat next to me and turn it on, the glow lighting up the interior. If I were smart, I would listen to the captain and leave this kind of trouble alone, but I remember Clara's ballgown and the way it swished as she walked away from me. No one is that smart.

My thumb hovers above the keypad. Clara is still bound to be at the dinner. Or at the concert, if she has more duties.

It's too soon to text her, and anyway, what am I supposed to say?

Nice meeting you. That was a big tiara.

No.

As I look down at my screen, a message from my mother pops up.

There's a picture from tonight on *PAPZ*—a flash tabloid site—of me entering the Ambassador's house. Some careful photoshopping shows Clara when she enters later. We are juxtaposed, and the headline is the motto of the Handsel Company: *Semper Prope*. Always near.

Three dots bounce on the screen and then Mama's text comes through.

"I vote yes on a future of pinching chubby royal grandbaby cheeks."

I grunt and turn the phone off, swiping my keys from the car and going into my empty house again. Thinking about Clara...*Vede*, she doesn't even have a proper last name. Her job title is literally "Princess of Sondmark." I ought to be telling myself that someone like that is too expensive to think about.

I stay awake all night thinking about her anyway.

In the morning, I force myself to think about something else for ten miles as I run the trails around the lake. Smuggling, maintenance logs, high seas piracy. I'm tired when I come in and open the fridge, leaning in for a nectarine. Juice runs down my hand, and I grab a cloth just as my cell phone vibrates. A notification that my eye exam has been rescheduled.

It's nothing, but try telling that to my heart, which is beating out of my chest. It's time to take my shot.

I hit voice-to-text.

"Hey, Princess—"

Delete.

"Hey, Clara. Remember me from last night? Max Andersen. I'm the guy..."

Delete.

I turn off my brain and type quickly.

Send.

7

HELLO, PEASANT

CLARA

My ears are still ringing from the concert after the ambassador's dinner. Because I am young and someone needed to represent my family at the late-night event, I volunteered as tribute. I'm paying the price now and smother a yawn behind my hand.

"Tired?" Her Majesty Queen Helena asks from across the breakfast table. Everyone else has slipped away, and though I usually make it a point not to be caught alone under her basilisk gaze, I was not fast enough this time.

I nod.

I love my mother. Let me repeat that. I love my mother. She is brilliant, strong, bears up stoically under intense pressure, and cares fiercely for her family. Winning her respect, a goal I have been chasing since I was a little girl, would be an enormous achievement. But she is not a comfortable person to disappoint.

"You looked exquisite at the dinner," she says, gently dabbing at her lips. "The Minister of Finance made a point of telling me how much he enjoyed your conversation during the cocktail hour."

This all sounds like good news, but I tense and my suspicions are justified a moment later when she spins a newspaper across the table at me. I capture it under my hand. The picture is of me and Max Andersen in the garden, captured by a grainy cell phone camera. *Flamen.* When did that happen?

Judging by the expressions on our faces, I would say it was while we were concocting an imaginary, if vomitous, menu plan, and I have got to give the man credit for consistency. He looks like he's about to propose each time a camera captures us.

"Is this something I need to worry about?" Mama asks, her eyes narrowing in speculation. It's not really a question. It's more like a word-scrambled version of a command.

I consider a flippant retort, but I am not Ella, needling the institution of the monarchy like a spinal surgeon checking for sensation below the waist.

"I stumbled across the gentleman," I say, carefully choosing words that make me sound like something from the last century. My mother loves anything from the last century. Jodhpurs. Knighthoods. Dynastic marriages. "I thought it would be good form to apologize for the publicity. Was I wrong?"

Her eyes narrow still further as she assesses me for subtle rebellion, and I can see she isn't being fooled by my pat answer. My mother hasn't become the premier power broker in the North Sea Confederation by being meek and naive, but by vanquishing her foes mercilessly. I drop my eyes before her penetrating look.

"Not wrong," she allows. "But if you were to indulge this flirtation—"

My eyes flash for the briefest moment. Flirtation? What I have with Lieutenant Commander Andersen hardly rises to the level of flirtation. Standing out there on the terrace had been more like proximate awkwardness.

"—it could only end badly. The young man performs a vital service in the Navy, I understand. His career could be damaged by this and any association with him would be unwise."

My brows gather. "What does the Navy have to do—?"

"The press picks heroes and villains, champions and losers. For now," she says, tapping the headline, "you're charmed lovers, something they've plucked from a fairy tale."

I glance down at the paper. "Romance Under the Stars: The Little Princess and Her Summer Sailor." With so little to go on, the narrative has already been framed, just as she says.

"When, in the natural course of things, a relationship fails to materialize, you will be recast as the spoiled young princess, too good for a plain, honest military man. 'Who does she think she is?' they will ask. 'Aren't we good enough for her?'" Her head tilts. "They will either cast him as naive and ignorant, or calculating and socially ambitious."

Heat rises in my face, and I swallow away a hard, bitter knot. It's such an ugly view of the world. There are many facets of my mother I want to emulate, but this extreme calculation is not one of them.

Mama takes a sip of tea and tilts her head in a gesture of maternal concern. "Your reputation is…-unstable, Clara. These tiresome stories trickling out of your time in college—" She sighs heavily, as though a picture of me in a chicken wing eating competition at a dive bar is equivalent to a naked billiards game in Vegas. "You can ill afford—"

Heat and unease spread down my arms, settling in my stomach. I think of my phone number sitting unused in Max's list of contacts. "Of course it's not going anywhere.-"

She flashes a brief, official smile. "Excellent."

Caroline Tiele, Mama's private secretary, enters and gives a picture-perfect curtsey in her beige court shoes, the primness of her work clothes—buttons that go all the way up the neck and all the way down each wrist—nearly putting me back to sleep. "The prime minister's office is on the phone, Your Majesty. They have several suggestions for your speech you will wish to address quickly."

Mama nods to Caroline and sweeps out just as my phone gives off a ding. My heart leaps into my throat, already overcrowded with fresh-baked bread and mortification. I swipe up.

Max.

"Did you survive the pickled herring? This is a wellness check."

I squeak, clapping the phone to my chest, awash in panic. Didn't I just tell Mama this was going nowhere? But what am I supposed to do? He's engaging me in witty banter. I glance skyward, accusing the Almighty. *If you had wanted me to block his number, Lord, you would have made him pretty but dumb.*

My feet do a little dance under the table. Be cool, Clara. Be cool. My fingers begin tapping furiously.

"Yes. I have a pulse and everything. What's up?"

'What's up' is cool. As in, "What is up in your neighborhood, Fellow Citizen?" I groan.

Three jumping dots. My eyes follow them the way a penned-up border collie watches a tennis ball.

"A quick bite."

A picture appears and I laugh out loud, quickly swiveling my head to make sure my mother hasn't swooped back in like a lady-vampire. He's sent me an image of his plate. Three eggs, Pankedruss (My college roommates insist that Sondish yogurt tastes like death but that can't be true. My people love it.), a handful of berries, half a pig's worth of sausages, and toast.

"A bite? That's what you get when you sack a whole English village."

"The seas were rough this morning."

I shoot another accusing glance skyward and begin typing.

"A raid at dawn clears your whole day. It leaves time for an afternoon of pillaging." This is going brilliantly.

"Or housekeeping. You headed to Podense?" The next message arrives almost immediately. "Posters were up on base."

Well, well, well. Looks like a certain officer is not above a little stalking of his own. I am, indeed, planning to meet with the *Meesterin* of Podense and her husband for a tour of the city hall and a walking parade through town (behind the brass band and in front of the horses, as one would wish) while my brother and sisters are deployed in different areas of the country for the day.

"Yep. I can pillage this evening. Hope the tides cooperate."

Three dots dance and disappear and dance again on my screen. I'm holding my breath when the text appears.

"You should pillage my fridge. Come over for dinner?"

"What are you waiting for?" asks a voice behind me. "Answer him."

I emit a tiny scream and whirl around, my pulse pounding furiously. Ella is grinning.

"What are you doing, sneaking up on people?" I hiss.

"Sneaking up on people," she says. "It's my palace as much as yours, and if you hadn't been so absorbed with your boyfriend—"

"He's not my boyfriend."

"Why are we whispering?" she asks, winding one of her ginger curls up and tucking it back into her messy bun.

"Her Majesty," I begin, waving in the direction of the Crown offices, "would have an aneurysm." I shove the phone into her hands, letting her scroll through. I will be telling her everything anyway.

"Aw. You guys are adorable. I'm already on Team Clax." She wrinkles her nose. "You know what? We're going to workshop that."

I tug the phone out of her hands. "Whatever you do, workshop under your breath, maybe? I don't need Mama to find out."

"Find out that you've got a man? You were bound to find one sometime, Clara, even with the pronounced overbite and the geyser of drool."

I snort out a laugh.

"Anyway, you're legal in every country I can think of."

That's not quite true. Thanks to the Marriages and Succession Act of 1798, the reigning monarch and parliamentary bodies must approve the marriages of the first five heirs to the throne, and you'll never guess which one I am. Lucky number five. It had something to do with the scourge of Papist Uprisings. At least, that's what my constitutional tutor said. Though it's not nice to call them Papists anymore. Come to that, I don't think it ever was.

"She assumes the press is going to paint me as Vlad the Impaler, looting the countryside and drinking the blood of peasants, if it turns into nothing."

Of course, it will turn into nothing. I can't even let myself think otherwise. With this tiny, tiny text flirtation, I've merely pushed back the nothing a few hours.

Ella rolls her eyes. "Eat an Affelworst at a Dragons match and you'll be back in their good grace in no time," she says. We know how the game is played. Which papers to call. Which pictures to leak. Which levers to pull and which dials to turn to manage public perceptions. As much as I hate Mama's doom spreading, I hate Ella's brand of skepticism almost as much. Still, she's probably right.

I look down at my phone. I don't want to end this. I don't want to manage this. I just want to do it. It's just one dinner—enough to get him out of my system—and Mama doesn't even have to know.

I type.

"Time?"

Send. Ella shakes my arm with excitement.

"6." He follows that with his address.

"Can I bring something?"

Ella gives two thumbs up and an encouraging, "Very cool."

"How about dessert?" He answers. "Something easy."

I like that.

"Pickled herring *oliebollen*, it is."

Ella squeals loud enough to shake the chandeliers, and I clamp a hand over her mouth, dragging her behind the heavy curtains. "This is a secret," I command. "No blabbing it to every courtier and footman you meet. No rubbing it in Mama's nose. I want your promise."

Ella releases an irritated breath before her pinky wraps around mine. "Not a peep or I'll spend a night in the family crypt." That's as good an oath as any Princess of Sondmark can make.

"What are you going to wear?" she asks, puckishness returning to her face. "The Lauza Erdo number with the hat?"

It's my parade uniform and for that, she gets a poke in the ribs.

"It's only dinner at home." I lived in the States for four years. I know what actual people wear to hang out in. Sweatshirts. Crop tops with big flannels over them. Jeans or joggers. Tennis shoes.

The question is, did I get asked out on a date or a hangout? A frown must have settled on my face because Ella chuckles. "Oh, my gosh. Look at you, you're so cute. You don't even know what to wear."

I shake my head. "You ought to know how important clothing is." The war Ella has been waging with our mother over the matter of stockings has been going on for nearly a decade. Mama, as ever, is immovable.

The queen says that clothes communicate everything even before a princess opens her mouth. National pride? There's an outfit for that. Official grief? There's an outfit for that. Dedicating a new car park? There's an outfit for that.

I pull Ella out of the dining room and towards the grand staircase. We pass Alma coming in from an early-morning engagement at a farmer's market, and Ella gives her a wolf whistle as she walks backward.

"Hot date, Alma?" she asks.

"I'm engaged, infant," Alma replies, and I drag Ella into my suite before she can draw a crowd.

I sit at my computer and pull up ThumTac, the lifestyle site. Because it has to do with computers, Ella immediately shoves me aside while I explain what I want over her shoulder. "I need something that says—"

Her voice drops into a husky whisper. "Hello, peasant. Can I sample your wares?"

"Should I have asked Freja for help instead?"

"She'd dress you head to toe in medieval garb." Her neck twists and she looks me over. "Maybe you'd look good in a wimple. I don't know your life."

"I need an outfit that says, 'Though our attraction is doomed, I want you to be haunted by this one night for the rest of your life.'"

"Tall order." She starts plugging in keywords, and within seconds I'm presented with an array of choices.

"It would be better if it were autumn," she says, echoing my thoughts. There's nothing more dressy-casual than skinny jeans, boots, a button-down shirt, and a chunky scarf.

"A dress is too much, right?" I say, wondering if I possess anything that would be as light and casual as the choices I see.

"Shorts?" she asks, punching in more keywords.

Our faces contort into twin expressions of revulsion as soon as the search results pop up.

"No shorts." In this, we are one.

8

THERE BE DRAGONS

MAX

It would be ridiculous to drive over to Podense for the parade, and it only takes twenty minutes of fidgeting with my keys before I arrive at that decision. I'm not, however, above turning on the live feed while I scrub the inside of my oven. My place is neat, but I'm imaging how it will look through the eyes of someone who lives in a palace.

The sofa is a hand-me-down from my brother, none of the lamps match, and instead of artwork, snapshots of my family line the mantelpiece. I picked up a bouquet from the grocery store while I shopped for dinner, but when I see Clara on the television accepting posy after posy as she walks a rope line I wish I hadn't.

After lunch, I hear car tires on the gravel drive and pull my head from the broom closet and step outside to see my parents have come.

"What are you doing here?" I say, kissing my mother on the cheek, nodding to my father.

"Can't a mother visit her son?"

Not during Queen's Week. "Aren't you supposed to be organizing a parade float somewhere?"

My mother is short and cuddly, camouflage for her formidable nature. Only a fool would underestimate her and, as she reminds me often, she did not raise a fool.

"Don't speak to me of floats. Or glue. We put the finishing touches on last night," she tells me, "and my fingers are still sticking together." She holds her thumb and pointer finger like the bill of a hand-puppet duck, the skin stretching as she pulls them apart.

I follow her into the cottage, wondering if I can execute a maneuver where I march with her and then manage to turn us about without her realizing it. In my ingenious plan, she'd be gone before she knew it. "What was the theme?"

She arcs a hand as she punctuates the words, "Three Glorious Grains of Sondmark. We made a ship out of rye, sailing on an ocean of wheat, populated with fishes of barley. The dust was unbelievable." She brushes her hands with a grunt. "I'm switching to white bread."

I choke out a laugh. "Why did you come?"

She lifts a brow, but by some miracle, she gets right to the point. "Why haven't you asked out that girl yet? Don't you care about giving me grandchildren?"

My mouth dries up, but I have to remain calm. "Grandchildren?" I look to Dad.

He's wearing his customary summer outfit. Golf shirt. Long shorts. White tube socks. Loafers.

"Don't drag me into this," he says, taking a seat on the couch and commandeering the remote. He doesn't shift the channel, only turns up the parade coverage. There is a contingent of ecological protestors with patchy beards holding a massive papier-mâché representation of the Sondish coastline, a brass band is playing a traditional Sondish waltz, and the boozy crowd is seeping into the parade route to stagger drunkenly into one another.

"How's Susi?" I ask, sure their trip this morning took them past my sister's house. I willingly throw her under the treads of Mom's advancing tank.

"That one—" Mom starts.

I have half an eye on the television, watching Princess Clara's party coming down the road when fear brushes lightly down my neck. That crowd is too big, too loud. It's beginning to choke off points of exit in the medieval town square. I remind myself that the princess has guards to handle these kinds of things—people paid to see she comes to no harm. What in the hell are they thinking?

Mom bustles around the kitchen, opening and shutting cupboard doors, her voice hardly a buzz in my ear. Clara's detail stops her at the edge of the crowd, and she is approached by a stooped old man wearing his corporal's uniform from the great war. His medals hang straight off his chest and his back is a bow, but he salutes her in a formal fashion, and she smiles, saying something the mics don't pick up. She waves off her attendants and then she curtsies when he raises his shaking left hand. She fits herself neatly into the shape he has made for her, and he sweeps her into an old-fashioned waltz.

For a few moments, everyone, even the unkempt protestors, is entranced by this unscripted scene. The men wearing beer hats and face paint lurch backward as magic fills the square, and the borders of the parade route are quietly reestablished.

The brass band finishes, the old man spins Clara away from him in a flourish and a swirl of skirts. It's over. The man salutes. Clara curtsies. The parade continues.

"Would you look at that?" says Mom. A muscle jumps in my jaw. I have been staring at the television with heaven knows what emotions written all over my face.

But when I turn, she's staring into the fridge, her mouth hanging open.

"Max Josef Andersen," she begins, her tone sorely tried, "child of my heart, sunshine of my golden years, who are you having over for dinner?"

Vede. I glance to my father for help.

"Run for cover," Dad whispers with a chuckle.

There is no retreat, not under my mother's piercing gaze. Like any good officer, I quickly begin to shore up my position. "My personal life is—"

"No, no, there be dragons," Dad mutters from the side of his mouth, of no help whatsoever.

"His personal life?" repeats Mom, her voice pitched high and quivering with outrage. She's talking to Dad now, and he shoots me a glare. "He was a four-and-a-half kilogram baby, and I have an entire parade ground of stretch marks from growing him inside my own body. I race to the bathroom twice a night because his enormous head crushed my bladder to the size of a thimble, and your son has the nerve to talk about his personal life?"

"It's only a date," I say, attempting to head off the meddling.

"Liva?" Even now, Mom is careful about Liva, trying not to let me see how she never warmed to my last girlfriend.

"No one you know," I assure her, feeling a twinge of guilt. It's not quite a lie, and maybe being vague will work for once.

But her eyes narrow into tiny, triumphant slits. "I knew it. You asked her. You asked the—"

"Princess. Yes. I asked Princess Clara out. It seemed the gentlemanly thing to do after groping her on live television."

Mom tsks at my language, but Dad lands a large hand on my shoulder.

"Nice."

"When do we get to meet her?" Mom asks.

"Meet her? No. You're not meeting her. Dad—" I say, looking for an ally.

He stuffs his hands into his extra-deep pockets. "Nope."

"It's nothing serious," I insist. "Dinner. We'll spend the whole time making uncomfortable conversation about how we have nothing in common. Don't get any ideas."

My mother lifts a glass dish from the fridge and raps it with her knuckle. "This is your grandmother's sacred pork roast recipe, Max Josef. I served your father this meal on the night he proposed. I don't need to get any ideas. You've got plenty for the both of us."

"I'm supposed to feed a royal princess chicken fingers?"

She looks around like one of those old-lady detectives on TV that pedal through small towns and stumble over dead bodies. She sniffs. "Your house is particularly clean."

"It's always clean," I say, hoping she doesn't check the broom closet. If she sees the state of my grout lines, she'll be shopping for her wedding purse before she gets home.

"Why can't he just say he likes her?" Mom asks Dad.

Dad shrugs.

When she sees she can't get anything more from me, I walk them out to their car and Dad gets behind the wheel. I open Mom's door, and she reaches up to kiss me. Mom is so small, I was towering over her at fourteen, and I have to stoop. When I'm out on deployment, this is what I miss the most.

"Clara is my favorite," she whispers against my cheek like a cold-blooded assassin, palm against my face with her sticky fingers. "If you hurt that girl, I will murder you in your sleep."

By early evening, I'm contemplating pulling my white shower caulking out with some needle-nose pliers and reapplying it. The conversation with my mother plays on a repeating loop in my head.

It's nothing serious. Dinner.

Over and over.

But I'm not acting like it's just dinner. I'm acting like I'm being handed one shot at the thing I want most in the world.

At six, I hear the crunch of wheels on the drive. A more ubiquitous car, a compact blue Fiio, would be impossible to find, but it's her. I lean against the entry and wait in the doorway, hoping that the jeans and button-up shirt with rolled-up sleeves strike the right note. The sun is still high in the sky and we've got a few more hours before it gets serious about setting.

She swings her legs from the small car. Sandals, a summer dress, her hair loose. I ought to be breathing a little more easily now that I know both of us dressed for the same event, but my chest tightens.

"You look nice," I say, glad she's not wearing a tiara this time. Those things remind me of the gold braid banding an admiral's uniform; the eagle mounted on the hat. I assume the effect is meant to be intimidating. "Did you drive yourself all the way over? The road on that last stretch is winding."

Her smile lifts on one side. "I spent four years driving a manual transmission around San Francisco. I'm the best driver in the family. By the way, my security detail was poring over aerial maps of your place and they set up a position at the end of your drive," she says.

I approve.

She hands me a box. "You can pop that into the fridge," she says, lifting her nose to sniff the aroma coming from the kitchen. I hope the scent of lemon cleaning supplies hasn't lingered.

"You actually cooked?"

"You doubt me?"

She slides into the house and through the narrow entryway. I open my mouth to explain, apologize, something. It's just a house. The land is good, but I'm not wealthy and the place isn't meant to be a showpiece.

"I'm sorry it's not—"

"Nice," she says, standing behind my sofa, perilously near the table that wobbles if there aren't thirty-three pages of a *Sondmark Sport Fishing* magazine tucked under one of the legs.

"Thanks," I say, moving to take her light jacket. It brings us close and suddenly she swivels her head. For a second, we freeze. I wouldn't mind being rooted here for the rest of my life, but she steps back and tucks her hair behind her ear, a gesture I've never seen before. The girl on the television and the one in front of me are like a double exposure. I can't quite reconcile them into one person.

She smiles. "Sorry, I'm a bit nervous."

The admission is disarming, and my own apologies seem to evaporate in the face of it. I try to bring my mind squarely to face the fact that she is only someone I've invited over for dinner. I try to forget that I made my grandmother's sacred pork roast because this girl makes me lose my head. She has since the first time I saw her.

I lean against the door and hold the back of my neck to keep from reaching for her hand. "What's there to be nervous about?" I look around the room at the modest furnishings. Maybe she thinks I might try to bury her in the woods.

"I haven't been on a lot of"—her hand flutters in the narrow space between us—"whatever this is."

"A date?"

9

SUPPOSING THINGS

CLARA

I exhale, nodding. "That makes me sound like a troll. I went out a lot in the States. Clubbing, midnight runs to Penny's for pie and greasy fries," I say, naming a super cheap American chain with sticky menus wiped down with a damp cloth only periodically. "And there have been official meetings with Archduke So-and-so and his eligible son." He frowns at that, I notice, and my stomach does a little flip. I like Max Andersen's frowns as much as his smiles. "But I don't go on dates. Not that many people ask."

"Got it." He gives me a soft smile, eyes lightly skimming my face, and folds his arms across his chest. "You're not a troll."

Max looks even better in jeans and a plaid shirt than he does in his uniform, and that ought to be scientifically impossible. He asked me why I'm nervous? Her Majesty would not approve of me being here; has already warned me away from him. But instead of driving on by, I'm cranking the wheel and peeling off the exit like the cops are on my tail.

There is a tattoo peeking out from under the cuff of his sleeve, winding across the inside of his forearm—

I blink hard and tear my eyes away, mentally adding his tanned, muscled forearms to the list of my top three favorite things about him.

"Do you have a washroom I could use?" I blurt, attraction threatening to turn me into an idiot. "I can help you in the kitchen."

He points to a door and I slip in, gripping the pedestal sink with both hands and leaning towards the mirror. I conjure Ella. What would Ella say?

Get it, girl.

Ella is not a helpful shoulder angel.

Freja. What would Freja say?

Nothing. Freja would raise an eyebrow and go back to minding her own business.

Alma? Help me, Alma.

For the sake of your country, Clara, show some self-respect.

Thank you, Alma. My oldest sister can be counted on to remind me of my singular duty: Not ripping Lieutenant Commander Andersen's shirt from his back.

I pump some foaming soap onto my hands and hastily wash up, checking the cabinet for methamphetamines and homemade bongs because Modern Dating. I am relieved to find a full complement of flavored flosses.

Putting a cool hand to the back of my neck, I give myself a silent pep talk, reminding myself over and over that this has to be a one-time thing, and enter the common room.

The kitchen comprises the back wall of the cottage and looks out on a lake. It's small but tidy, and there is a pocket-sized table with a sharply pressed tablecloth set under a bow window.

"What can I do?" I ask, looking around. The smell from the oven, an aged and polished Aga, is making me drool.

He's standing at the stove stirring a pot and a hand towel is flipped over his shoulder. I wonder if he's a good cook or if he knows one dish and cooks it for every date. It seems forward to ask those questions.

"You can mix up the salad," he says, not relegating me to being a bystander. I unhook a tea towel from behind the back door and tie it around my waist, open the fridge and pull out the butter lettuce, cucumbers, tomato, and assorted other vegetables.

He hands me a large wooden bowl, and I dance around him to the sink, rinsing the greens and shaking them out. When I return, a knife is sitting next to the cutting board and he's bending into the fridge. I look to the ceiling and mouth my thanks. Max retrieves two bottles of berrybeer, popping the tops off with a flick of the bottle opener.

I accept one, trying not to let myself be affected by the simple contact of his fingertips brushing mine. There is a gold foil wrapper around the neck. "Royal label, huh?"

"Worse," he says, his eyes crinkling into a smile. "They're from Vorburg."

He takes a pull and I watch his neck, the swallow, feeling it in my toes. I am reconsidering the wisdom of handling a knife, but I remember Alma's imaginary exhortation and thump my drink on the counter, turning to address myself to the carrots and striving not to sever my fingers off by a lack of attention. A few minutes in, I've found a rhythm only by pretending that I'm in front of an audience talking about the importance of early childhood nutrition. The crowd is riveted and vows forevermore to limit certain simple carbohydrates. National healthcare costs plummet.

"So you went to Stanford," he says, and my hand slips, the blade landing hard on the cutting board. Heat rises in my face, but I try to answer briskly.

"Yeah. My brother Noah went to Yale and then into the military. Alma went to Harvard and spent another two years at the Sorbonne. Freja went to Arnhuis University and finished at Cambridge. When Ella went to Stanford, I followed her."

"But Ella and Freja are the twins, yes?"

I hate this. Hate it. My voice is as clipped as this knife. "Yes."

"Look," he says, putting his spoon down and turning to watch me butcher a cucumber. "I don't mean to pry, but it's weird to pretend I don't know things about you. If there's something I ask that's out of line or—"

"You weren't out of line." This cucumber is going to be juiced in another minute. A cord seems to run down my neck, tightly tied to another one binding my shoulders. I've spent the last year within the royal bubble, and I've forgotten how instinctive it is to curl up around my secrets like a hedgehog.

"I don't want you to get the idea that I'm fishing for information."

"I don't think you are," I murmur, lying. I set the knife down and turn only to find that the kitchen is even smaller than I thought. I could reach forward and hook a finger around his belt loop and tug him closer if I wanted to. A well of resentment floods through me. Why can't this be a normal date? Why did I have to arrive with all this baggage—Mama, the press, all those people back in California willing to sell their piece of my story. Why can't this be the start of something instead of the end?

"Don't you?" he asks, and he gives me a soft, undemanding, unhurried smile.

It's second nature to a Sondmark princess to be private—only trusting each other to bear our secrets. How do I explain that I have been betrayed by friends at school, teaching assistants, and roommates when the press comes looking for a story? It would be so much easier for me to handle this like I'm working a rope line—cheerfully royal, carefully remote. I can imagine pasting my smile on and skating through the rest of the night like it's an interview. But I can't imagine doing it while I am standing a foot away from him.

"I'm bad at this." My hand sketches the air in the little room.

"Making dinner?" He laughs, maybe offering me a way out of this awkward moment.

"Going on a date with someone I haven't known from the time I was toddling off to primary school. It's strange."

His stance is relaxed but I can feel the tension in his muscles. "I'm strange? Wait. Is this slumming?"

"That's not what I meant." I exhale impatiently. "I just—you know things about me that I don't know about you yet. And you found out those things from reading the tabloids or watching the news. Those aren't me."

This officially feels like the most pretentious thing I've ever said, and I once instructed a footman on the proper use of an epergne. It feels like the right time to pray for a sudden earthquake to open up the ground under my feet and end my misery. Is mortification a strong enough force to shift the tectonic plates? Probably.

He turns around to take the roast out of the oven, popping in a meat thermometer and grunting before setting the dish aside under a foil tent. It can't possibly taste as good as it smells. It'll be dry and overdone, despite looking so delicious.

He gives the contents of the saucepan a stir and turns around again, the plaid shirt stretching over his muscles. Those have been such nice muscles to be adjacent to for a time. I will miss them.

Max clears his throat. "I met someone and thought she was cute, so I googled her to make sure she wasn't an ax murderer. The good news is that she doesn't have a criminal record. I also know that she's twenty-four, looks exceptionally good in cardinal red, and has a few siblings. When I got the chance to ask her out, I took it. It's not a big deal, Clara. Only dinner."

He's putting me at ease, but I can't help feeling like a punctured weather balloon, slowly losing altitude. I feel stupid.

"You aren't stupid."

I blink. "Did I say that out loud?"

He laughs, the sound of it filling up the room. Mama's voice tries to crowd the sound out of my head. I can hear her telling me to march my Gucci handbag right out of there. I can hear her telling me that the press will make him look like a fool. But the laughter pushes her out instead. It's loud and real and not what I was expecting from someone who looks capable of launching a one-man amphibious assault. Though I thought his digital trail could tell me who he was, it didn't tell me everything.

"You finish the salad and I'll set the table," he says, bumping my arm. The gesture, offhand and friendly, seems to unstick the last of my reserve, and as we sit down and dish up the meal, my constraint slips away.

"This," I say, talking as I chew—groaning. My fork taps the plate several times and my eyes close briefly. "This. How—? Where—?"

He smiles. "My grandmother on my mother's side. You have her to thank. No matter how clumsy in the kitchen, every Henstrom learns this dish."

"The Henstroms," I repeat, diving in for more, "were culinary gods?"

He gives a short laugh, watching me eat. "Military. Long before Napoleon marched through Sondmark and back out again. Army, then. Navy now."

"Your father?"

"Oh, Dad's an insurance salesman," he answers, smiling as I drag a potato through this heavenly sauce.

"Much more comfortable for your mother."

He touches the tip of his nose. "I think that's why she picked him. Your brother served?" he asks, and this time I don't tense up or wonder what he's heard.

"Army. He served in Cherkout but he doesn't talk about it much." And that is an understatement. If Freja has unusually good boundaries within the family, Noah has an entire border wall. "The logistics it took to make sure he could serve with his unit as an ordinary soldier..." I spread my hands. "The press hasn't forgiven us for being so tight-lipped about it. Since he turned thirty, Her Maj—my mother," I correct but it's too late to head off his grin, "had him scale back his military work and has been having him do more work for The Shop."

Max takes my plate and stacks it with his by the sink. He grabs me another berrybeer (which is delicious, I am annoyed to find—nothing good ought to come from Vorburg) and leads me to the couch where I scoop up the pillow and sit with it on my lap.

I am not at all comfortable. My stomach is full and there are butterflies in any empty space. I wonder if there is anything in my teeth. But I am loving every second of this.

He settles on the other end of the sofa, crossing his feet and setting them on the coffee table, heedless of provenance, age, or the dead master artisan who created it.

"The Shop?" he prods me back to our conversation.

I smile. "The family business. That's what Ella calls it. She says living in the palace where we host official engagements isn't so different from living above a shop."

"She's the one you're closest to," he guesses and I tap my finger on the tip of my nose.

His eyes crinkle in appreciation. "And how do you like the family business?"

I get asked this a fair amount. People are curious, wondering if I'm like an elephant bred in captivity and oblivious to the tourists tapping against the glass. They think I'll tell them what it's really like. It's rare that I do.

I sit up very erect and say in a careful and cultivated voice, so at odds with our easy banter, "It has its challenges, certainly, but I am proud to carry on the royal legacy of service and sacrifice for my country." I slump back against the couch with a grin. "That's what I say if any cameras are pointed at me. The truth is a little more nuanced."

"Try me."

"King Frederick VI once beheaded an entire town of recusants—and, statistically, probably a few Protestants. The legacy hasn't always been one of self-sacrifice."

He chuckles. "Why sacrifice yourself when you can make some other poor bastard sacrifice himself?"

"Practically Frederick VI's motto."

He touches his forehead and begins mumbling. I catch on after a few beats and we recite the rhyme together.
Harald Dragonslayer, he was first
Then Fredericks one through five
Louis the Squat, we stopped at one,
Malthe came next, contrive
Two more Malthes, that's enough
Frederich the Wary was next
Freddy VI made up for that
Papists made him vexed...
We laughed our way through it, finishing it with:
Magda's son, he wed a cow
And went to chew his cud
The Crown passed down to Good King George
A prince of royal blood.
Queen Helena...
We stop at the same time, laughing a little awkwardly over the fact that, though we are sharing a bit of common history, the rhyme memorized while playing hopscotch or jump rope, Queen Helena is a real person to me in a way she has never been for him. The chasm between us opens up, but he does not let it remain wide, the wind whistling through the gully.

He taps my knee with the back of his hand and there are a series of tiny explosions under my skin, each nerve alive to his touch. "You were telling me about the family business. Do you mind the rules?"

I comb my fingers through my hair. "Not as much as you might imagine. Most have reasons for existing, and I've made peace with them. But the layers of protocol can be suffocating. Stand in such a way, dress in such a way, say such and such thing, don't say such and such thing. My mother is..." I search for a word to describe my dynamic, opinionated, epic mother who might, like her grandmother, earn the epithet 'the Great' before she's through. "She's from the old school. She likes things done in a particular fashion."

"But that isn't how Clara would do it," he observes.

"I'm not the queen."

His eyes narrow. "Is there any room for innovation?"

I bite my lip, really thinking about the question. Is there room for innovation? Ella fights for it. She's like a caged tiger, pacing along the wall of her pen each day, waiting for an opening, pressing against the bars. That's not me. I have a chance to make a difference in my role, and I don't want to waste it.

"I'm new to this full-time royal business," I answer. "I should learn the ropes first, right?"

He takes a pull on his drink, and I lose track of what I was going to say, awareness of his scent and proximity narrowing my vision to just him.

"I saw you today," he says. "At the parade."

My stomach clenches, but I toss the pillow into his lap. "Were you skulking in the crowd?"

He points to his enormous TV. "You were impressive. That crowd was getting out of hand, and dancing with that man was clever." At my skeptical look, he lifts several fingers and ticks them off. "You provided the crowd a locus of attention, highlighted a veteran, and gave your team time to reestablish order, all without saying a word. It was genius."

I'm not sure he could have said anything that could please me better. Mama delivered a scold when I returned to the palace today, asking what I would have done if the man had stumbled and broken a hip. But I stood there absorbing her words, unable to believe my instinct had been wrong. Max is confirming it.

"They're fortunate to have you." There is a tight, expectant silence before he grabs my drink and heads to the kitchen.

"Don't you dare wash up without me." I kick my sandals off and curl my feet up on the couch.

He calls from the back garden where he's scraping the plates. "Wouldn't dream of it. I want to know what you brought."

"I told you, pickled herring *oliebollen*."

"You wouldn't dare."

I giggle. "How are you hungry already?" That roast is settling into my tummy like a hiker in a toasty mountain hut.

"I'm a Navy man. We burn a lot of calories. What's in this box?"

I pad across the pine floor, knotted, scraped, bearing every scar of its existence, and swipe the box from him. "I wanted to make something myself, though, I warn you, if you hate it, I'm never going out with you again," I say. Then my rigorous training deserts me and I blush to the roots of my hair. I'm supposing things I shouldn't be.

The air between us is charged, and I wish for a time travel device that will reset the last ten seconds.

His gaze is heavy and intent. "I promise to like it." He swipes the box back.

I cannot breathe and then I start babbling. "It's chocolate tarts with raspberry sauce. We have a patisserie chef who huffed from the other side of the stove the whole time I was doing this, so I hope it's worth upsetting the entire staff just for your dessert."

I flip open the box and wait for his verdict. The tarts have suffered from the car ride and the whipped cream has completely slid off. I've never seen anything so ugly.

He gives me a wolfish smile and slides one tart into my hand, the other into his. He digs around in the utensil drawer for a couple of forks and hands me one. We're standing, in our bare feet, in his kitchen, scooping chocolate ganache into our mouths, getting it all over our hands.

"Thank goodness," he says, stabbing another bite. I raise my brow. "I don't have to lie."

10

— § —

NOTHING SERIOUS

MAX

I lean against her car, the deep bowl of the night sky curving overhead. The sun set so long ago that there isn't even the slightest rim of orange gilding the horizon, and light spills from the open door of the cottage. There isn't any breeze at all.

She reaches for her car keys, jingling them in her hands. "I had a nice time," she says.

I glance over at her profile and my heart rate kicks up another notch. It hasn't been nice. It's been hours of existing in a state of hyper-awareness and potential danger, each nerve stretched taut as all of my senses overload me with impressions and feedback. It's been like a man-overboard drill in the middle of a squall.

And I want more of it.

For a brief moment, I try to remember how it was with Liva—if I felt this way about her in the beginning, too—and discard the thought. Liva believed that if one of us was right, the other had to be wrong. No matter how inconsequential the topic, she had been unwilling to let each of us go our own way.

In these hours, I have found that this girl has a curious mind—uncertain, exploring, persuadable, and persua- sive. Attached as she is to such an entrenched institution, I expected Clara—my mind searches for a surname to attach to her—to be far more set in her ways.

"What did they call you at school?" I ask.

"What do you mean? I didn't have an anonymous identity. Lots of people knew who my mother was. Usually, at the beginning of the semester, someone would give me a hard time when I raised my hand in class, asking for silence for Her Serene Most Precious Highness or something. But that died down quickly. It was fine."

"No, I mean what name did you sign when you turned in your papers?"

"Oh. Clara Reike, after the duchy. It's customary."

"And your sisters?"

"Goodness, let me think. They are Alma Lowenwald, Freja Piskmont and Ella Sorstorm." She tips her head to the night sky, the light from the cottage a soft glow against her neck.

I can't take my eyes from her and my voice sounds rough in my ears. "And your brother?"

"He's the heir, so it's a little more straightforward. His military patch read 'Wolffe'."

"Was that strange? Not having a proper last name?"

She laughs, the low sound carrying in the night air. "Inconvenient for credit card applications, I understand, but a secretary sees to that."

Secretaries, a duchy...I think of my grandmother's recipe—of how much time and attention it requires to get just right; of how rich it is. In the Andersen family, it's meant to mark special occasions like the birth of a baby or a job promotion. If I had it twice a week, I'd get sick of it. My eyes stray to Clara again. It should be easier to remember what my captain said about promotion boards.

"I'm glad you came over," I say.

"I am too."

Her hands are positioned in front of her, clasped as though she is waiting for a basket full of violets to distribute, and the thought runs through my head that my job is not simple. Sometimes I'm at sea for weeks and months at a time. I don't draw a paycheck that allows for many luxuries, my ship is often involved in dangerous mine-detonation missions, we encounter traffickers, and occasionally come under fire. Every girlfriend I've ever had has found it impossible.

The thoughts come faster and more insistently, and my lungs constrict. My mother, bred into this kind of life, ran as far and as fast as she could when the chance came to her. A princess would run faster.

I catch my wild thoughts, curling my hands over the window frame, and take a deep breath. It's too soon to think these thoughts. It's too soon. I'm already looking down the road with Clara, seeing what it could be, wanting it. If I stay on this path, it's going to hurt.

Her hand touches my forearm. "There's the Big Dipper," she says, pointing to the constellation. "It's so bright out here."

"Big Dipper," I grunt in mock disapproval, wishing her hand would stay where it is. "Imagine a princess of Sondmark calling *Karlswagon* by an American name. The scandal it would cause if such a thing got out."

Her cheek curves with a smile. "I used to imagine Karl had his cart heaped with gold. What did you imagine it was carrying?"

She turns her gaze on me so quickly that I cannot think for a moment. "I wasn't dreaming of gold. I was dreaming of the sea." I lean nearer so that our shoulders touch and raise my hand, finger tracing a line from the back of the wagon until I reach Polaris.

"The North Star?" Her breath is warm on my cheek.

"It brings every sailor home." I forget all the things that worry me about us and speak. "Are you free on Friday?" I ask. "We could go to the—"

"Max," she shifts away and boosts herself onto the hood of her little blue Fiio. "I can't do this again. For one thing, going out with me in public is a circus." She sighs and there is no breeze to carry it away; it envelops us in sudden heaviness. "We're already in the newspapers. If we're caught in a pub or at a game, speculation will only ratchet up."

"You never go out?"

"When I do, the press has me married off within the week." She smiles in a self-deprecatory way. "That's a lot of pressure to put on kebabs and chips, and before you know it, it's all the press will talk about. You would be in the newspapers constantly and I can't believe your captain would approve. I have my mother to worry about. If I'm in the press every day, there won't be any focus on the engagements the Crown is sending me on or the people whose achievements deserve to be highlighted."

"Attention doesn't stop your brother. He must go out with dozens of women a year. Maybe he's got the right idea."

"What?"

"You should make them so numb to your dalliances that they stop paying attention. I could be the man who gets you started on the right foot."

Her eyes crinkle in amusement and then she tips her head. "I've been handing out violets since I was sixteen, Max. I could do it in my sleep if I wanted." The smile shifts, and though her lips have hardly changed shape, I can see the sadness in her expression. "My mother keeps giving me these make-work assignments, and if I want more responsibility, I have to earn it. So," she lifts a shoulder, "for the next few years, I can't afford more stories about my personal life in the papers. Even coming here once was a risk."

What are we supposed to talk about the next time Queen's Day rolls around and she's handing me flowers? The thought of being trapped into small talk on a parade ground with this particular girl is a nightmare. Silence lapses between us, and when it grows too strained she hops off the hood of her car. "I did have a nice time, Max. I don't get many nights as easy as this."

She fumbles for her keys and I take a gamble, unable, at this point, to calculate the cost. "What if we don't *go* out?" Her head jerks up, the keys are forgotten. "What if we *hang* out?"

Her eyes narrow. "What do you mean?"

I hook a hand in my pocket, an arm resting along the roof of the little car. I look as casual and off-hand as a naval officer can. I gesture to the cottage with my chin. "You don't want the pressure of being in public, but you like...slumming."

An outraged sound escapes from the back of her throat. "I did not call it that. There's nowhere for me—"

"I'm not asking you to complicate your personal life or do anything to get you full coverage in *The Daily Missive*. I'm asking if you want more nights like this one."

Her head tilts and her eyes shift as she considers my proposal. Her question is tentative. "Food and talking? What do you get out of it?"

"It's isolated out here." My eyes arc across the lake and into the deepness of the woods. I try to look unsettled by the fact, haunted. "If you come, I get some company. I get to make conversation with someone who doesn't have to salute me when it's over."

She chokes out a laugh and I know I'm winning.

"Come on, Clara. I'm offering to let you put your feet on the furniture and teach you mysteries all the peasants know. We never need to go out. Just dinner. Just friends. Nothing serious."

She opens the car door, sliding behind the wheel. The light illuminates her features and shows me a car that is devoid of even the smallest sign that it has ever been driven before. No dirty dog paw prints covering the rear seat. No wurst wrappers wadded up in the console. I have died and gone to heaven.

"No one has to know?" she asks, gripping the steering wheel. I lean over, resting my arms against the window frame.

I don't like this. I don't like secrets and I don't like loose ends. I don't like stepping into a situation with so many unknowns. But I like this girl and maybe that's enough. For now.

"No one has to know."

She nods once, intently. "Friday. I'll do it, I'll come. On one condition."

Having won my point, I am in the mood to negotiate. "Name it."

She looks up. "I'm making you dinner."

"Done." I lean into the car and brush my lips against her cheek.

Nothing serious.

11

—:—

CHOCOLATE CAKE

CLARA

Ella leans over my bed, her curly red hair tickling my nose. "Did he make a move?"

Early morning light slants across my eyes, and I shove her back, pulling the covers over my head so I can go back to thinking about last night.

"Not really." My voice is muffled.

She jerks the entire blanket from my bed like a nosy matador. "I thought this was a binary choice. Yes, he made a move, or no he did not?"

"He kissed me—"

"Yes!"

I shake my head which shuts her up. "—on the cheek. Like, an *Oh you forgot your umbrella. Here it is* kiss."

"No." She says it like water circling a drain. Nooooooo.

Ella flops back on the bed, jostling me.

The night was so good, but there is no way I could take his kiss as anything more than a polite salutation. Compared to Americans, Sondish people greet each other with kisses a lot, but compared to other Europeans, we do it very rarely. Perhaps Max comes from a kissing family. Perhaps he fell into the car and tried to make it less awkward. Discovering an answer to his motives feels harder than calculating the average airspeed velocity of a laden swallow.

I shake my head and slip from my bed. It's good I wasn't firmly kissed. I probably, almost certainly, very likely don't want that. I told Max it would be better if we became friends, and that wasn't a lie. It *would* be much better for my mother if Max were only my friend. But it wouldn't be better for my lips.

Padding over to the chair, I shove my arms through an oversized robe as Ella sits cross-legged, watching me. "When is the next date?"

"Who says there's going to be a next date?" I ask. It's an obvious diversionary tactic, but I majored in international relations, not theater performance.

"He didn't ask you out again?" Ella arches a skeptical brow, enjoying my one-man Liar McFibber Show.

"He asked," I concede.

"And you told him no?"

"I told him the truth. I told him that dating is a bad idea and that I didn't need the press attention on my social life right now."

That sets her back. She can't sense a lie because I haven't told one.

"Did he talk about football the whole time? Did he go on and on about his ex? Does he have bad breath?"

A smile steals over my face as I remember the floss hoard and his lips, soft against my cheek. When I arrived at his house, Lieutenant Commander Andersen's breath was like flying over a field of mint growing through the icy tundra.

"You are killing me, Clara."

"Friday," I say, and she shrieks. I do a running tackle, clamping my hand over her mouth. "It's not a date, and you can't breathe a word."

Her eyes are enormous, and she gives me a scowl before she nods her head. I don't let go until she raises her hand and gives me her pinky.

I return the vow.

"Friday isn't even a week away," she says, dropping her voice into an intense, high-pitched whisper. "He likes you."

I let her words settle against my intentions, absorbing them, wondering which of them is strong enough to dissolve the other. And then I stop wondering and repeat his words. "It's only dinner. We agreed that we're just going to be friends, and he said he needs company." Ella rolls her eyes and I whack her. "What? It was nice to go someplace the press doesn't follow, and it's not like I'm going to marry him or anything."

Ella laughs at the bare mention of the idea, and I cannot help the feeling in my heart—like a splinter being brushed the wrong way.

"Oh my gosh," she gasps, "can you imagine what Mama would say? I'll tell you what she'd say. She'd say, 'Is this why your great-uncle abdicated the throne? So the royal family could drag home every no account commoner who crosses its path?'"

The specter of my great-uncle hangs over the family, reminding us of our fate if we don't fall in line. Horst married a twice-divorced—and common—socialite and paid the price with his crown.

I frown at my sister. "And that's why she doesn't have to know."

Ella's expression shifts into one of dry skepticism. "Clara, she's the head of state. How do you expect to keep this friendly dinner club a secret?"

"I won't be taking a table at Minty's, waiting on the curb for the paparazzi to snap our picture."

"Okay, fine. You hide away in your culinary love nest—"

"Friend nest." We both grimace at that. 'Friend nest' needs some workshopping.

"But when you run out of things to say and meals to cook?"

I'm getting angry with her. "Then he can go his way and I can go mine. Not every relationship has to lead to booking Roslav Cathedral and getting parliamentary dispensations."

Mama has spoken endlessly about our duty to the Crown and what we owe our position. An alliance with a commoner has never been on the table. Max does not have a hereditary title or a museum named for his family. He hasn't saved the nation from mortal peril. Mama would never allow me to have him. I should be clear-eyed about that from the outset. I've done the right thing in limiting myself to Max's friendship. It is like sensibly taking one tiny sliver of chocolate cake instead of scarfing down the entire thing in one sitting.

Ella's brow lifts, and her mouth splits into a grin. "All right, this is a fun little game. You're just friends and it's just dinner. So, tell me it doesn't mean anything more. You've only been to his place once so far, and it shouldn't be hard to do."

It's impossible to do. I wondered if, after seeing him once a year and meeting in an official capacity for only a few moments, I would find the actual him a bit of a letdown. Imagination can run away with itself, I told myself on the drive over yesterday, only to discover, after a few hours in the homeliest circumstances, that my imagination hadn't done him justice. Max Andersen is the whole chocolate cake. No, he's the whole *flamen* bakery.

Instead of answering her challenge, I look her square in the face.

"Don't tell Mama or Père or Noah or Freja or Alma. Since you disapprove so heartily, forget you ever heard it."

I stalk into my closet, and she calls after me. "I don't disapprove, sister. I'm wild with approbation. I think it's the best thing you've ever done. But you're kidding yourself if you think—"

"Shut up, Ella." I poke my head out of the closet, tugging a sports bra over my head.

After spending several miles jogging around the palace grounds, I wind up at my godmother's cottage for breakfast.

"Come in, *elskede*," the old woman calls through the open window. Lady Greta is nearly a whole generation older than my mother and served as her chief lady-in-waiting for more years than I can count. She suffers from dementia, and these days, she keeps close to her cottage. "Maren made an English breakfast for me, and I had her set aside the fried tomatoes for you, in case you came."

I whip around to the front door and enter her morning room, sitting as primly as possible in my trainers and workout clothes. It's Freja who likes the fried tomatoes—and the blood sausage, come to that. But I don't correct her, only making eye contact with an apologetic Maren when she sets the tomatoes—somehow crisp and slimy at the same time—in front of me. I reach for a roll and begin to butter it.

"What are you doing today, Godmama?"

"I have an engagement with Her Majesty this morning at the—" She's silent for a long moment, snapping her fingers. Then she laughs. "It popped right out of my head."

It's one of Godmama's bad days. "That sounds fun. What are you wearing?"

"I'll wear a dusty rose coat dress and a flying saucer hat," she begins, eyes flashing with wicked amusement. "Not to be unkind, but Her Majesty is wearing yellow. She'll look like an overripe banana, but you can't tell that woman anything."

I bite down on the crusty bread and smile. Godmama's memory must be more than twenty years old. Mama's royal dresser hasn't brought the queen anything yellow in decades, and there are whole fashion websites devoted to solving the mystery—imputing political messages into the lack of that color in her wardrobe. I wonder if it's because Godmama did let it slip—the bit about her looking like a banana.

"What are you wearing?"

"Am I coming too?"

Godmama's utensils clatter and she gives me a fierce look. "Monarch, lady-in-waiting, security and private secretary." She stabs the air with the last, pointing her fork at me. "All essential. You're not trying to get out of an official engagement, Miss Hansen?"

Miss Hansen. A former private secretary. Again, Maren's eyes meet mine and I tighten my smile, absorbing the rebuke and taking on the persona of a stranger for the duration of my visit.

I gag down a quarter of one tomato and excuse myself, returning to the main palace for a quick shower before presenting myself in the conference room not far from the Queen's offices. It's an awkward but necessary meeting, the one time during the week Père can't avoid Mama and vice versa, pretending even to us that things haven't gone very wrong between them.

Caroline places agendas at each seat, organizing the staff to bring the preferred beverage for each member of the family. Coffee for Mama. Cappuccino for Père. Nothing for Noah. Sparkling water for Alma and Freja. Vestfyn for Ella. Iced Diet Coke for me, a habit I picked up in the States.

Noah comes in from Lily Cottage wearing Armani and a sober silk tie. He has dark hair like our father. The authority that must come with being the crown prince, as well as a soldier, sits comfortably on his shoulders.

The servants evaporate, and save for Mama's secretary taking up a seat in the corner of the room, there will be no equerries or comptrollers—only the family talking amongst ourselves.

The family being all together should create an environment of candor and ease, but there is the customary tension when my mother takes her seat at the head of the table. Père, his dark hair winged at the temples with a brush of gray and wearing his suit with the effortlessness of a man brought up on the shores of the Mediterranean, sits at her right hand. I try not to notice that he's got a faint, sardonic smile on his face as he stares at the middling landscape framed on the opposite wall. When was the last time they looked at each other? Public appearances do not call for shows of affection, and only within the cloistered walls of the palace do we know that they began keeping separate quarters last year after Grandfather died.

"Let us review the week," Mama begins, launching quickly into her agenda, listing off successful engagements and feedback.

"The burghers of Aunslev sent a note about your brooch, Alma." She picks up a hand-written card and reads, "How lovely to see the Princess Royal wearing a piece of jewelry created in our province, gifted to the Crown on the occasion of Queen Magda's coronation. Throughout the engagement, Her Royal Highness showed her care of the people of Aunslev in every gesture and represented the interests and concerns of Her Majesty with unparalleled grace."

Mama doesn't even need to say that Alma is flawless—she's glowing with approval. Her satisfaction in her children continues down the line. Noah hosted a luncheon with a group of business leaders group in Handsel and *BQ—Businessman's Quarterly*—has asked to feature him on their cover in the coming months. Ella watched an exhibition football match of urban youth. Her photograph in the local paper—appropriately hosed and shod—wins a rare smile from our royal parent. Mama asks if Freja's stamina was taxed by her visit to the Culinary Institute.

"Not at all," Freja assures her.

Mama concludes with, "Clara caused the only contretemps of note." Freja sends me a look of sympathy from across the table. She would literally prefer to be knee-deep in fragments of a medieval manuscript than hear our mother list our wrongdoings. "It was my wish that you keep a low profile, but there was that second picture in the papers as well as the dance along the parade route. Does anyone wish to share their thoughts?"

I'm always impressed that though her chair theoretically has the power to swivel, it stays absolutely still as she turns her head from one to another of us. Just as a petroleum magnate would solicit solutions for an oil leak, she serves me up as a problem to be solved.

"The dancing was charming," says Ella. "The press ate it up."

"It certainly diffused a tricky situation," agrees Alma, and I smile at her. Alma is engaged to Pietor, the Hereditary Grand Duke of Himmelstein, who is richer than Zeus. Mother matched them two years ago, and Alma has been dutifully preparing herself to be the next Hereditary Grand Duchess of Himmelstein, working to become fluent in the obscure, guttural dialect. She is the perfect princess—relentlessly proper—but doesn't let it get in the way of being a decent human being.

"Charm is not my concern. Popularity is fickle," Mama counters, and I mentally recite the proverb along with her, "but decorum is not."

"It would have been far less decorous to have a drunken reveler sweep me into his arms and spill his beer down my dress," I reply, borrowing a little of Ella's courage and a bit of Max's certainty that I am an asset at this table.

Mama's brow lifts in surprise. "That may be so," she agrees, and I wonder if Caroline Tiele is noting this in her minutes.

10:45 AM: Her Majesty Helena, by the Grace of God Queen of Sondmark and the Sonderlands, considers that Her Royal Highness Princess Clara might not have been at fault.

10:46 AM: Statement is greeted with shock.

Père looks proud—anyone willing to throw even the tiniest spanner into mother's well-oiled autocracy pleases him—as does Ella. Noah looks like he hardly notices the undercurrents. Village parades are well below his pay grade.

"Nevertheless," says Mother, sweeping my little triumph away, "we'll spend the next few weeks repairing your image. If you appear in the press, it will be because we wish you to. Press is a necessary evil as long as we're the ones in control of it. I expect a recommitment to discretion and prudence." She reaches forward with her pen and ticks that item off the agenda.

Though she doesn't say so, 'repairing your image' means she will instruct Caroline to give me only the most pedestrian and PR-friendly assignments for the immediate future. That means dedicating car parks and touring animal rescue centers. I am on probation. A lead weight hits my stomach, but I push it aside, vowing to redouble my efforts to win her trust.

Mama continues. "Celebrations conclude tomorrow night with the starlight parade. Alma will be joining me in the viewing gallery..."

She has moved on to more important things.

12

HER COMPANY

MAX

I work the next day and overnight, sleeping on a narrow bunk and slipping seamlessly into the rhythms of ship life. Stores must be replenished, a survey of repairs must be taken, a plan to address them sketched out. My hours are busy, and I return to my home on the lake to perform similar tasks for the little cottage. Replenishment, repair, and planning.

But this time as I navigate the green and blue border between worlds, Clara crosses over with me and back again, the thought of her like a spirit hovering over my shoulder. I save up interactions and observations, picking them up like a soft-edged seashell to be examined in an hour when we are together again. I look at my occupation through her eyes and wonder what she might be curious about; wonder if she will find it strange and unendurable.

And then I wonder if, like a child's pocket after a day at the seashore, the shells and sand will be dumped out and forgotten or saved in a glass jar with other keepsakes. Clara has been honest about what she wants—a little friendship, some light relaxation, a bit of easy companionship. I'm the one lying here, saying anything to secure another date when my feelings are—-well, I managed to keep myself from proposing as soon as she got out of the car, so that's a win.

Clara had worn a summer dress that skimmed her long tan legs, and when she'd taken her sandals off and padded barefoot into the kitchen to serve up dessert, I'd almost laid all my worldly goods at her feet: the keys to my well-kept, 15-year-old hatchback and the mortgage to a remote cottage that will need a new whitewash before the summer is over.

My brother Hals gets a couple of tickets to a Dragons game, and we join the stands, choking on red smoke bombs and chanting for our team. I get a few lingering looks and have to remind myself I've been in the papers recently. It will pass if I keep my head down. Hals asks me how things are going during halftime, and I shout back that I'm fine. The Dragons lose. I ride the light rail north, disembarking at my nearest car park. Two fingers brush a bronze plaque as I round a corner, tracing the name of my princess.

I spend the rest of the day working on the tumbledown rock wall around the front garden. No mortar, just muscling the rough stone into place, adjusting it until the fit is right. Clara joins me again, in a spectral sort of way, and I imagine her perched on the stone wall, her ankles crossed, telling me how to do things.

It doesn't matter that I stretched the truth about wanting nothing but a little company. The important thing is that I got her to agree to come back to my house. I grunt as the rock shifts, pinning my fingers. I jerk them free and nestle the stone where I want it. If I'm only going to get a few dinners, just as friends, I'm going to make them count, I think, putting a knuckle to my mouth before I reach for the next stone.

I finish repairing the section of the wall I've been working on. I run before dinner. When night falls, I can't help myself from picking up my phone. I've gone as long as I can without talking to her.

"Hey," I type. "You should know I only have one oven. You might have to bring that seven-course meal down to four."

Half an hour later, she shoots back, "I'll take the *Spicy Ostepops* Pork Rolls off the menu."

"I must have those."

"Lost. Lost forever."

"How dare you dangle sketchy processed foods in front of a military man?"

It's late now and I'm lying in bed, hitched up on one elbow as I read. The lamp casts a small pool of light, and I can hear frogs out near the lake. This is why I live here—the solitude, the silence—but here I am, reaching for her company.

Three little dots drum on the screen and I grin.

"Quick Q. You have a sterling silver shrimp peeler, yes?"

"Do I look like a man without a sterling silver shrimp peeler?"

"And a pair of shark-mesh oven gloves?"

"What have you been googling?"

"Only 52 *maarke* with shipping!" The message comes with a picture, and I enlarge it. Clara's excited face, her finger pointing at the sidebar of her computer screen. There's a photo of a shark biting on the hand of a smiling chef who is also somehow holding a hot roasted chicken. In the background, I can make out an antique table and lots of soft green and creamy white.

I roll onto my back and touch the phone to my forehead for a moment. Now I have somewhere to imagine her, which should help me sleep.

"How was your day?" I type.

"Research, online shopping for a few events. You?"

I snap a picture of my scraped knuckles. "Working on the cottage. We're still on for tomorrow night?"

There is a longer pause this time. "See you then."

13

— : —

BLURRY ABS

CLARA

His knuckles look bad, but the blurry abs behind them look very, very good. For a second, I'm tempted to call Ella in so she can work some of her computer magic—sharpen the lines, clear up the cloudy graphic, project the image on the massive palace wall like some tourism advert. *Visit Hot, Hot Sondmark.*

I'm still thinking of them in an unfriendly way an hour later, and I kick off the covers, grabbing a robe. I could press a button. Someone from the night staff would answer and bring me a snack, but this kind of wide awake, overheated restlessness can only be assuaged by digging through the freezer and stumbling on the ice cream bars at the back myself.

The kitchen is down a couple of flights of stairs, and my fingers brush the polished mahogany handrail. Unlike the chipped and rusted metal railings at Stanford, these probably won't leave a swipe of dust across my backside. At the head of the last stretch of stairs, I crane my neck, eyes narrowing on the dark hallways. I see no security guards. There are no disapproving courtiers. I hop on, and in a whoosh I'm bumping off the bottom and landing on my feet. I've still got it.

Lights flicker to life in the kitchen, and I bend over the icebox, grasping a box of fudge and hazelnut chocolate bars, when a laugh spins me around. Alma. My oldest sister appears regal even in her nightclothes.

"What got you out of bed?" she asks, her blue silk robe billowing behind her like a cape. If only the paparazzi could get this picture. Slay, queen, indeed.

I shrug and lift the box, tipping the opening to her.

To my surprise, she nods, and I toss one over the silvery workbench. She catches it neatly, though I'm puzzled by her presence. Did she hear me creeping down the hall and follow after me? Were there worries keeping her up as well? Alma is easily the most self-contained of my sisters, and it is difficult to imagine her indulging in tears or contemplation or midnight chocolate, but here we are. We drag a couple of stools across the tile floor and sit side by side, eating our ice cream—me licking steadily at the drips and her taking dainty bites. I finish before she does and I drop my wooden stick in a nearby bin.

"What brings *you* to the dungeons on a night like this?"

"Nothing," she answers, quickly. I sense her breathing shift, her shoulders relax. "Nothing. I have a long week coming up, and I can't get out of my head."

"Nightmares of pickled herring getting you down?" The Vorburg state visit this February will demand a lot from the House of Wolffe, requiring events and study for months ahead. The whole autumn and winter filled with choking down their treasured national dishes, training herself to tolerate them without a grimace, will be enough to haunt the dreams of any self-respecting princess.

She stifles a laugh. "Something like that."

"Is Pietor coming for the state dinner?" It's the least he could do. A less attentive fiancé would be difficult to imagine. Pietor is currently spending weeks rowing across the Atlantic with a crew of schoolmates in aid of heaven knows what. The Society to Prevent Plastics Pollution, maybe.

She nods and then her wooden stick follows mine into the trash. "Don't let Mama make you feel bad about that officer," she says, and the blurry memory of super-hot manly abs clouds my vision for a second. Just dinner, I remind myself with a mind's eye spinning and whirring the dials to get them in focus. Nothing serious.

I'm happy where I put him—in a box labeled *Friends of Clara*—but I am anxious about the packing tape securing the box. I'm worried that it rattles and claims my attention. Everywhere I look, there are scissors to slice it open.

Alma is still talking, and I jerk my focus to her. "It's that she imagines a scandal hiding around every corner."

"Can you blame her?" I ask. "All those notorious uncles. The House of Wolffe came very late to the respectability party."

"And brought the gin," she laughs.

It's only then I realize how rare the sound of her laughter is these days. I pick up her hand and examine the antique opal monstrosity that is her engagement ring. I wonder if she's happy about the choices she's made—the careful engagement with a wealthy scion of a noble house. The amount of space he gives her—whole oceans, sometimes. I wonder if Pietor has any abs worth losing sleep over. Maybe a few after all that rowing, but Himmelstein is known for dense facial hair. There are national songs about it. I wonder if Alma cares.

A long silence stretches between us, and my sister stands, tugging me along and out of the kitchen. "You don't need to worry about finding your place in the family. Jump through Mama's hoops and it'll come."

"Thanks," I whisper, the glow of hall lamps making golden lily pads of light against the crimson carpet. When she turns to her room, the blue robe is billowing again, and it's hard to remember I wasn't walking with a queen. I return to my room and lie awake all night.

On Friday, I wake early, going on a run through the wooded grounds of the Summer Palace. Too many white-tailed deer dot the misty parklands, and I enjoy the sight with a little twinge of guilt. The herd is due to be culled, the venison sold with the Royal label in upmarket grocery stores—an idea thought up by Noah. Unlike in the days of Harald Dragonslayer, the Royal family doesn't use the massive medieval kitchens or need to feed an entire court each day. The deer will remind people of their heritage as well as go to funding maintenance costs. That's what the Bambi-slayer says.

I pop in on my godmother for a few minutes, watching her deadhead a pot of geraniums in the bright sunshine with hands that have forgotten nothing. She tells me to fetch Ansgar, and I wonder if that's a former gardener I'm meant to remember. I spend the rest of the morning reading materials on an upcoming engagement in Vaado—memorizing the history, innovations, and pertinent facts of an auto manufacturing firm.

Her Majesty is hosting a garden party, and in the early afternoon, I present myself in a tea-length gown and Prada block heels on the steps leading down to the wide lawn as a celebrated pop star does her best to soften the national anthem. Noah gives a short speech about Mama's dedication to Sondmark, and I notice Père's jaw tighten. The press hasn't caught wind of that rift, but I feel the sword swinging above all of our heads.

Courtiers and guards walk ahead of each one of us as we cleave through the crowd, guiding us to selected guests. We are introduced, exchanging a few words, and I find myself saving up impressions to give to Max. I meet an heiress in shocking headgear (a bedazzled trucker hat, complete with plastic size-adjusters at the back) who runs a charity devoted to beautifying abandoned land between the highways by planting native wildflowers. She presents me with several seed packets, and I hand them off to a courtier discreetly. Then there is the man who arrives in full court dress...from three centuries ago, his curly mane of hair almost certainly a wig. My heels manage the spongy garden grass very well, and I plan to tell Max all about that too.

The whole thing passes so quickly that I'm shocked when a courtier whispers in my ear that it's time to retire.

"You did very well, Clara," Mama says, slipping the gloves from her hands and striding through the great hall, slightly ahead of the rest of us. Père is ignoring the pace that she has set, and he is strolling along on Ella's arm, laughing at some joke she's told. Mama's clicking heels halt, and I catch her watching my father with an intent, almost stricken, expression. I feel my hand lifting to touch hers in silent sympathy, and then she blinks, hardening her gaze and turning it on me. She looks fully in command again. "I like to see such single-mindedness."

My smile doesn't reach my eyes, my hand drops, and my insides squirm with guilt. Single-minded? Yes, I am exceedingly single-minded.

Visit Hot, Hot Sondmark.

14

LUTHERAN BABIES

MAX

When she arrives at six I want to lean up against the door frame and kiss her until her shoes come off. Six is exactly on time. She can't know what punctuality does to me.

"I thought you brought dinner," I say, craning my neck to look behind her.

She pushes a button on her key fob, and the trunk pops. "Help me with the boxes?"

I expect to see pre-packaged dishes—pressed sandwiches and salad with hand-carved carrots, purchased from Bette's food hall—but I lift my box, inspecting the contents. "Are we making paella?"

She looks over her shoulder as she goes up the garden path, the sun turning her hair into the color of one of my mother's Glorious Grains of Sondmark, and gives me a smile. "Something like that. It's a dish from Pavieau. My father taught us all to make it when we were children."

Pavieau. There is no good response when she brings up her father's family. The history is well-known. The small country on the Mediterranean coast was ruled by a military dictatorship for the better part of thirty years when the generalissimo reversed course and reinstalled the old king to the throne. Protests and riots broke out in Handsel when young Queen Helena honored the marriage contract with his second son, Prince Matteo, making him her consort. Even now, you'll hear old people mutter that they thought they were getting a homeless prince and got a fascist puppet instead. Poor Queen Helena, they said, and the parliament made an addendum to the ancient coronation oath.

Talking about my grandparents is not so complicated. They live on two sides of the same city, giving each other grief about opposing football teams when they meet for weddings and baptisms.

Clara sets her box on the counter and busies herself with unloading it, not meeting my eye. "The food there is good."

Her words rush from her mouth, and I feel guilty, wondering if she felt the need to justify something as simple as love for her father. I shift the box and set it down beside hers, eyes widening.

"I was only kidding about having a sterling silver shrimp peeler, you know," I say, lifting a bag of shrimp.

She laughs, the thin film of tension between us broken by a strange kitchen utensil. "I never travel without one. Have you ever used a shrimp peeler?"

"I'm in your hands."

She grins at that, pulling me to the sink, demonstrating the process with a neat flick of the wrist. Then she sets the peeler in my hands and pulls a new dishcloth from the drawer. I look away from the sight of her tying it around her waist and fumble with the task.

She chokes out a laugh. "This way," she corrects, hands guiding mine through the mechanics. I am completely useless with her so near and I'm tempted to keep getting this wrong so she can keep teaching me.

"You've got it," she pronounces, turning her face up to mine. "Can you do it?"

I take a sharp drag of air and wonder if I could convince her that friends kiss now and then. She begins to set out her supplies, moving around the kitchen, but every atom I've got is aware of her.

"Music?" I finally ask.

She nods and I wipe my hands. Going to my dad's old hi-fi set, I slide an LP from a stack and slip the record on the player. Soon, the room fills with the soft scratch and smoke of Miles Davis, settling like pliable mortar into awkward silences. I can breathe again.

"Did you always want to live in the country?" she asks, dumping the shrimp, rinsed and patted dry, in with shallots and garlic. Her hands move competently, and a hiss is followed by a fragrant cloud of steam. I lean against the counter and watch for a while, wishing that we could skip to the part where I have the right to slide up behind her and kiss her neck.

"Max?"

Vede. Who knows how this will last? Who knows how long she will be in my cottage, calling me by my name? I can't afford to skip any parts.

"What?"

"Why don't you live on base or have an apartment in Handsel near some bar?" she asks, turning to me.

I pull the dishcloth off my shoulder. "You know those garden plots by the central train station?"

"The allotments?" She brightens. "Yes. My great-grandmother started that scheme."

Of course, she did.

"Well, my great-grandfather bought one. The Andersen family allotment has a shed that has been yellow, orange, purple, and then yellow again, and we are in a long-standing boundary dispute with the Maagensens. Every year, my mother plants enough potatoes to get us through another world war and puts up jars of produce. We tidy it up for winter and go out too early in the spring to tidy up again. In the summer, we sit beside fires and listen to the trains coming in from across Europe. When my parents give it up, it will go to my older brother."

Unexpectedly, she giggles.

"This is my great tragedy." I give her a mock-wounded expression, but she continues to laugh, her words breaking with amusement.

"I didn't know the laws of primogeniture applied to garden plots."

"Five years to get another, Clara. Five years on a waiting list for a plot without a yellow shed, or encroaching grapevines, or neighbors I've known since I was born."

She smiles. "Is it a hard thing to be a second son?"

"Is it a hard thing to be a fourth daughter?"

Her smile checks and the bright resonance of jazz trumpet plays in counterpoint to the meanderings of a piano. It isn't awkwardness between us now, only the magic of finding things in common where we least expect it.

"So, faced with the prospect of your ancestral lands entailed away to another..." she prods, and I flick her elbow with the towel.

"I went off to make my fortune. When this cottage came up for sale, I was fortunate to have saved enough money. I didn't have anyone to consult, so I jumped on it. My family has a place to retreat in high summer, and I can grow a few things."

"Your own kingdom." A dimple tucks her cheek, and she turns back to her big pot of 'something like paella', stirring. "Oh," she starts. "I brought you something. It should be in the bottom of that box."

"Isn't there a rule about royalty giving gifts?" I say, pawing through the container. I wonder if her royal status is like snake venom; if you can build up immunity with enough exposure. Perhaps, soon, it won't even register that she's headed home to a palace or likely to be discussed on the morning news.

She laughs. "There are only rules about receiving them."

My hand closes around something slim. Seed packets. I hold them up with a question on my face. When she nods, I read the quote on the label.

"Wildflowers on the Verge: Filling the in-between spaces with beauty."

"It's a charity that spruces up neglected areas. I didn't go shopping or anything," she hastily assures me. "I only got them from this absolutely mad woman at a garden party today, and I thought they might look nice along your wall."

I press a palm to my chest. "It's wonderful for taxpayer morale, knowing you re-gift things."

She grins. "Noah does so like it when we're thrifty."

"And you were thinking of me," I say, trying to work out how many steps were involved to make this happen. Princess receives the gift, aide whisks away the gift, princess requests the gift, princess brings the gift along, princess proffers the gift with suspicious casualness. One, two, three, four...

She raps the wooden spoon briskly against the skillet. "You'll have a fat head if I say yes."

I already have a fat head. Clara was thinking of me, and I can feel the carefulness in her manner. I'm trying to be careful too, feeling along the border of what this is and could become. It feels like friendship but also like I'm holding on to a downed power line, jolting with an electric current.

It is not simple and it is not clear, but I lean in, moving slowly enough that she'll have time to rap that wooden spoon if she wants. But she doesn't. Only holds perfectly still and closes her eyes as I kiss her lightly—my lips landing half on her cheek, half not. In between.

"Thank you," I say. I'm fascinated when color runs up her cheeks as I straighten. "What's the rule for receiving gifts? I suppose I'm not allowed to give you a yacht."

She turns back to the not-paella and stirs, pulling the spoon out and letting the drippings run off. She puts her finger against the spoon and licks her knuckle. I want a do-over of that kiss now. "Pepper?" she asks and I hand her a pepper shaker in the shape of a Delft windmill.

"Do you want to give me a yacht?" she asks, smiling.

"I've got a little sailboat out there—"

"It's not the size of the gift that matters. You could offer me a lifetime loan of a tiara, an entire estate for peppercorn rent, and so on, but the catch is that you can't expect anything back. No invitations to the Summer Palace, no access to the Queen, no hospitality or services that would place any member of Sondmark's Royal Family under obligation to the donor."

"Quite official. Is that in writing?"

"It is, actually. We have something called The Red Book—tooled leather. It smells heavenly. It's a sort of how-to guide to ruling Sondmark and goes back to Malthe III. Every generation adds to it."

"The same rules exist for the Navy," I sigh, sliding the seed packets across the counter. "I'd have to report this to my Captain and..." I shrug helplessly, but my smile has something calculating in it. "It's out of my hands. Nothing to be done."

"You have rules about receiving gifts in the Navy?" She slides the packets back, leaning against the counter, chin propped in her hand.

"It's a matter of national security." I hunch over, crossing my arms, getting down to her level, and slide the packets across again. She slaps her hand down over mine and now we're touching.

"Strictly speaking," she says, a wicked glint in her eyes, "this isn't a gift. It's a few homeless seed packets."

"Homeless, huh? Sounds like we need to work out a joint custody arrangement."

The not-paella is a little overcooked. She says I distracted her at a critical moment and it's my fault the bottom of the pot is covered in scorched rice. But we take our dinner onto the back patio, and I light a blaze in the fire pit so that we can eat in deep plastic chairs. She holds her bowl like an oversized mug of hot cocoa with her legs curled underneath her.

"What are your plans?" I ask, returning from the kitchen after refilling our bowls. She lifts her brow and I explain. "The Navy is straightforward. I work hard, keep my record clean, and in a few years I'll get a command of my own—small crafts at first, larger if I do well. What's the career path for a princess?"

She bites along her lip. "The eternal question." Her fingers trace the faux-grain of the plastic. "A few hundred years ago, it would have been more straightforward. My education would have been good, but probably not as good as my brother's. When the time came, I would be betrothed to a foreign prince. Likely, I would have sailed away from Handsel and left my family forever, writing to my parents often, and spying on my new husband and his court full of intrigue and perfidy." I nod. "An alliance would be strengthened, and I would continue serving my purpose by making lots and lots of Lutheran babies."

"My niece is a Lutheran baby. I'm quite partial to them." With a laugh, she kicks me lightly, but I capture her heel, setting it on my knee. She leaves it there and blood warms in my veins. "If that's not your path, what is?"

"That remains to be seen. Mama only has one sibling, and up until a few years ago, we leaned hard on Uncle Georg to help shoulder the duties of the Crown. But there are five of us now—all adults. A lot of patronages were handed out while I was busy growing up, and I'm not sure how much they need me, trailing at the end, having not yet been taught everything my siblings already know."

"Not everything can be taught," I murmur, recalling the way she interacts with a massive unit of sailors every year, managing to make every one of them feel like he's an admiral of the fleet. I tug the laces on her sandal. The knot springs free and I give her a look. "Massage?"

She smiles, wiggling her toes. "Is there anything you can't do?"

I slip her sandal off and work my thumb up the narrow channel in her foot. She sighs, the sound of it like an ember spinning up from the fire, extinguished in the soft, night air.

"I don't need paid employment, heaven knows. I aim to find a charity that needs me and speak about it as loudly as I can for as long as I can."

"Your whole life, then." I move on to the ball of her foot and she sinks back, her eyes drifting shut. The careful friendliness slips from my face, and I look my fill at her features picked out in the firelight.

"The press won't be interested in me that long. Noah will have a family someday, and I won't be so close to the Crown. I can expect a momentary spike of interest for every scandal I'm involved in, another spike when I marry, and smaller ones with each Lutheran baby."

I smile. Eyes closed, she smiles. My hands still. I want to pull her out of her chair and into mine, but I don't trust plastic Scandi engineering.

This wasn't supposed to happen. I was supposed to remember that my commanding officer has the power to sink my career, relegating me to a future of obscure commands and insignificant clerical work, if I don't stay out of the press. I was supposed to get Clara to the cottage and find out that she's like a fish out of water—find out that she tiptoes around my house and sniffs at my hand-me-down furniture until she can make her excuses and go. I was never supposed to forget she is a princess. But the truth is that she treats this place like she belongs here.

She opens her eyes, and I hastily rearrange my features. She glances at her watch, tugging her foot from my hands.

I want to touch her again, maybe in a bout of arm wrestling, but she swiftly ties the laces of her sandal and stands. "I have to get back."

"Do they pull up the drawbridge at midnight?"

She pulls me out of my chair, walking backward towards the house. "Help me with the boxes?"

It's friendly but I'm still holding that live wire, tense all the time and aware of every breath she takes, frustrated out of my mind.

"When are we going to plant the flowers?" I ask as she slides into the driver's seat.

"We have a bunch of preparations for the state dinner with Vorburg."

"That's not for months. February, right?"

"You wouldn't believe how much there is to get ready," she says. "If I could come in the morning sometime—"

Hell, yes. "Wednesday. Sunrise."

Her brows lift. "That's five o'clock."

"Oh, I see. You're one of those soft Handselites."

She rolls her eyes. "Five it is. You'd better feed me breakfast."

15

JUNIOR ASSOCIATE

CLARA

I glance at the time on the dashboard, my fingers drumming anxiously on the steering wheel. I didn't mean to stay so long. There's a logbook in the gatehouse that switches out at midnight, and I am bound to be the first, obvious entry if I don't hurry up.

Maybe these gymnastics are silly. My security team also knows exactly where I am, with whom I spend my time, and how long I'm out—there's no getting around these frustrating realities unless I take Ella's advice and entirely bypass the security system. But, I remind myself, pressing down on the accelerator, no one (by which I mean my mother) will go snooping over the records and asking awkward questions about my movements as long as I don't give them a reason to.

I am cutting it close.

As I pour out of a roundabout, I remove my earrings, snatch a make-up removing towelette and scrub it haphazardly over my face. At a stop, I pull my hair into a ponytail and grab the linen bag with the bright logo emblazoned across it from the floor and plop it conspicuously on the passenger seat. When I slip the car into its slot in the old stables, I shoulder the bag and follow the illuminated path towards a side door of the palace, my heart thumping out of time.

"Hey."

I yelp, adrenalin surging through my veins. My breath breaks from my lungs when I see it's only my sister.

"Oh. Hey, Freja. You startled me."

"Gone shopping?"

With clammy hands, I lift the bag, full of books from a recent trip to the Handsel booksellers market. They aren't for show. I did buy them. I will read them. No lies have crossed my lips.

"Going out?" I ask.

She shakes the short, auburn hair from her face. "I needed a walk. The final review for my exhibit proposal is tomorrow."

Instantly, guilt shoves my worries away. Freja hasn't been able to talk about anything but organizing an exhibit of Sondish Romantic painters for months, and I've been tuning it out.

"Of course the museum board will sign off on it. Who would say no to a princess?" I laugh. "Especially one who works for free."

She doesn't laugh with me. "You're right." I catch a certain wistfulness in her voice but she is half in shadow, her face hidden from me. I should drag her under the pool of light and make her talk, but she turns crisply on her heel. Then, a few paces away, she looks back. "The book stalls closed hours ago. Next time think of a better excuse for being out late."

I make it to my suite before anyone else sees me and draws all the right conclusions. I toss my bookbag on the bed, glaring at it. Maybe if I had more girlfriends living in Handsel, I could credibly use one of them as a cover ("I'm binge-watching *Five Minutes to Marry* with Brigit tonight. Wine and cardigans..."), but all my closest friends are in America.

I flop backward on the bed. Maybe that's all this thing with Max is—loneliness and pent-up frustration. It's hardly surprising that I feel at such loose ends when I spent four years immersed in rigorous studies and campus events only to return home and feel under-used and itching for a challenge. Maybe this interest in Max can be chalked up to the sudden deflation of going to places where I *am* the event, meeting people who come to glimpse a tiara and look vaguely ill-done-by when they don't.

Ping.

Like a zombie rising from the grave, I lift my phone.

"We left your shrimp peeler in the sink." He has attached a photo.

I make the image larger, propping myself onto my elbows to get a better look.

Just as I thought. There are some nice, Sondmark-grown abs reflected in the kitchen window. I release my fingers, the image returns to its original size, and I flop backward again. If it were anyone else, I would think he was doing it on purpose. I expel a breath like an old woman at a Lars Velmundson concert. The sliver of abs was just that. A measly sliver.

"I had fun," I type, padding to the closet for a change into my nightclothes. "No problem if Wednesday doesn't work out."

It's a pleasant text. Noncommittal. I don't want him to feel like he has to have me over. It must be difficult to navigate a relationship—a friendship, I remind myself for what feels like the millionth time this week—with a member of the royal family; difficult to create healthy boundaries when he pledges an oath of allegiance to my mother.

Healthy boundaries. I return to brushing my teeth with more vigor, a line forming in my brow. Nearly everywhere I go, people thrust bouquets into my hands, and I am treated like, well, a princess. If Max were one of the *adel*, it might be different. The hereditary nobles of Sondmark are the worst, most stuck-up, self-regarding club in the world. They don't think being a princess is anything special. At a guess, I'd say they even pity me, knowing that they can splash themselves all over social media, live on a yacht for three-quarters of the year, and name their children Guava or Hum without answering to anyone.

If one of those peacocks said he wanted to spend time with me, I would know he meant it. But does Max have much of a choice? Is he thrusting bouquets at me? Metaphorically, an inner voice reminds me as I floss.

Ping.

"Soft city girl. 5 isn't too early. I want to see you."

I stare at the message for what seems like a long time, mechanically walking around the room and switching off the lamps, slipping between the sheets.

"Clara?"

"Go to bed, sailor." The word is supposed to sound like a gentle insult, but it takes the complexion of an endearment and I draw a breath, knowing with sudden clarity that I'm not lonely and this has nothing—hardly a sliver, really—to do with his abs. I like Max Andersen, and I will like him in five years and ten and twenty. More, even.

I'm not laughing but an unaccustomed feeling of laughter runs from the tips of my fingers to the pads of my feet as I struggle to hold on to my intentions. Friend. Max is my friend. But my neck is warm, and I am smiling in the dark as I finish my message.

"I want to see you too."

Morning dawns with an unseasonal thunderstorm, the sound of it rolling over the distant ocean, rippling with white-capped waves. I've been thinking all night, and I reach for my phone, pulling up my contacts, and prod the circle next to Madam Secretary.

"Good morning, *Vrouw* Tiele," I type. "If possible, might I arrange a meeting with my mother today? Alone. A quarter of an hour would suffice. Regards, etc., etc."

Though it's shockingly early, I don't even have to wait two minutes before Caroline pings me back with a time, accompanied by the suggestion that I arrive a little beforehand. "Her Majesty will fit you in between a meeting with the ambassador of Zouvier and a conference call with the trade commission."

This is her code for telling me that my meeting will not be allowed to go a second over.

I spend the morning working out in the gym, keyed up and oddly annoyed at Max. He didn't prod me into confronting my mother, but something about the way I feel when I'm with him makes me chafe against Mama's glacial timeline for bringing me fully on board the family business. I was content to wait for her pleasure before Max came along, filling my head with ideas about my talents and gifts.

As the hour to meet my mother approaches, I arrive in the administrative wing wearing low heels, stockings, and a conservative skirt and blouse. My hair is coiled neatly, and my make-up is giving me a precise and radiant glow. I wish things were different. I wish that I could breeze into the kitchen and have a chat with my mother while I rummage through the fridge—but even at her most casual, I know that business questions must be addressed in a business-like way.

Caroline is at her desk in an anteroom—a door to her right leads to the Queen's office and a door to her left leads to the Queen's formal receiving room—and greets me with a pleasant smile, indicating a chair.

"Her Majesty will be a few minutes, Your Royal Highness. May I get you something to drink?"

I shake my head as I subside and look around, not often finding myself in this corner of the palace. Caroline's office looks exactly like her. A couple of terrified potted plants grow on a ledge by the window, careful not to overstep their bounds, and a discreet copier/printer looks as elegant as possible perched on a William and Mary side table, the power cord apologetically slinking off behind some drapery.

Caroline herself has managed a wardrobe even more modest and self-effacing than my own. A dark blazer is draped on a thick wooden hanger, ready to be donned in an instant, and she is wearing an uncrushable jersey dress in muted tones. Her shoes are black, and her make-up is so unobtrusive as to be almost non-existent.

I am stirred from my examination when a tiny light on her desk flashes and she touches a button, dousing it. On goes the blazer. On goes a bland, pleasant smile. Out she goes through the door on her left.

Mama breezes through the small anteroom a bare minute later, Caroline on her heels. One of Caroline's small nods tells me that I should follow my mother into her office, and I do so without any fuss, closing the door behind me.

Her Majesty sits behind her desk. Rain lashes the windowpanes, and I dip an unconscious curtsey, waiting for her to begin.

"What is it, Clara?" she asks, unceremoniously.

My words to Max tumble in my head, just as they have all night. It was so easy to tell him what I thought. I can't wait for a patronage that matters. If I only have a few years to carve out my role in the royal family, I need to start doing more than absorbing the spillover from events no one else wants or attending engagements to which I have no connection. I have to find work that will sustain me for years.

I want to say all this, but the words are thick on my tongue.

"It's about a patronage," I manage, and Mama brings her hands to the desktop, lacing them together. Does she know that she looks like the famous Dragon of Sondmark when she stares at me like that? "I feel it's time to take on an assignment."

Her brow notches. "The charities are divided between working royals, and there are no patronages to be had, at present. A review is not scheduled until next year."

I am tempted to apologize for taking her time, but I think of Max—of the family garden promised to his brother and five years on a list to get an allotment of his own. I think of circumstances beyond his control and how he found a path to get what he wanted anyway.

"I would like to research the patronages and—"

"How would it look," Mama begins, "if a charity were simply tossed from one member of the family to another like a hot potato? Would it look like we had its wellbeing at heart or our own?"

"I didn't mean—"

"No one expects you to know." She smiles and I feel five years old again, standing on a tarmac with my hand tucked firmly in Lady Greta's, waiting for my mother to finish being the queen. "You are getting something no one else got, and goodness knows I could have used: Time to acclimate yourself to your role before taking on the burdens of it. I was your age when the Crown passed to me, and it's a wonder I wasn't crushed. You have a rare opportunity to find your feet and prepare yourself for when the moment arrives. I'm certain you will make the most of your time."

I've binge-watched all seven seasons of *Chicago Law* three times. I know this is the kind of speech a partner would give a junior associate, hoping to squeeze 80 hours a week from her subordinate. Yet her words also make me feel uniquely qualified for my present position. Honored by my mother's consideration.

I curtsey.

Only when I'm standing on the plush carpet of the hall do I realize I haven't gotten even a sliver of what I came for.

Wind rattles the glass door at the end of the hall, and I brush shaking hands against my sober skirt, lifting my chin to return to my suite. I pass officials and courtiers, housemaids, and distant family members. My mother shut me down so effectively that I'm half impressed. The other half of me is shattered.

I think of Max and wonder what it would be like if I ever stood in front of Mama and told her I wanted him.

16

Hot Skillet

MAX

A car has been on my tail for the last kilometer, at least. I adjust my rear-view mirror, pulling up at the base gatehouse.

"Identification," the guard says and I present my badge, eyes scanning the road behind me. Green Ciprio. Older model. This is the third time I've noticed a car like that following me into base. It's gone, disappeared up one of the side streets before the gatehouse and I shake my head. A few clandestine dates with Clara have made me paranoid that someone will find out and alert the papers. But it's hilarious to think that a quiet dinner or two would make the news. Our last appearances in the press had the novelty of highlighting fashionable public events.

The barrier lifts and I drive through, parking my car and heading to the HMS *Thetis*. Before I'm halfway up the gangplank, I smell the aroma of fresh paint and spot some sailors with long-handled brushes working near the water line, evidence that my orders have travelled successfully in a line from myself to the lieutenant, chief, ensign, and sailors.

After mustering the crew, I meet with my department heads on the helicopter deck, as far removed from the memory of last night, of the mellow warmth of the fire and the girl with laughing eyes, as it is possible to get. Inspections commence in a few days, and I dole out assignments to each department to inspect a counterpart's area.

"I'm coming on those tours," I announce and watch the lieutenants sit up. There's no shifting or nervous looks jumping from person to person, only curiosity at such an unusual order.

"So you'd better get your *riv* in gear," a voice barks. The scrape of folding chairs echoes in the large bay as we stand and salute. The captain dismisses the heads who have, by now, begun to exchange nervous glances, and I follow him up to his office.

"At ease," he waves, sinking into his chair. "Inspection tours, Andersen? Bit beneath you."

"I don't know this ship like I need to, sir," I answer. I've only been aboard a year. There's a lot to learn. "The crew don't have anything to fear in my oversight. I trust my lieutenants to see that my orders are carried out."

"Trust," Captain Dusstock laughs. "We don't 'trust' in Her Majesty's Royal Navy. We stand over our sailors until they make a deck so clean you could serve your Sunday pot roast on it. If they so much as sneeze, your job is to put the fear of God in them."

He scrawls a note across a paper and looks up, regarding me from a brown, weather-beaten face. His gray eyes are the color of the ship he captains. "There are dozens of lieutenant commanders looking to make commander in the next few years, and I don't like your chances. The ocean doesn't say please, Andersen. It doesn't have manners. Carrying lieutenants around in woolen mittens won't prepare them for it, and holding everyone's hand on an inspection tour is a waste of time." He tosses the pen down, and it bounces before it settles. He flicks his nose with his thumb and crosses his arms.

"The promotion board is going to rake over your record with such a fine-toothed comb that they'll find the socks you left on the bathroom floor last week. You give them anything—you give *me* anything—scandals, your name all over the tabloids, soft crew management, the smallest whiff that you don't have 'Navy' tattooed down the length of your lower intestine, and you'll find yourself steering a river patrol for the rest of your career. Am I clear?"

"Yes, sir."

Still, I spend the week poking my head into every supply closet, wardroom, berth, and canteen the ship has, poring over engineering drawings after hours. I wake Wednesday morning in my cottage, half expecting to see a late-night text from Clara bailing on me. It's 4:30 AM and I kick the blankets off, throwing on a t-shirt to go downstairs and start the coffee the way my mother insists is the only right way. She might actually die if she sees what passes for coffee aboard the ship.

Slicing several pieces of dark rye bread and taking a couple of eggs from the fridge, I lay them near a pan before jogging through the back door and into the pre-dawn stillness. I trace my footsteps down the familiar path, hearing the soft thumps of the sailboat bumping against the dock. In moments, I bait a hook and cast a line out over the smooth water. Now I only have to catch a fish before the sun comes up.

The flashlight is my friend, and I feel a tug not much later, just as I hear the crunch of gravel on the drive. Clara finds me on the dock as the sky is lighting, though the rim of the sun is still sunk below the horizon.

"Mmmm. I love fish," she says, leaning over my shoulder, her hand wrapping my bicep. The way her breath stirs against my ear threatens to overcome me. I inhale a lungful of air. She's only wearing a pair of jeans and t-shirt, I remind myself. Nothing to cause this reaction.

"Do you love to catch them?" I ask, offering her the pole.

I don't expect her to take it, but her grip is confident and she bounces the rod lightly. "Two kilos," she guesses.

This woman. We are lucky she knows how to do this. I wouldn't be able to maintain a posture of disinterest if my arms were wrapped around her, guiding her movements. "I'll start the eggs and toast," I say, hands in my pockets.

Clara's green eyes dance. "We're having *smorebrod*? Ah, Max, that's my favorite."

I nod, jogging back to the cottage, each step loosening the band around my lungs.

After reeling in the catch, Clara follows me into the kitchen and asks for a knife.

"There's a flat rock out there I use for cleaning," I say, handing it off by the blade, a little surprised a princess knows how to gut a fish.

"I saw it." Even when I'm not looking at her, it feels as though my body has developed the senses of a bat, locating her position in the room and the curve of her face when she answers.

I toast the bread, and she brings in two slim, white filets to lay into the hot skillet. They only take a few seconds to brown and serve up.

She eats in contented silence, adding dollops of sour cream to each bite. "Do you do this a lot?" she sighs, popping the last bit of egg into her mouth. "Fish for your breakfast."

"To tell the truth, it's usually toast and *Supernuss*."

She sighs contentedly and carries our plates to the sink where she turns on the tap and leans back, craning her neck.

"Under the sink." I brush crumbs off the table with my hand and she finds the scrubber.

She says over her shoulder, "I didn't expect—Max, I could get used to this," like I've given her a kingdom. I want to step behind her and hold her around the waist, fitting my chin in the crook of her neck. *Friends.* The word is like a cul-de-sac. There's no going through it to some other destination. So I dry the plates and put them away.

When we move to the garden, I hand her a battered shovel and an old pair of gloves. "I haven't prepared the ground at all. Work has been—" My hands spread.

"Wisely, you waited for an expert," she says and when I raise a brow she transforms before my eyes. Gone are the work jeans and t-shirt. It's like she's standing in heels and a dress as she poses, hands resting lightly on the shaft of the shovel, camera-ready smile, the firm plunge of the spade into the soil and a quick flip.

She dusts her hands. "There we are. I've just inaugurated the Historic Andersen Cottage Wildflower Gardens. I hope you put up an enormous plaque to commemorate my visit."

"Historic Andersen Cottage, huh?"

"Won't you be making history out here?"

I like that, the way she has of expanding the borders of national tradition to include something so small. I nod at the overturned dirt. "That was impressive."

"Maybe you could tell my mother that?" she murmurs, turning the soil over in earnest as I work on my section. "You could offer a testimonial. Review me on the internet or something?" Her words are amused, but I detect a trace of frustration underneath them.

"Doesn't she think you're impressive?" I grunt, working at hacking at a ball of roots and earth with the sharp tip of the spade, giving her space to decide whether or not to answer me.

There is a long silence, broken by the bird calls churning the air near the woods and the steady slip and slice of our shovels. I let it be and continue down the line of the wall.

Clara works behind me, taking a finer, secondary slice at the clods, finally saying, "Sometimes she looks at me like she thinks I'm the one who's going to single-handedly take down 800 years of rule."

I lean an arm across the head of my shovel. "You never put a foot wrong."

She shakes her head, unimpressed by my clever reference to her stuck shoe. "You are hilarious."

I grin. "If anybody is likely to bring it down, I would think—" I halt.

She shoves her tool into the earth with a thunk, leaning her elbow on the top, hand dangling, just as mine is. Her slim wrist is a feminine contrast to the old leather gloves, and I spend a second imagining it set against the back of my neck.

The look crossing her face is a playful threat. "Don't you dare, Max Andersen. Tell."

I can't resist her glowing skin and the martial glint in her eyes. It is good that the morning is cool because I am already too warm for comfort. "My money is on Princess Ella."

"Ella?" Her brows wrinkle. "Ella wouldn't hurt a puppy."

"She looks like she's plotting."

"No more than seventy percent of that expression is plotting. A solid thirty percent is because Mama won't let her wear glasses out on official engagements. The contacts bug her."

I turn to my work with an amused grunt. "Myopic royals. They're just like us."

Clara tosses a bit of earth across my boots and her laughter drowns out the birds as we set to, spading around the base of the rock wall I built with my own hands.

"How's work?" she asks, returning to the point where I spread my hands and didn't answer. Now it's the easiest thing in the world to tell her about the captain who wants to drum me out of the Navy and the long hours spent going over engineering plans. It solves nothing, but it feels good.

"Enough?" she asks when we come to a bend. The sun slants over us, running her shadow into mine.

I draw the seeds from my back pocket and toss a packet to her. In a few moments, we've shaken them over the ground and walk, pressing them into the earth. I fill a plastic watering can and hand it off to her.

She stares at the abomination. "The watering can is in the shape of a pig, Max."

"I know it's a pig, Clara." It's so bright and pink that national defense satellites have probably picked up on the fact.

She tips it forward and bites her trembling lip when two thick streams of water come pouring through the snout.

"My niece uses it when she visits."

She only grins and hands it back, boosting herself onto the rock wall, making real my daydreams. I can feel her eyes on me as I finish my patch and stow the garden tools. I return, leaning at her side, arms resting across the top of the wall. The exhaustion of the week is seeping from my bones, the air fizzing like carbonated water.

"Do you know how mad my security team was when I asked to be covered for this time slot?"

It's not even six yet. I lift my brows, and she makes a volcano noise, her hands an explosion of fire and ash. I choke on a laugh.

"How many people know about—about this?"

She gives a throat-clearing cough. "Three security personnel and Ella. Five if you count Freja. She caught me sneaking back the other night, and I had a streak of eyeliner smeared all the way to my temple. I think she suspects something."

"You know it's ridiculous keeping an activity as wholesome as sowing wildflower seeds a secret."

"Hey," she bumps my shoulder with her own, "aren't *you* keeping...this," she pauses at the word, "secret?"

"This?" I ask, stepping closer, treading on the delicate seeds that haven't even had time to take root. The laughing smile slides away from her mouth as awareness threatens to surface. Even though we don't say it, we know that there's a silent conversation between us that runs in tandem to everything we say and do, making the air hum and crackle with electricity every time we're near each other.

I open my mouth, not even knowing what I'm going to say, but she hops from the wall. Our eyes lock. Somehow over the last few weeks we've lost the uneven balance of a scale. I sometimes forget she's royal. Maybe she forgets that I don't have a trust fund and a title. We're people who have a 'this' and the right to know what it is.

But the look in her eyes. Uncertain. Unready. I can't press her right now. I give a short nod and she slips away.

17

Historically Speaking

CLARA

I slide into my seat at the weekly family meeting with seconds to spare, damp hair curling at the ends from my hasty shower. Mama is still conferring with Caroline, sparing me a glance as I reach for my glass.

"Have you been out running?" Alma murmurs. "I'm looking for a partner—"

"Not it," I say, touching my nose quickly.

Across the table, Ella giggles and touches her nose. "Not it."

Freja looks confused, but everyone knows not to rope her into anything that requires a partnership of any sort. Alma shakes her head at our antics, and Mama calls the meeting to order. For the first half-hour, she covers a slate of the usual news, sprinkled with a few events in conjunction with the Vorburg Embassy.

I peek under the agenda to my calendar. Once again, my portfolio of items is thin. Mama didn't hear a word I said this week.

Ella doesn't bother to leaf discreetly. She paws through her papers and lets out a groan. "Lepus Leaping? You're sending me to Lepus Leaping. *Stultes es*, I've seen that on the internet," she says, crashing her head on the table and beating it a few times over and over. "Why does Vorburg have to be so weird?"

Mama gives a tight smile. "We don't call neighboring countries about to drop their trade tariffs in a historic deal *weird*, Ella," she chimes.

"If you can't call rabbit show jumping weird, then the word is meaningless."

"It's also no concern of ours. If you feel you cannot maintain an attitude of polite interest while observing a cherished national pastime, I'll give the engagement to Clara."

I perk up. My schedule is certainly open even if she has made it sound like I'm the last resort.

Ella's face is still buried in her notebook, red curls muffling her words. "They're going to make me try to get a rabbit to jump something. At least let me wear tennis shoes."

Mother's smile is as smooth and tight as the series of dams holding back the North Sea. "You will wear court shoes and stockings. Now," she dismisses my sister, "Clara, you're slated to deliver a speech on solar power this week. I don't have to tell you that it's an opportunity to test your mettle."

Solar power. It's not my favorite topic, but I give a nod and begin to scrawl notes, ideas already forming in my mind. The sun is warm. It makes me think of coziness. I can dig up a quote from Copernicus. "I'll write something up."

"No need," comes her brisk reply. "I asked Caroline to compose a suitable address. It's quite short. You only need to read it."

Père makes a small growl at the back of his throat, and I glance over towards him as Mama's secretary leans forward and slips the transcript of the speech next to me.

Though I am irritated and resentful that, once again, Mama seems to be tightening the bolts on my training wheels, I'm too shocked to linger on the feelings for long because while Caroline Tiele is leaning across the table in all her beige glory, Noah is noticing her, looking at her like I admit that I wish Max would look at me. Noah. His Royal

Highness Crown Prince Noah. My brother who attends international events with a rotating cast of women who model for Gucci and Dior when they're bored and survive on a diet of cigarettes and the smell wafting off freshly-baked cookies. That brother. My mouth drops open.

He's looking at her legs, I want to shout, running around the room and grabbing arms, shaking them. Our Bambi-slaughtering, fiscally-prudent, granite plinth of a brother is looking at the court shoe-wearing secretary's stocking-clad legs.

"It's nothing you need to worry about, Clara," Mama murmurs, mistaking my expression. I snap my mouth shut and avert my eyes before Noah can catch me staring. I blink the shock from my face. "Don't be upset."

That's right. I'm supposed to be irritated that, once again, I am denied an opportunity to show her what I'm capable of. But it's like I'm running across a swamp. My shoes are sucking in the mud, and everything is happening in slow motion.

The harsh sound of Père scooting his chair back draws all eyes. "'Don't be upset.' You may take that as a royal command, daughter," he says, the remnants of his Pavian accent furring his words. He gives the briefest nod in the general direction of the head of the table, collects his informational packet, and saunters out without a backward look.

Such a tiny gesture of defiance, but in the restrained, mannerly atmosphere of the Summer Palace, it has the effect of a bomb detonating. My sisters and I exchange sharp, darting glances. It's hard to breathe. Mama watches him go, lips compressed, sinews tightening in her neck. Then she, too, blinks her face into its official mask.

"I think that will be all," she says, setting down her pen and skipping almost a third of her agenda.

"Clara," she says as the others file out, "I'm sure you'll do a fine job." She sweeps from the room, and Caroline, carefully juggling three binders and her laptop, follows.

I collect my papers, hurrying after Ella, wanting to drag her into my room and inform her that the man breaking hearts all over Europe is ogling our mother's uptight secretary. My sister is going to die.

The notion of watching her face as I tell her has me walking at a brisk trot down the main hallway of the administrative wing. I take a shortcut through the ballroom and skid to a stop at the bottom of the grand staircase when one thought catches me.

I remember this morning, hopping down from that rock wall and turning my face up to Max, unable to look away as the cool morning air swirled between us. The soft atmosphere had been one of expectation. An unresolved chord.

"This" he had said, and I hadn't needed to guess what he meant. I knew. Though I drew a line for us days ago—a bright, friendly line—it has blurred since then. I'm conscious of how often I want to push my hand across it, erasing its presence altogether.

The thought of Max and me being fodder for laughing, back-channel family gossip—each conversation weighing his suitability in Mama's eyes and finding him wanting—makes me feel a knotting aversion. I don't want to turn our soft summer nights, and one sparkling morning, into one more thing my family has the right to have an opinion over. I can't have that, not when I'm not even sure what I want.

I hear the gentle click of a door shutting along the upper hallway. I'm not going to chase Ella down, I decide. If I deserve some privacy, Noah, despite being gripped by some inexplicable, beige-curious madness, deserves his. And I bet Caroline would be horrified if she knew the crown prince was having amorous thoughts about her figure.

So I wind up alone in my suite, reading quickly over the text of the speech Caroline has written. It's correct, just as everything she does is correct.

"...innovative technologies..." "...providing support to critical infrastructure..." "...owe it to these scientists to provide..."

This is all Mama thinks I am capable of—something short and rote. Two brisk paragraphs, complete with stage cues. Raise glass. Pause. Nod left and right. Take my seat.

I scrub my face with my hands and try to remember my mother's prescription for getting more meaningful assignments. Serving the Crown is not about what I want for me. It's about doing what needs to be done. I know it. I set the text on a music stand and position myself in front of a full-length mirror. "I am delighted to be here with scientists and innovators in the field of renewable energy..."

I go over it again and again, until the delivery is smooth.

When my throat needs a rest, I ring for a snack. When it arrives, I wander down the hall to knock on Freja's suite. There's no answer, but I follow the music into her office. This is one of my favorite places in the palace. Instead of the bright, Scandinavian atmosphere found elsewhere, Freja's office has been fitted out like a dark, cozy British library. Rich, subdued jewel tones thread the carpet, finely aged leather covers deep chairs, stacks of books and paper litter every surface, and she's got too-loud Italian opera playing as she works. I switch off her sound system and she gives a startled, "Oh."

"I could have murdered you and you'd never have known it," I say, offering her a roast beef sandwich. Within the family, we've nicknamed Freja "The Lone Wolffe." She would have starved until dinner if I hadn't come, bearing protein and carbohydrates to sustain her through her studies.

She eyes the food with delight. "What an upsetting thought."

Tipping back in her chair, she tears the crust off and places it neatly to the side. "What brings you to my lair?"

I'm chewing away at my sandwich, remembering fresh-caught fish and dark rye bread—the man who made them for me. "What did you think of the meeting today?"

"Père leaving as he did?"

I nod. During my years at Stanford, the subject of royal marriage did not concern me overmuch, but I am older now, far closer to the time when Mama will introduce me to the heir of some ancient, hyphenated duchy and expect me to do my duty for Sondmark. Other royal houses have love matches, but not ours, not yet, and realities must be faced.

"No one's screaming and none of the heirloom china is being smashed, so that's good," I say. I can't even imagine such a thing happening within these walls. Mama and Père are in a cold war.

Freja wipes her mouth, and I'm always impressed by her ability to look like a magical woodland creature even while consuming a roast beef sandwich. "It might help to remember that, historically speaking, their marriage isn't at all bad. Frederich the Wary chopped his queen's head off while she was sleeping."

I give her a dry smile. "Her head might have led a coup against him. One has to be sure." If there's one thing our bloodline has taught me, it's that there are few acts so gruesome that five hundred years can't turn it into a joke.

"King Victor," she moves forward several centuries, "had fifteen illegitimate children...that we know about. His poor wife hardly got a look in. It was three decades of violence and war until the succession was settled."

She has me laughing and then we catch each other's eyes and subside into twin sighs. Beheadings and war. These disasters are what we're comparing our parents' marriage to. "Were there any good marriages?"

"A few," she says. "Queen Magda—"

"No, no, no. We're not counting the marriage with the prince consort who had a love nest inhabited by a string of actresses for fifty years. That's not good."

"He kept it secret," she chuckles.

"How gallant." I feel an exhausted wave roll through my shoulders, down to the tips of my toes. It was an early morning, I could say, but this exhaustion is more spiritual than physical. "So what do we do about it?"

She lifts her shoulder. "They have to work it out in their own way."

That's Freja. Giving other people space. Quietly, calmly in command of her own. The girl may look like a fairy princess, but she holds her boundaries better than any walled city under siege.

I nod and pluck up her serviette, depositing the crumbs in the trash.

"Anything else you wanted to talk about?" she asks, her eyes tracking me around the room.

I thought there was. Père is on my side, but I don't want to seek out more overt help in case it makes things worse between him and Mama. I was looking for an ally in Freja, but she's already given me what I needed to hear. Just like my parents, I have to work this out in my own way. This. I'm not sure if I mean the patronage or the secret trips I'm making to the edge of a lake, a little north, to spend time with a man I'm not supposed to care about.

I give a glancing smile and return to my two paragraphs, determined to nail them.

18

—:—

OPEN ACCESS

CLARA

I send him a picture of the sign to the public bathrooms at the palace. Instead of stick figures of a man and woman, we have a prince and a princess, complete with robes and tiara. The wallpaper is a stylized version of the family tree with modernist portraits in pen and ink.

Another time he messages me, "I found a missing storage room."

I'm on my way to a distant province to visit an animal shelter and my brow furrows at the text. "I am trying to figure out how that is possible."

"Simple. Each department has a number of rooms assigned to it, and each must undergo inspection. Follow?"

"Follow."

"They're scattered all over the ship, not localized in one area. So, you don't go down a hall, opening every door, but ping pong all over the vessel. Follow?"

"Follow. But how could you lose a room? This isn't Harry Potter."

"Someone dropped it from a department list years ago, and I found it by cross-checking the engineering plans."

"Great! You have one more place to put puzzles and extra rolls of toilet paper."

"Not great. The sailors have been using it as a rec room, renting it out for sexy times, flicking cigarettes into the ventilation shaft..."

"Shut. Up."

"Guess what's in the room next door?"

The car I'm travelling in moves like a cloud, even at 130 km/h, but my nerves feel like I'm in a rattletrap. "What?"

"A ton of refrigerator oil. A stray cigarette butt could have ignited the entire store."

I grip the leather seats. The idea of it—a blazing inferno on a ship in the dark of night, Max being the one responsible for all those lives, putting himself in danger—makes me ill. "Captain must be glad."

His three dots bounce for a long time.

"Not glad."

When the day arrives for me to deliver my speech on solar power, I have memorized every word. To keep my restless mind occupied, I make my way to my godmother's cottage to give Maren a respite. I bring along a deck of cards, and Lady Greta's face, surrounded by a halo of well-kept white hair, brightens with a warm smile.

"I haven't had a good card game in ages," she chirps, though I know good and well that Maren gives her a game as often as she likes.

Playing with my godmother takes every speck of my attention as the game shifts from a kind of whist to *Hjerterfri* to poker. She pops a caramel, one of our wagering chips, into her mouth and corrects me. She leans around my fan of cards to select my discards and keep me in line, slapping them down on the card table between us like a hardened gambler.

"And how are things with you?" she asks for the fifth or sixth time. It's a friendly, noncommittal question, the kind which must have served her well as a lady-in-waiting when she used to meet hundreds of people a day. She returns to it like a touchstone, finding her bearings as she navigates interactions that must feel bewildering.

"I'm seeing someone," I say, making a discard that has her frowning. "No. Not seeing exactly." I'm telling her about Max because I am desperate to be honest with someone and I know she'll forget.

"He's nice," I say. "He lets me come over and fish."

"I fish," Lady Greta informs me, pleased to find a common connection; forgetting that her sure hands taught me how to cast a rod and forgetting, too, the hours and hours we spent together on the banks of a river.

"Max cooks for me, and he likes records."

"I like records," she replies, picking up the discards pile and sorting through it until she hits upon a card she likes. "You know I was the inspiration for a Herb Gurtling and the Handsel Brass album?"

"No." I draw the word out. No one spills tea like my godmother.

"They called it *Toffee-Nosed Dame* and kids used to do a swivel-hipped dance to it."

She stands, the cards forgotten, and juts her arms out in front of her, snapping her fingers as she, indeed, swivels. I rise and try to mimic it, laughing.

"What else about Max?" Lady Greta asks, dropping into her chair with a happy sigh.

"He doesn't seem bothered by my title."

"Why should he be? Being the Queen of Sondmark and the Sonderlands is something to be proud of. What are his titles, compared to that?"

I ignore the fact that she thinks I'm my mother. "Max only has his naval pay and a cottage."

"A cottage?" Godmama catches me by the wrist, her blue eyes bright. "If he's not noble, *elskede*, better let him go. The people won't stand for it. Bad enough when your eye was on that homeless princeling, it would be far worse to marry a commoner."

I smile. "He's only a friend." A super-hot friend I can't stop thinking about.

Godmama snorts, muttering about handsome sailors being no friend to any maiden, and lays down a jack of hearts, a six of spades and a ten of clubs.

"Better luck next time," she says, scooping wrapped caramels into her pile of winnings.

I return to the palace to shower and dress, presenting myself for my mother's inspection before we leave. She runs a cursory glance over my person, gives a nod, and leads me to the car.

When we arrive at the Guild Hall, members of the press snap pictures as I emerge from the Bentley behind my mother, but it's nothing like the night at the ambassador's house. No one is shouting questions about Max. Having given it no fuel, the tiny scandal has fizzled out. A nine days' wonder. My smile widens with secret knowledge.

We accept the small curtsies and sober half-bows of men and women who have surely been practicing for weeks and make light conversation in the dusk before we move within the hall. I try not to allow thoughts of Max to distract me. Dusk is our time. And dawn. Hours stolen away from our duties.

I am paired with a grey-haired gentleman for dinner and find, to my surprise, that he is a Naval officer—a submariner.

"What was the longest period you ever spent below the surface?" I ask, peppering him with questions.

"Sondmark doesn't have nuclear subs that stay under for months at a time. We've got fast-attack subs. I stayed under forty days. As long as Noah rode the flood, seeing neither land nor sky. You should have seen us," he laughs with the memory, "running into the arms of wives and sweethearts, blinking against the sun, skin as pale as newborn babes."

I giggle and my mother shoots me a bland smile—the best she can do under so many eyes—and I apply myself to the chicken breast, cutting microscopic pieces and chewing discreetly.

"There is nothing like it—of being gone and catching the first glimpse of my wife in the reception area, ringed about with babies in the old days. Kissing, kissing, kissing. Touching each small head and wondering if they grew. Of course, every time we returned, the mariners all caught colds," he says, eyes twinkling.

My brow furrows. "Why 'of course'?"

"Those kisses introduced the first new germs we'd seen in a month, and we kept going back for more."

I have to bite my cheek to prevent myself from laughing out loud. My shoulders are shaking from the effort at control. Has Max had such meetings—a girl lifted off of her feet and kissed until she couldn't breathe? An eruption of jealousy coats my insides, splashing through my limbs and shocking me in its intensity. Jealousy is an emotion I have no business having, and mine is like eyeliner on a 13-year-old girl—strong, dark, and messy. I refuse to imagine him kissing anyone else when he comes into port.

"...invite Princess Clara to say a few words."

I jerk from my focus back in time to hear my mother, magnificent in sparkling white, introduce me at the podium. I get to my feet, taking one slow, cleansing breath, praying that my preoccupation doesn't show on my face. Standing with a glass of champagne half-raised in my hand, I recite Caroline's precise, appropriate phrases in a clear, carrying voice. Noble service. Innovative work.

"To the men and women who dedicate their time to so great a cause." I lift my glass, and others follow suit. I take the tiniest sip. It is done.

As a rule, Mama tries not to speak until the Bentley swings through the gates of the palace on the principle that the press employs lip-readers and photographers that make one look "as though one has been scowling mercilessly at a peasant."

It doesn't help that she has resting 'Scowling Mercilessly at a Peasant' face.

"You did well, Clara. The speech was flawless."

But. I wait for it.

"You were having a rather voluble conversation with Admiral Raukema."

That's it. Nothing more. But she leaves me with the impression that the whole evening would have been less upsetting if I had been as still as the statue of Magda the Great in the forecourt. Still, she touches my face before I turn to go up to my suite. "You're working hard."

I give a tiny nod. Yes. I'm working hard, I think, slipping into my suite. But I'm working in the narrow little channel she has set for me, racing and racing like a greyhound after a rabbit dummy. If I catch the prize, there are no guarantees that it will be satisfying.

Ping.

I am halfway out of my stockings and I stumble-hop over my shoes and across the dressing room to answer it.

"I saw you were having dinner with Admiral Raukema."

The hose are abandoned, one leg turned inside out and the other rolled down to my knee as I give over to typing. "Were you watching me on Open Access?" I ask, naming the Sondmark public television station. "That's weird."

"It's weirder that you were *on* Open Access. Anyway, I watched Open Access before you were on it."

"You and three old women from Durmstein."

"We have a club."

I grin, peeling my stocking free and tossing it in a corner. The shoes I treat reverently, placing them in the appropriate cubby in my closet.

"Your boss was nice."

"The admiral is not my boss. And he is not nice."

I google the Naval chain of command, snap a screenshot, draw a line between lieutenant commanders and admirals, and add 'boss' with the design app. Send.

"You did well," he writes, and I scowl at my phone. What am I supposed to say to that? I know I did well. I was like a trained seal barking out the answer to a math equation on an episode of *Sondmark Has Flair*.

"Clara?"

"???"

"Come over."

Warmth flickers through me and my heart begins to race. Unconsciously, I start doing the math. Time to change, plus the time to drive, minus the light traffic at this hour of the day. By the time I get there, it'll be ten. Not too late to see a friend. Friend. But the feeling I have is one of intense craving. We haven't seen each other in days.

"Coming."

I move fast, scrubbing off my gala makeup. I pull on black leggings, shove my feet into a pair of trainers and toss on a Stanford sweatshirt.

"Where are you going?" Alma asks as I encounter her in the hall. "Need some company?"

Vede.

I hold up my phone and dance past her, not stopping. "Not this time." I don't know what she's supposed to infer about the phone. That I'm doing research? That the prime minister is on the line?

I register that she looks disappointed, but there is no time to confirm. I jog out to the Fiio and soon I'm flying past the gatehouse with a spurt of gravel.

19

---:---

ABOUT BUTTER

CLARA

It's twenty-four minutes from the time I send the text until the time my car pulls into the drive.

"Security?" he asks.

There's a twinge of guilt as I bound from the car, tossing the keys on the front seat, but I shove it away.

"They'll just have to be furious," I say, passing him, catching his hand, pulling him into the cottage as I walk backward, "but you're a trained military professional. I'm sure you can vouch for my safety."

His hand is rough and calloused and I'm suddenly conscious of the fact that, though our text messages have blazed a fiery trail from our phones to distant satellites these past weeks, we have rarely touched. I'm conscious as well that this started as an attraction—despite this friendship we've decided to have—and he is too busy trying to hide his interest in me to do things like check the perimeter.

I should withdraw, slipping my hand away and socking him in the arm or something, but I'm still chased by the thought of some girl waiting for Max's ship to come in, being caught up and kissed; still fighting off the visceral realization that I want it to be me.

Clearing his throat, he asks, "What do you want to do?" He scratches the back of his head and looks around. "We could watch a classic movie or I could make a fire or—"

"Classic movie?" I ask, swallowing back my first answer to the question. I put some space between us, kicking off my shoes by the door and taking up my spot on the sofa. "What kind of classic movie?"

He picks up the remote and clicks, displaying a drop-down menu. "Lots to choose from."

But I see it's mostly old Sondish black and white films featuring witchcraft and angry Protestants or mid-century cinema with games of checkers played out on empty beaches.

"Do you have any of the Aksel Kroner comedies?" I ask, tugging him down beside me.

He laughs. "Like the one where the penguin has an office job and delivers his reports by vomiting them up?"

Was that a dismissive laugh? I toss the pillow at his head, and he catches it, setting it on his lap, giving it a pat.

Oh good. I swing my legs up for a foot rub. My polish is chipped, but he runs his finger over one of my pink painted toenails. I force down a shiver.

"The dress code is closed-toed shoes at evening events so it doesn't matter—" I scrunch my face. "I know it's strange that my mother sometimes gets to decide how I dress."

He scratches his neck, the short bristles of his hair fading down his scalp. It's a Navy-approved haircut. "Yeah. Totally bizarre."

Just like that, he's narrowed the gap between us. I smile, pushing my feet under his hands. "You like some dreary films."

"They're all in the International Benchmark Collection," he counters, kneading his thumb into the arch of my foot.

I close my eyes, a jolt of desire blending with self-derision. *This is only a foot rub, Clara.* Obviously, I have been single for too long.

He laughs, the sound of it touching my skin, whispering over its surface. "Perhaps you don't appreciate your cultural heritage, princess."

Blindly, I reach for the other pillow and give it a toss. I hear it land on the floor with a thump.

"I'm worried about us, Max." His thumb stills. "If we can't watch anything on television together, we'll be fighting for the remote until—" I almost choke when the realization of what I've suggested hits me. My face flames.

I tense, waiting for this overfilled reservoir of attraction between us to burst its dam, wreaking havoc downstream, taking out a couple of villages.

He clears his throat. "So you don't like my old movies."

Instead of bursting, the water slowly circles down the drain, making gurgling noises as it goes. He was right to ignore me, and on the upside, I can breathe again.

"I bet you like that one where butter melts for three hours."

"*Consumed By the Sun*? The cinematography—"

"The title is grossly misleading, Max. It should have implausibly handsome people yearning for one another, secret babies, a shortage of buttons. Passion. There isn't a hint that it's about butter."

"It's not *about* butter. It's about unspoken repression in rural villages. It's an allegory—"

This feels like a safe topic, and I lean into it. Opening my eyes, I shake my hair away from my face, hitching myself up on my elbows. "Do you know what else is an allegory, Max?"

My question is supposed to be light-hearted, but his expression sharpens, and I feel the reservoir filling again—plink, plink, plink, one fat raindrop at a time. I lose my train of thought. A kidnapping gang of Vorburgian ninjas could break in right now and I'd never notice.

I blink, swallow hard, and will myself to be a sensible creature. "Penguin vomit."

"Mm?"

"Penguin vomit is an allegory."

Drain.

His gaze softens and shifts, and he lets me choose a Kroner film—all slapstick and sight gags—but twenty minutes in, his hand resting across my ankles isn't enough. I shift, rotating until I'm tucked up at his side. Friends do this.

Then he moves his arm along the back of the sofa, and I scooch closer. Friends do this, too.

He doesn't say a word about the cinematic genius of Aksel Kroner, but I laugh so hard I cry, pulling up the cuff of my sweatshirt and wiping away tears. We talk through the credits and talk until the screen goes blue.

"My godmother loves these movies. We used to watch them together."

"Used to?" His fingers comb through my hair, lifting the strands and letting them fall against my back.

"She's—" What do I say? My godmother isn't gone. I'm lucky so much of her is left. "Her memory isn't—sometimes she still calls me Clara but usually not."

He pulls me closer. I brace myself, my hand resting over his heart, and every centimeter of my skin is alive to his nearness. He places his palm over it, his breath matching mine.

"How's her health?"

"Mostly good. She has a little cottage on the palace grounds, and it's calm for her there, unchanging. It's ideal when you consider how many people have to live in care centers or nursing homes." I shake my head, desperate to stay focused. "I'm not saying that some of them aren't quite good. I toured one last year with my sister. Vorburg has a lot of innovations in that line."

"Vorburg? Something good comes from Vorburg?"

I give a little laugh, and kneeling on the sofa, I pull away. My glance catches the TV. A clock is bouncing slowly from one corner of the screen to the other. 2:14 AM. Security will be livid. I give Max an apologetic look. "I've kept you awake."

"Isn't that just like royalty," he says, lacing my fingers in a loose grip, "always thinking they're the center of the universe. I called you, Highness. I kept you up."

"Next time you can choose. We'll settle in for a night of burning Protestant Reformers. I'll even bring the licorice." Our mouths are keeping things light and friendly. The rest of our bodies are having another conversation entirely.

"I love licorice."

I glance down at our hands, at the slow drag of his fingertips across my palm. I've been so good for so long. So good. It's no wonder I'm slipping now. No wonder I'm slipping with him. "Why did you ask me to come, Max?"

He smiles a lopsided grin. "I didn't know your taste in movies was so bad."

I wrap my arms around him. "I wanted to see you too," I say, the words muffled against his shoulder as he returns my embrace.

This is dangerous. I've walked so far down a forbidden path tonight that the usually deafening roar of royal duty and my mother's wishes have been drowned out by how much I want him to kiss me. Still, I haven't said anything I can't take back. I haven't said anything I can't hide under the broad umbrella of friendship. I'm still safe.

His heartbeat is strong, and I hold my breath in case moving triggers another look at the clock.

He rests his head on mine. "Rough day?"

I nod.

"Mine too."

My arms tighten around him, and I smell his particular dusky citrus scent. I'm convinced I could pick him out of a crowd of thousands blindfolded.

"Max?" I ask.

He takes a breath. "What?"

The reservoir is spilling over, water cascading down the dam, ominous patches developing in the earthen embankment. The ground is practically shaking. I have been so good for so long. "We're friends, right?"

"Right."

Do I sense a hesitation?

"Have you ever wanted to kiss me?"

20

Sexy Pirate

MAX

It is like a piece of the International Space Station has smashed into my chest. Air disappears from my lungs, and in the beat before it comes rushing back, Clara shifts on the couch to get away. Elbows and knees bump. We've become so tangled up that it gets worse before it will get better.

"I'm sorry," she says, stumbling through her words as she scoots away. "I shouldn't have asked. What are you thinking? No, no, no, don't tell me that, either."

"Clara," I say, hands settling on her waist. She stills, halting her retreat, bracing herself against my shoulders. When I know I have her full attention, I answer. "Yes."

Her breath hitches and the pulse at the base of her throat is visible. I imagine the sequence of events that might unfold if I allow myself to brush a knuckle against it. I would tug on her waist, my hand turning to push through her hair, following the curve of her bones.

It's easy to imagine because it's not the first time my mind has chased down this path. It's not the first time today, even. And, as with those other times, I force myself to remember that Clara doesn't want this. Not now. Not really. She laid out her plans to me weeks ago, and they don't include a serious relationship. I have to keep my mind focused on that.

Suddenly, Clara swallows and gives a brief nod—a sign she has come to a decision. I wait for more apologies and an awkward dive for her shoes.

Instead, she says, "I've thought about kissing you, too." Her green eyes shift away, and I feel myself turn to stone. *Don't move, Max.* But my mind is like the bridge of a ship in the middle of a dangerous maneuver—loud alarms, tense orders, and 4,000 tons of steel to navigate in a precise and pinpoint way.

She bites along her lower lip. "Maybe...maybe we could just get it out of the way, relieve this tension, and then forget it ever happened?" she finishes, the sound of my refrigerator humming softly in the background.

My eyes widen slightly. Clara has said the stupidest thing I have ever heard in my life. Stupider than an Aksel Kroner movie, even. My gaze shifts to the bouncing clock on the television. It's The Witching Hour for Stupid Things. There is no way I could ever forget her kiss. No way I would let her forget mine.

But my imagination grabs me again, and it's a testament to how much strain these last hours have put me under—with her ratty sweatshirt, chipped polish, and shifting on the sofa, getting closer and closer and closer each time—that I reach for her bit of faulty logic like a life preserver.

"Definitely."

She smiles but it disappears when I tug her slightly towards me. Her hands slide off my shoulders and land on the back of the sofa, bringing her lips closer, her breath mingling with mine. My smile evaporates, too, but she gives a shaky laugh and suddenly I close the distance, stilling her warm mouth with mine.

There is no going back and choosing the wisest course—the slow, gradual incline of friendship. We cannot un-kiss.

For a half-second, I plot out my path through to the other side of this minefield. I should make sure she enjoys this and leave her wanting more. I'll be in control. I won't let her see how much—

She drops lightly against my chest, fitting in my arms as though we are two pieces of the same puzzle, and the emotions I've been holding in check for weeks pour through me, searching for release. *Keep it light. Keep it easy.* Thoughts chase through my head even as I run my fingertips over her waist.

Then she lifts her hand and wraps it around my neck, brushing her palm against the short-cropped hair, stroking the bristles, and I know I am lost. She is soft, sweet, and feels exactly right. I lift my hand but halt it in midair as a final thought burns through my head. Though I could deepen the kiss, taking everything I can from this single encounter, I don't want it to be the last. I don't want a single kiss. I want her.

My chest tightens painfully even as I savor the last moment.

Then I lift my head, drawing a broken breath. Clara's eyes are glazed, and I ball my hands into fists, fighting off the urge to pull her back.

"Is it out of your system?" I ask, my voice sounding winded to my ears. She gives a husky laugh, resting her forehead against my own. Our breath mixes, and for a wild moment, I wonder if she's changed her mind about us.

I loosen my grip so that my fingertips are barely grazing her waist and the soft curve of her hip. Then she leans back, giving me a nervous glance as she slides from the sofa and gets to her feet, eyes avoiding mine. A wobbly smile is aimed ten centimeters above my head. "You should hire out, lieutenant commander. You're more reviving than a shower and good night's sleep."

She regrets it. Damn. "Clara—"

She rolls her neck, stretching, and my hands tighten. She has got to stop doing that. Then she gives a quick, bewildered lift of her shoulders. "Kissing was a bad idea."

"Bad?" I ask, a smile tucking my cheek. *Keep it light. Keep it easy.*

I can see the panic in her eyes and an echo of it tightens my stomach. I've moved too quickly. I've scared her off.

"The problem, Max, is that it wasn't bad." She shakes her head and I see my opening. "You don't look like a Navy man when you smile like that. You look like a sexy pirate."

"You've obviously not met very many real pirates." She punches my arm, but an arrogant certainty has hold of me now. She wants to kiss me. I can save this mess.

"None rate an invite to my mother's garden parties," she says, hooking her shoes onto her feet and walking to the door. "Anyway, I shouldn't have kissed you, not if we wanted to be friends. I've ruined it."

She's right. It is ruined. We crossed a line tonight, and no matter what fiction we decide on in the next minutes, I could never settle for friendship now. The risk of losing even that pushes me forward.

I lift my shoulder and hope it sounds like this is just another back and forth about pig-shaped watering cans. "Kiss me, don't kiss me. Be friends, don't be friends. Those are unimaginative choices, princess. You had your way with my lips tonight, got it out of your system," I wait for a contradiction that never comes, "but I'm still planning to press-gang you next week into painting the cottage. I'll even call you lazy royal scum if you like."

She laughs, the sound filling up the tiny hall. "Paint the whole thing?"

I grin, dialing back to half-pirate. "Have you seen the peeling? I'm not about to lose free labor by becoming awkward over a kiss. I can't afford to."

A brow lifts, but she gives a tiny nod to this bit of ridiculous logic. "I'm worried. If the press gets a whiff of this, all my hard work to impress my mother might go up like a puff of smoke. And I had to complicate it by kissing you. Do you really think we can go back to how things were?"

We can never go back to how things were. But I say, "Easy."

Another smile, this time more firm. "I have to get back to the palace, Max. I should have told the guardhouse that I needed a security detail. I should have—" She exhales a long breath. "I don't know what I'm going to tell security to get me out of this."

I nod, trying not to think about her lips on mine; of how easy it would be to drag her back to the couch and lose another hour or two. "They don't behead princesses anymore."

Her nose wrinkles. "I'm trying to prove to my mother that I can be responsible, and I shook my security detail. It can't happen again."

"No texting you to come over, last minute?"

Her eyes shut. "This must sound so stupid to you."

I get close, closer than I should in light of such friendly talk. "When I'm on deployment, you'd be surprised by how much warning I have to give before I'm allowed to leave."

She smiles at that. "I like it when you do that."

"Do what?"

"Make me feel like my life is normal." She touches my hand. "Still friends?" she asks.

"Still friends," I reply, fingers twining with hers, brushing her palm, communicating the things I can't say.

"And nothing that happens tonight has to change things?"

"Nothing."

A tiny nod. "Good," she answers and goes up on her tiptoes, pressing her lips softly against mine, lingering.

I take it from there. Friends don't kiss like this.

21

DISPUTED TERRITORIES

CLARA

I don't sleep. I don't even try. I spend the whole night clutching my phone, swiping it on and off, waiting for Max to text me. What is he supposed to say after I threw myself at him? What do I want him to say?

Officially, we agreed to kiss and forget, but I see that this was a ridiculous vow made when I harbored the faint hope that he would kiss like the guys I knew in college—boozy and distracted by mastering a kill move in *Fourteen Nights to Die III*. Instead, Max kisses like he's been dispatched by the Royal Navy to claim disputed territories or die trying. (In this metaphor, my lips are the disputed territories.)

The night is long, and I have plenty of time to draw increasingly strange parallels.

If my feelings are a mimosa, the remembered delight of those kisses would be a tall flute of champagne, while the guilt would only be a tiny container of orange juice wafted from an adjacent room. For blowing off my security detail, however, I feel genuine remorse. At first light, I throw back the covers, determined to prostrate myself to the head of security.

Nils Helmut is composed of equal parts spit and polish. I'm hoping that a hot Danish and fresh coffee from the palace kitchens might buy me forgiveness for this one tiny lapse, and I set off, armed with the peace offering.

It's just my luck to run into Noah as he's returning to his cottage, wearing worn tweeds and a dress shirt open at the neck. His biscuit-colored dog is busy sniffing the petunias in the garden bed. He raises his hand in greeting, and I jog over, the paper sack and lidded cup feeling conspicuous paired with my jogging clothes.

"Good morning," he murmurs. Sounds travel far in the wide-open meadow of the palace grounds, and we've mastered the art of pitching our voices low enough to allow for privacy. "What gets you out of bed so early?"

Does he suspect me? My answer is careful. "It's not that early. You're up."

He regards me for a moment and then I see that famous smile—the one hidden under the dark, three-day whiskers; the one plastered on a semi-permanent basis across every tabloid in the North Sea Confederation. There are women across Europe who would sell their grandmothers for that smile.

"I didn't get in at three this morning."

Vede. My eyes narrow. "I'm already on my way to apologize to the tattle-tale," I say, lifting the bag. "Do you think he told Mama?"

"He should have." Noah gazes over the parkland. "It's not my business, little sister, but..."

I'm too old for these lectures. "You're right. It isn't. Any more than the way you look at Caroline Tiele is mine. You're not my lord and sovereign yet, brother."

His smile vanishes and his jaw tightens. Blast. This isn't his fault. I expel a short breath. "I'm sorry. I shouldn't have—"

His hand comes up between us. It's not a Sondish gesture, this way of touching the tips of his fingers as though he is cupping a golf ball in his palm, but one that he inherited from Père along with his Mediterranean coloring.

"It's nothing, Clara," he bites out, his voice a sharp contrast to the cool morning air. Though I don't know what I've said to deserve such a reaction, I can't remember a time when I've seen him so coldly furious. I lift my shoulder and dart past him, wondering what he means.

Is my rudeness nothing? My sneaking out? His unlikely attraction to Caroline?

I don't have much time to mull the question over before I'm tapping on the gatehouse door. It swings back quickly and Nils waves me through with a jerk of his head as though he expected my visit. That's the thing about the longtime staff. I can't rely on the mystique of my princessness to garner any measure of respect or awe when these same people recall me wearing orthodontic headgear.

"Coffee?" I say, and he gives me another jerk of the head so that I know to place my offerings on the tidy desk. I stand like a naughty child, hauled before the headmaster of a boarding school.

"Would you care to know how many protocols you broke last night?" he asks, his tone mild.

"Three," I answer promptly, lifting my fingers to tick them off. "Failure to notify security of plans twenty-four hours in advance. Failure to sign out in the logbook. Failure to notify security of destination."

"Four," he corrects me. "Failure to wait for security to accompany you on your ill-advised jaunt across Handsel at all hours. You peeled rubber, Your Royal Highness."

Four. I should have brought a whole cake.

"The cheese Danish is piping hot," I breathe, prickling with shame. I know without him having to tell me that his job is important; that he would take a bullet for me, for any one of us. The enormity of that cannot escape me, and the least I can do is honor that sacrifice. "I am so sorry," I repeat for the second time that morning. "It will not happen again."

Nils grunts and scoops up the bag, sniffing the contents. "You were easy to find," he says. "You haven't been anywhere else in weeks." He removes the lid of the coffee cup and sniffs again. Perhaps he's looking for foreign objects; something he can put in a chokehold. "I hope he's good enough."

I am forgiven and relief touches my mouth. "Too good. We're only friends."

He gives another suspicious grunt.

Max still hasn't texted by the time I have my first engagement of the day. I'm off to inspect LED light fixtures retrofitted in an elder care center by a state-sponsored energy conservation scheme. I arrive in my court shoes and stockings before noon, pleased that I'm not looking too tired. There is one press photographer and a few women and children holding bunches of supermarket tulips near the security barrier to watch me greet the delegation, and I pause to chat briefly before being swept inside. For forty-five minutes, I am treated to a presentation on the inner workings of the electrical grid, walking the corridors and tilting my head to look (photogenically) at bright marbles of light dotting the ceiling.

We finish in a common room where I am invited to take tea with a table of elderly residents, all with matching bobbed hair. Over thick ceramic mugs of rich tea and a plate of caramel waffle biscuits, they tease me about finding a handsome prince. A gentleman shuffles over and tells me he can't imagine what a headache wearing a tiara must be.

"A couple of painkillers beforehand and the proper placement help," I smile.

"Placement?"

"Like this," I say. Placing my thumb in the dimple of my chin and the pad of my index finger on the bridge of my nose, I then slide everything up until the thumb is between my brows. My finger is buried a couple of inches past my hairline. "Voila."

Morag, a lady with fluffy white hair who reminds me of Lady Greta, laughs and says that she'll have to save that tidbit up for her great-granddaughter when she comes in her plastic crown.

"When will that be?" I ask, and I know immediately that I've said the wrong thing. Her smile slips. The human being inside me wants to reach for her hands and ask her more, but the princess knows that stepping too far outside official lines is dangerous. I may get an answer I can't solve with a government initiative or walking tour.

So, instead, I turn the subject, gesturing towards a wall, broken by a series of doors. "I've been passing those doors all morning and can't understand why they look that way. Where do they lead?"

Each door has a different full-sized decal affixed to it, but instead of a decal of famous art or billowy clouds, these doors have decals of other doors so that they appear to lead to a cottage in the country, a high rise city apartment, or a small house in the suburbs. On the clinical tile in front of each one, there are decals of a variety of welcome mats.

"Those are for our dotty patients," Morag says. "The staff prints up pictures of their actual doors—house numbers and potted plants—which makes them feel like they're going home at the end of the day."

"Dotty. You mean dementia patients?"

She shrugs. "If you know you might end up there, you get a little less precious about it."

I want to tell Max about this. This is one of the good senior care centers, and looking around the table, I wonder how many of my new acquaintances will end up in the dementia wing.

Before I leave, I meet with the administrative staff and thank them for their welcome. I ask them about the doors and drive away, deep in thought.

My phone vibrates, and since I don't wait until I'm at the gates of the Summer Palace to wear expressions, I dive into my purse, swiping the screen.

My heart speeds up when I realize it's a picture from Max. After it loads, I laugh, causing the driver to tilt his head towards the rear-view mirror. Max has sent me a photograph of a ladder stacked next to large buckets and painting supplies.

Three text dots bounce.

Hey, friend. I'm ready to paint my cottage.

I tap my reply.

I don't know how to paint.

I am not joking about this. My painting history includes painting a single room in college—door, walls, and ceiling, all black—when a sorority sister was going through a breakup.

Allow me to introduce you to a valuable apprenticeship opportunity. What day? I'm off on Tuesday and Wednesday.

I'm smiling. He promised me the kiss wouldn't ruin our friendship, and he doesn't break promises, no matter how awkward it will be to see each other again. I pull up my calendar and look for a free day.

Tuesday? I have an evening event, but my morning is free.

Done.

We're super friendly.

22

ACT OF WAR

MAX

Tuesday is hot. I'm outside after breakfast, mixing the paint, when I hear her car drive up. It's impressive that I don't rush to the front door, instead keeping my hands involved in the task, but I've had a few days to talk myself down from the nerve-destroying heights of movie night. I've resolved to be calm.

"Out back," I call, swirling the stirrer through the thick liquid. I am not at all calm.

The door creaks open, and I hear, "Max." My breath gusts from my lungs. It's not her at all. I wipe the wooden stick across the lid of the paint can and set it aside, turning to greet my mother.

"I brought you some cherries, peas, and raspberries. Left them in the kitchen. They're good this year," she kisses the tips of her fingers. "Composted manure came through for me."

Mom glances over the wall I've prepared. It means something when she gives me a nod of approval. If nothing else, decorating parade floats year after year has made her an expert at large projects and small details.

"Nice that you're finally getting this old place painted," she says, padding over in her flat cork sandals, each of her toes painted a different color. That's the work of a four-year-old. My mother will do anything for her only grandchild.

"I like your nails, Mom." I kiss her cheek and she pops her knee.

"Ava set up a salon in the garden plot last weekend, and I let her do them any way she liked. It made a dreadful mess."

"Nice of you to humor her," I say, giving Mom a hug and steering her through the house. "I can't chat today. Lots to do. Are you on your way to Susi's house?" My sister lives a half-hour up the motorway. Though mom often pops by, this unexpected visit is particularly ill-timed. Clara is ruthlessly punctual, and the clock is quivering near the top of the hour.

"She wanted me to teach her how to hem some curtains."

"Teach, huh? Susi's going to find a way to make you do it. She'll impale her index finger or something and end up with stitches."

Mom jabs me in the ribs. "I said I would teach her, and I meant it."

We're through the front door now and I kiss her, hoping it feels like a period at the end of a sentence. "Sounds like a long day." Better get to it.

A furrow lines her brow as she reaches for the car door. I can taste the freedom, but then she spins back to me. "I'm worried about you, you know."

I expel a small, silent sigh and place my hands on her shoulders. "You always worry about me. It makes more sense to do so when I'm in the middle of the North Sea than when I'm sleeping peacefully in my own cottage."

"You usually come into town for dinner, but you haven't been in ages. We've hardly seen you at all since Queen's Day."

The morning is silent, but I can practically hear Clara's car speeding down the drive. Tension tightens my stomach. "There's a lot to do with the house." I play her off.

She gives a dissatisfied sigh. Not silent. Her gaze arcs over the roofline of the cottage lit with morning sun. "You work too hard. If you waited until tomorrow, your dad and I could—"

She's like a barnacle and I have to scrape her off. "Things are fine, Mom. I need to get going on the painting."

"Is it to do with Princess Clara? I never asked how things went."

"I know," I say, opening the door for her. I grin. "I didn't think you had it in you."

"Max," she chides, sliding into the driver's seat. I shut the door and breathe a little more easily.

"Mom," I answer and she tugs the front of my shirt and then my ear, bringing me down to her level so that she can kiss my face.

"I'm sorry it didn't go well. But you can lick your wounds just as easily over a pot roast with your family as you can out here."

"There are no wounds." Not yet.

We smile at each other, and I can see that she doesn't believe me. She pops her sunglasses on, making her look a little like a middle-aged Brigitte Bardot, and turns the key, pulling away to the sounds of ABBA.

Safe. I'm safe. I am already congratulating myself on the near-miss of my worlds colliding when she slows to navigate around a nondescript blue Fiio at the neck of the drive. My stomach drops.

Clara continues, but Mom hits the brakes and leans her head out the window, tipping her glasses back. "Never mind about the pot roast," she shouts.

Clara slides out of the car. The embarrassment and awkwardness we ought to be consumed by has been displaced by my mother.

"Pot roast?" Clara asks, the commonplace question papering over memories of being tangled up on the sofa and in the tiny entryway of the cottage.

I close my eyes for a long moment. It didn't paper over all the memories.

"You just met my mother," I say, whipping my phone from my pocket and tapping out a message.

It's nothing. Also, you're allowed to tell Dad but not another living soul.

Send.

There is no sense in locking Mom all the way down. If she couldn't talk to someone, she'd be like a pressure cooker, in danger of explosion and taking someone's head off—my head. Better that my love life stay quiet.

It's not a love life, I remind myself. That's what I've promised Clara, but the memory of her low laughter against my lips tells another story.

"She won't tell anyone but Dad," I assure her, tucking the phone in my pocket again and swallowing away the urge to pick things up where Clara and I left them. She's here to help me as a friend.

On the chance she didn't have the right clothes for painting in, I have a neatly folded pile on my bed—an old pair of jeans and one of my shirts. I open my mouth to make the offer when I notice.

"You're in shorts." The words are jerked from me as she brushes past.

"*You're* in shorts," she shoots back.

I'm in painting clothes. A Navy t-shirt, a pair of ratty football shorts, and paint-splattered deck shoes. Clara is wearing all the proper lengths, but it's much tidier.

"I've never seen you in shorts."

"Shorts are an abomination, but they have their place."

"That is a very specific opinion."

"And stop looking at my legs."

I grin. "I'm famous for looking at your legs, Clara."

Her eyes crinkle in laughter, and I lead her through the cottage, past the box of produce my mother left on the counter. She snags a handful of raspberries and pops one into her mouth, following me out the back door.

I was worried that we would never be able to get back to our friendship when I kissed her, but the first hurdle has been taken. It can't get more awkward than it was going to be when we first saw one another. But we're laughing together, and it feels like a return to normal, albeit a normal that includes wanting to taste raspberries on her lips.

I clear my throat and drop into lieutenant commander mode, giving her a few pointers on how to pour out the paint and load the brush. "I'll do the window casements and you can do the stone," I explain.

She cranes her neck and squints at the wall. "Unfair. There's a lot more of the stone," she counters.

"Edging is for experts."

She laughs at that, and within a few minutes, we're working side by side. She is daubing the white paint in broad strokes, freshening up the dingy look of the old wash while I trim the windows in black.

I talk easily, smoothing over any lingering unease she might feel with pedestrian observations. The difficulties of using the power washer, the success of a fishing trip on the lake, the work aboard ship.

"Did you find any more lost rooms?"

"Thankfully, no, but I'm going over the engineering plans with a fine-toothed comb. Someone has to know that ship inside and out."

"Your captain must be pleased."

"Not that you'd know it. I don't know how a man can be so good at seafaring and so bad at people."

We round the corner of the cottage, the view of the lake spreading before us, a lonely craft bobbing in the distance, and I tug my shirt up to wipe the sweat away from my face, ignoring the buzz my phone is making in my pocket. That will be my mother with a litany of questions.

"And what have you been up to?" I ask, bumping her elbow when it looks like she's frozen. She jerks her head back to the wall and I turn, swiping neatly down a line of the woodwork.

"Oh...Oh, this and that. A charity performance of *Tales of the Sonderlands*, an award ceremony for my brother's architectural preservation scheme, and I went to this care home."

The words seem to tumble from her lips, tripping over themselves, and she becomes absorbed in recounting her visit. "The admin said there's a model town in Vorburg—fenced so no one can wander off—just for memory patients. They can shop in a grocery store and sit on a park bench and visit a pub. A little like ordinary life."

She starts to talk about her godmother—about how her memory flags and how she could be one of the ladies on that ward, so easily.

"I prepared myself for unending tragedy when she started slipping. I thought that I would be sad all the time, but if I meet her on whatever ground she's standing on, we still laugh."

She stops her recitation, and her mouth bunches on one side. She blinks rapidly and I see the tears threatening to fall. I set my brush down, and she walks into my arms. I rest my cheek on the top of her hair, and the soft breeze blowing in from the lake wraps around us.

"This is a friendly hug," I say after a long time. "You're not allowed to grope me."

She gives a watery laugh, rubbing the palm of her hand across her cheek, and steps back, her heel catching the can. It tumbles over, sending the lid flipping into the air, and splashing white paint down the both of us. I right the pail quickly but there is a long river of paint oozing into the soil.

"It's eco paint," I say, "We can cover it with dirt." When we're finished, swaths of chalk-white paint are smeared up and down our arms and legs. Dirt is caked into our hands and knees. Her pristine palace clothes are wrecked, and I try to imagine her getting into her car like that. "Do you know how to swim?"

"Of course," she answers.

"Do you have any electronics or valuables on your person?" I ask, slipping my phone from my pocket and shucking my shoes from my feet.

Her brows lower and her answer is drawn out in confusion. "No."

"And you'll have time to shower when you get home?"

"I had planned on it. What—"

I grab her around the knees and toss her over my shoulder, striding down to the dock. Hooking the backs of her shoes with my finger, I peel them off as I go. They land with a thunk on the wood, and she shouts my name.

"This is very friendly," I tell her and she's difficult to keep hold of because she's laughing so hard. I pause at the end of the dock, pulling her down into my arms, my breath catching for a second before I begin rocking her. The plan was to pitch her in, but she takes me with her, and we fall together, the cold water a shock in the hot sun.

We crest the surface at the same time, drawing air and shaking the water from our eyes.

"That was an act of war," she gasps.

We're treading water, circling each other. Then her fingertips brush my waist and mine graze the length of her arm. Her hair is smoothed back from the crown of her head, and I can only see brilliant green eyes in a tan face. Staring at one another, we slip for a brief moment into a deep pool, the sparkling holiday mood submerged in awareness and wanting. Her palm rests against my chest.

Then she laughs, kicking away from me and pushing a wave of water into my face. I retaliate. She shoves me underwater and I grasp her ankle, tugging her with me. The play goes on until I roll onto my back and grin. The sun on the water is blindingly bright.

After the cool water, we dry out on the dock. I wring out my shirt, draping it on a pylon, and we lie on our stomachs, arms pillowing our heads and letting the afternoon sunshine bake into our limbs.

"You were at the care center to talk about dementia?"

Her nose wrinkles. She has that warm skin of her father's that tans easily, but I am close enough to see that she has freckles. "No, actually. It was something to do with the environment again. Energy conservation."

"You've had a lot of those assignments recently?"

She nods her head. "It's very important, making sure the planet doesn't burst into flames, but—"

"It's not the one you feel passionately about."

"Yeah," she emits a small sigh. "I know I should just do what my mother assigns me to do. Maybe you could teach me how to follow orders."

"No," I answer, reaching across the old wooden dock. She reaches too and our fingers lace together. Friendly and not. "You should find something you love."

"Easier said than done. I'm not even certain where my interests lie."

I stifle a yawn, wishing I could stay just like this, her hand in mine, the sun baking us into crisp *kyriekager*, fresh from the oven. "You don't know what interests you? You've been talking my ear off about your godmother, those doors, that village in Vorburg. Why don't you ask for that?"

Her hand tightens on mine.

23

— · —

Clash Horribly

CLARA

I'm a mess even after the dunking, and Max sends me into the cottage for a change of clothes. The stairs leading off from the kitchen are steep and narrow, the landing tiny, and I follow his directions left to his room, finding a pair of soft old jeans and a worn t-shirt folded with military precision on the bed, a belt coiled nearby.

I pick them up and pivot slowly, not above a little snooping. There is a white down coverlet on the bed, a spare birch side table with a clock, a snapshot of his family, and a book. I shuck my dripping shorts and, bending to tug on the oversized jeans, read the title. *Sondish Seas: The Legends and Poetry of Native Sailors*. A desk sits under the eaves, covered in engineering prints. A childish finger painting of a gray blob on blue water is taped to the wall. I work my way out of my top and don the loose t-shirt, giving the detergent a sniff. Citrus. That's one of Max's smells.

"Did you find everything?" he calls from below, and I spin, picking up my soaking clothes and the belt before making my way to the kitchen.

"You're a giant. I'm drowning in these clothes," I say, finding him rinsing produce at the sink.

Such a pedestrian activity. I suppose I should be thankful he's wrung his shirt out and put it back on since

I can feel my IQ nosedive every time I see his abs or the breadth of his shoulders. But it's nosediving now, too.

He smiles. "Let me introduce you to the genius of the woven belt." He plucks it from my hand and threads it through the loops, the back of his hands brushing my sensitive skin. His absorption in his task has brought his neck within kissing distance. I can't step away, so I close my eyes and hold my breath until he slots the prong between the weave and cinches me up.

We eat our lunch standing in his kitchen, spitting cherry pits out on paper towels, and finish a third side of the cottage before I look at the time and give a yelp. I will be cutting it fine if I don't leave this second.

"You can clean up?" I ask, wrapping my brush in a damp rag. Max is on a ladder, swiping the white paint more skillfully than I had been able to manage. A muscle in his arm rolls, an interesting new shape forms, and I want to trace my fingers over the path. Only friends. We have affirmed it several times today, but the first glimpse of his hard stomach had me trying to wriggle out of my good intentions.

"Go," he says, crossing his wrists and leaning over to look at me. "I'll finish up tonight."

I fight the longing to climb up and steal a kiss from him. I have to run now, or I'll be late.

I fight heavy afternoon traffic, and by the time I'm waved through the palace gates, I have to race for my suite, my progress so swift that I don't have to answer awkward questions about why I'm wearing these clothes. I jump into the shower, scrubbing the sweat and grime away and stepping into a silky cocktail gown in pale peach. My skin is practically glowing as I descend the stairs and meet my family in an anteroom outside the long gallery.

Père kisses me gently on the cheek. "Lovely, *Clarita*." His Pavian accent is faint but unmistakable, and though his Sondish is excellent, I always wonder if he has held himself back from perfect proficiency just to remind his adopted people that he doesn't belong to them entirely.

I hold his hands and step back, inspecting his magnificence. He's in his favorite tuxedo, an azure sash forming a bright line across his shirtfront, and two ribbons—orders of merit—are pinned to his breast. One of them has my mother's regal face painted on a miniature lozenge of ivory over his heart, but the real Mama is in deep discussion about last-minute details with Caroline, notebook and pen at the ready, and hasn't spared us a glance.

"You are dashing, as ever," I tell him, going up on my toes to kiss his whiskered face—first on one cheek and then the other. He *is* dashing. Not yet sixty, the years have been good to him. I can see the young prince in him still, who stood so straight next to his young bride and made answers which were clear and calm in the face of strong public outcry.

"I wish I could wear peach." Ella joins us, instructing me to turn around. Mama has forbidden that color for her because her curly red hair is not friends with peach.

Friends. I almost giggle. Max has filled that word with such shade and nuance that each reminder that we are friends is enough to make me laugh.

We kissed, sensibly setting that aside, but what we've reverted to is not the chummy, shoulder-punching friendliness of a platonic relationship. Instead, we are having an intense, unspoken flirtation—a dangerous, unsustainable game that feels like walking an impossible tightrope between friendship and love. This sliver of space can't last forever—at my most self-reflective, I know that. If we linger on it too long, there won't be any going back to "just friends". No return to what we pretended to be before.

I've spent the last hour racing to get here, but Max's words, the ones he spoke to me as he lay on the dock, soaking in water, warmed by the sun, have followed me. *Why don't you ask for that?*

I meet Mama's basilisk eye and wonder. Why can't I ask about a patronage to do with memory patients? There is a rightness to Max's suggestion which is making my fingers tingle.

Caroline rings a small bell, and we line up in order. I step into the last position, mentally scrolling through the list of patronages I know about, wondering if there's already one made to order. The doors at the end of the room swing back, Mama is announced, and we enter, ready to mix with artists and entrepreneurs, leaders in our country.

Mama gives a few brief remarks, and I go from group to group, welcomed so easily, the circle widening to include me, guests leaning forward a little to answer my questions. Any one of these people deserves what I have—the palace suite, the lovely clothes, and attentive company—far more than I do.

I speak with a man who started one of the largest toy companies in the world and discover that my brother has talked him into donating classroom supplies for every primary school in the country. Another entrepreneur speaks about how Noah got him to start sponsoring wheelchair basketball teams for wounded vets.

Making connections and highlighting causes are some of the things the royal family is supposed to be good at, and I'm pleased to see evidence of it. If I get to practice this skill with something I care about—again, I feel my fingers itching to grab up the nearest pencil and sketch out some of my ideas.

The thoughts and questions follow me into my suite at the end of the night. I unzip the lovely gown and step out of it, replacing the priceless earrings in their case. I glance at my phone with a smile. It's a message from Max.

Home, sweet home.

There's a picture in the deepening gloom, gold rimming the horizon. He's standing in front of his cottage, arm outstretched. Finished.

I look over the palace suite I've occupied for several years, fitted and decorated by the best artists and craftsmen in their line. Odd that I should prefer his cottage. Odd that I should feel more content within its stone walls. Odd that I wish I could hear the sounds of the lake. It's a thought which sends me off to sleep.

A couple of days later, we have another family meeting. I arrive early and find Noah sitting at the table already, staring at the landscape painting, his mouth set in hard lines. Who put the galliwasp down the back of his business suit?

Then it dawns on me. Caroline is pottering about the room, straightening portfolios, tidying away her notes. Back and forth she paces, and Noah's unblinking eyes bore into the painting as though he would light it on fire if he could. My brother is not known for his constancy, and I thought his interest would have faded by now. I wonder how long it's been going on. I wonder what could ever become of it.

"Am I early?" I ask, a glimmer of amusement in my eyes. Whatever my brother is gripped by, he'll have to get over it. My mother does not countenance HR violations, and if it's a choice between her right-hand woman and her heir, Noah might find himself pitched out of the family.

Caroline glances at me. Is that relief I see on her face? I have inadvertently stumbled upon this sinking lifeboat with my rescue helicopter.

"You're right on time," Noah says, getting to his feet and pulling out my chair. His manners are courtly and old school, and I should rise to meet them.

But before my manners rise, I ask, "Who was that you were out with last night? The one with the startling brows. I can't remember seeing her before, but there are so many."

He glares at me, tucking his tie against his shirtfront as he takes his seat.

"I liked her dress..." I lift a shoulder. "I mean, I liked the half of it she was wearing."

Caroline retreats into the anteroom and my brother leans to me, voice low and intense. "Stop it."

At his rebuke, it's as though he's taken my football and drop-kicked it into the ocean. Still, I nod. It is a great pity that Noah is not as fun as Ella.

I leaf through the itinerary until the others arrive and the room is filled with a murmuring family bustle as Caroline returns and sets the refreshments out.

She places the sparkling water, cap removed, next to a glass for Alma.

"Do you have to do that?" Noah snaps, and I blink in surprise. Everyone in the room blinks in surprise. "You're not a maid. We could serve ourselves for once."

Caroline's cheeks leach of color. He's hurt her. But then her expression retreats into the serenity so habitual to it, and I'm no longer sure of what I've seen. Mama leans forward with her fingers tented together—always the lioness ready to bat down her upstart heir.

"Thank you, Caroline," Mama smiles, her manner clearly meant as a model to her son. "You serve us so beautifully. I hope we deserve it. Now," she says, reaching for her coffee, beginning her recap of the week's events.

Finally, she looks at my sister. "Freja will lead us through the next item on the agenda."

Freja's proposal has been accepted. The National Museum will stage an exhibition of Sondish Romantics with several items to be lent from the royal collection and a few more brought over from England.

"We should keep the paintings once they're here. The British raided our national treasures, you know—overindulged noblemen bought them on their Grand Tours," Freja says, as heated as I've ever seen her. "Carried off our heritage for a song."

"Do not press it," Mama says, holding her hand up abstractedly, already moving on. "They will be bound to bring up the Viking raids and then where will we be?"

"Comprising six percent of their native DNA," Ella chimes in. She raises a Viking fist and giggles, her mouth unable to hold a bloodthirsty snarl.

Arrangements for the royal family photocall is next on the agenda—a supposedly casual opportunity for the press to snap pictures of the family together. The sun will be too hot, the angles all wrong. Either we will be accidentally too coordinated (as in the picture almost a decade ago when three sisters chose a similar single shouldered top) or clash horribly (as in the Year of the Great and Terrible Plaid Pants), but the event, the last official family event before the August holidays, allows us to have more freedom than many royal houses in Europe. By giving the press a little extra access a couple of times a year, the deal is that we can walk into bookstores or attend picnics in the park with less intrusion than one might expect.

The problem is that that agreement has grown fuzzy over the years. Noah and Alma were left alone for a long time, Freja and Alma got a smaller window, and I've been tabloid fodder since my teeth were straightened.

"I'd like to add an item," I say, anxiety churning my stomach.

Mama removes her reading glasses, dropping them on the table. This is an interruption, a deviation of the plan, and Mama looks at me like I'm an indelible spot on a silk blouse.

I imagine the sun on the dock, a sheen of lake water on my arms, and Max's fingers woven in mine. I take courage.

"I'm researching patronages," I begin.

Mama glances heavenward. "Clara, we've been over this."

I resist the impulse to apologize and desist. "I'm merely researching." This is not a lie, but the hefty stack of notes I've collected this week contradicts my apparent breeziness. "I wondered if anyone has a relationship with a dementia ward or works with memory issues?"

There is a flutter of interest along the table, but Mama reaches for a paper tucked lower in her stack. "As I said, this isn't the time for reviewing patronages, particularly in light of recent scandals. The internet is currently roiling with a conspiracy theory about your fingernails, Clara."

"My fingernails?"

She tilts her head as she puts the glasses back on. "I didn't want to bring it up, but there are scores of ReadHe threads about 'the white crust at the base of Princess Clara's fingernails'. They took a poll. 56% think you're doing cocaine."

"That's insane. ReadHe posters are gossip-peddling trolls." Everyone knows that.

She gives a tight smile. "There are pictures of you from the gala event."

My heart thuds as the paper is passed down the length of the table, and I swallow thickly when I see the nails. Sure enough, there's a swipe of white paint along the outside of my hand—a place I didn't even think to look—and tiny crescents of white at the base of a couple of fingernails. Barely visible. The photographer must have been part eagle.

Cocaine. Honestly. What am I supposed to say?

"I didn't see the residue. It won't happen again."

The room erupts with talk until Père slams his hand down. "It was nothing. Show some mercy, Helena."

The wrong words. Mama looks flinty. "Someone has to pay attention to these things. It takes so little to topple a monarchy, darling. You ought to know that." Then she stands and collects her things, striding from the room with Caroline following behind like a balloon attached to her wrist.

The room is silent in her wake until I speak. "She was right. I was a mess."

"We saw you before we went in. Ella did, too," my father says. His smile is encouraging. "We didn't notice."

A growl erupts from Ella's throat. "Someone ought to compromise that photographer's hard drive," she mutters, stabbing a finger at the picture.

"Oh yes, that would make it better, Ella. Illegal activity by a member of the royal family." Noah pushes a hand through his hair. I disregard his frustration. I suspect it has almost nothing to do with me, anyway.

"It was not a problem," Père repeats. He fixes me with a look. "Unless you *are* doing drugs? Cocaine?" He runs out of ideas and snaps several times. "What else is white?"

"I'm not doing drugs. It was a little paint. I thought I'd gotten it all off."

"Paint? I knew there was something you were hiding." Freja looks earnest. "But art is nothing to apologize about."

I bite my lip to stop laughing. My sister has decided I've got some hidden garret in the city and spend my time toiling over canvases.

"It's hard," Alma murmurs, "feeling like you're constantly falling short of perfection."

What would she know about that? Alma never puts a foot wrong, never steps off her pedestal, but I appreciate the support, and a portion of my courage returns.

"Since everyone is still here," I say, "I'll repeat my request. Does anyone have a patronage that fits my requirements?"

"I might," Alma says. "You can look into it. I'll email you the details this afternoon. Good?"

Hardly anything about this meeting has been good. Making the queen storm off in a fury has not been good. But I can't regret speaking up for myself. I'm proud of that, and I think Max would be proud too. I feel the warmth of the sun on the dock, all over again.

I nod. "Good."

24

RESISTANCE FIGHTER

MAX

I ask Mom to pass the potatoes, and she gives me an arch look, as though I'm a member of the Resistance and she's hiding a refugee and a ham radio in her hay barn. *Your secrets are safe.*

Ava scrambles onto my lap, and I smile when she shoves a glazed carrot into her mouth, another in mine, and scrambles off again.

"When is your next trip to the sea?" my brother asks, getting the terminology wrong, no matter how many times I correct him. I expect I'm no better when it comes to asking him about dental procedures.

"Late August," I answer, a twinge of unease catching me off guard. I haven't told Clara yet. "Though he hasn't informed the crew. The captain likes to spring these things on us. He thinks it makes us more ready."

"Does it?" Hals grins and catches his wife Rita's smile.

I give an equivocal shake of the head and my mother, silent too long, pounces. "You'll be gone for how long?"

"Almost a month."

"A month," she mutters, slicing into her pot roast and smearing a piece with savory brown gravy before popping it into her mouth. "A month in those metal coffins you call beds."

"Berths."

"How can you stand being away so long?" She gives me another arch look. The villager with the ham radio is offering to shelter the Resistance fighter, too.

"What does he have to leave behind?" Susi asks, tossing her head, patterned earrings brushing against her cheek. "Work, work, work. At least at sea, there's a breeze."

"Max has a very full life," Mom insists. "Hobbies. Friends."

Hals tosses a cherry at my head, and I catch it. "A girl?"

"Max is not seeing anyone," Mom says a little too emphatically. The villager is blowing it for the Resistance fighter. I shake my head infinitesimally but Rita catches the gesture.

She gasps, her chair rocking as she sits up. "Max has a girlfriend."

Now I'm too emphatic. "Not a girlfriend. Honestly, I don't."

But Rita is unswerving. "This makes me very happy and very sad. Do you know who I always wanted to see you with? Don't laugh." Rita jabs a finger at me. "Don't. Laugh. Princess Clara. You would be so good and, Max, your chemistry..." She trails off, eyes widening. "*Vede*—"

Hals slaps a hand over her mouth and nods towards Ava playing on the floor. She peels his hand away and drops her voice. "That's it. Oh my gosh, Max." She smacks her hand on the table. "Tell me I'm wrong."

"Not a girlfriend," I repeat.

Hals grins. "Right. Okay. Not a girlfriend. Lay the facts before us, little brother, and let us judge."

"She comes over sometimes. That's all." My grudging admission makes it sound like a book club.

"What do you do?" Susi's eyes are gleaming. I can see she's happy that for once, it's not her love life anyone is dissecting. Glad she's not the one twisting in the wind.

"Dinner, breakfast—"

"Hey. Hey. Hey," Susi laughs, even as Mom frowns.

"Nothing untoward. She comes over for breakfast."

"Untoward," Rita howls, twisting to look at her husband. "Remind me to get untoward with you later on."

He leans forward and kisses her soundly.

"Some fishing," I persevere. "Some work in the garden. We painted the cottage this week. We're only friends."

Rita gives a deflated sigh. "This is disappointingly thin beer, Max. You had a shot of giving Ava royal cousins—"

"Of letting me be the bridesmaid Crown Prince Noah disappears with at the wedding reception—" Susi continues.

"Don't be inappropriate," Mom says. Susi's brows lift, and Mom explains. "It's inappropriate to fantasize about your future king."

Susi snorts, but Hals is an unexpected ally. "The royals aren't normal people. They're trussed up in suits and crowns half the time. All those perfect pleats. Can you imagine wading through all that pomp and actually kissing one?"

Susi's eyes glint wolfishly, but I feel my neck redden. Mom squeals. The Resistance fighter is being marched off to his doom.

Of the number of shouted questions that follow, I answer only two.

"No, we are *not* dating and no, you can't tell anyone. What happens in *Huis* Andersen stays in *Huis* Andersen."

I rise, gathering dishes, pointedly clearing the table as the Andersen womenfolk erupt in a chorus of groans.

After a few minutes, Hals joins me, getting a dishcloth while I fill the sink with soapy water. I make short work of the plates and he speaks in a low voice.

"I would love to give you a hard time about this, Max—I'm dying to—but I won't if it's really something."

"It shouldn't be," I say.

"So it is."

It's more than something. I'm not sure when I realized how serious I was. Halfway through that stupid penguin movie? While I found myself looking up the public broadcast station program guide so I could catch a speech on solar panels, maybe?

"It hasn't even been two months. We agreed to be friends."

"And she buys this friendship *probish* you're peddling?"

I grin, pulling the plug from the drain and scrubbing the sink. "So far."

"How long can you keep that up?" Hals has dried the last dish and leans on the counter, watching his wife in the next room help Ava build a tower out of bright, interconnected blocks. They've been married six years, together far longer than that. I can hardly remember a time when Rita wasn't in the family.

My parents are tucked on the sofa doing a Sudoku square together and listening to old Eurovision tracks. They'll sing when ABBA comes on. They always do. *My my, at Waterloo Napoleon did surrender...*

How would Clara fit in with this? I know what I'm supposed to think. That she would sit primly on a hard kitchen chair, a tight, attentive smile pasted on her lips. That she wouldn't have anything in common with us. But that's not how it would be. Clara would like them. They would like her.

"I don't know," I answer my brother, bracing myself against the counter and unrolling my shirt sleeves. "I keep telling myself that it's fine the way things are. No need to complicate it."

"Complicate it with honesty?" he says with a smile.

"Complicate it by asking for something she's not ready to give," I correct.

"You kissed her. That seems a little complicated."

"She asked for it."

"Better and better." For that, he gets an elbow in the ribs. He rubs the spot. "You come to these dinners, Max, and I hear how you're navigating the problems at work, treating your men well but worried about your captain. Diplomatic, not entirely straightforward. You and Clara—I can't believe we're talking about a princess—you and Clara are in a relationship, even if you've decided to call it something else. You should have that talk with your girlfriend and find out where you stand."

"After two months? It took you a decade to propose to Rita."

He puts a hand on my shoulder. "Propose, sure, but I locked her down the same day Valdemar Kestler tried to come between us—I knew three weeks into autumn semester that she was it for me."

"You were fourteen, Hals." I shake him off.

"Affairs of the heart, little brother, are evergreen."

I punch him in the arm. He punches me harder. I punch him harder than that. He tells me he needs that arm to perform a root canal in the morning.

25

STILL FRIENDS

CLARA

There are no plaid pants this year. Ella is wearing a striped seersucker sundress that looks amazing on her. I am certain Mama has notes. Seersucker never looks crisp or pressed, but these are the breaks of the casual Wolffe family photocall.

High, billowing thunderclouds have given the gardens of the Summer Palace good light, and we stride across the lawn to the bank of press photographers stationed near the decorative bridge. As we near, a no-man's-land five meters wide is maintained between the camps, and Queen Helena offers the welcome. It's friendly and laughing and nothing like how she really feels about these things.

The senior royal reporter—an elderly man with a deferential attitude—has a handful of questions he has collected and asks on behalf of them all.

"Your Majesty, what are the details of the new economic policy with Vorburg? Will the wall between our two nations come down?"

Mama beams and responds that the prime minister will be announcing developments soon. And the wall between Vorburg and Sondmark, she reminds them, is little more than a stone gate in the eastern forest.

"Prince Consort Matteo, your brother King Gilles of Pavieau has recently spoken out against the very junta which reinstalled your father so many years ago and removed several officials from that time. What are your thoughts?"

Père grows still. "I trust that His Majesty can rule his country far better than an exiled prince. I haven't had anything new to say about Pavieau in many years. I wish my homeland the best as they work to re-establish democracy."

It's the line we knew he would take—indeed, the line he has taken for years—but there is a note of bitterness I haven't heard before. Père hasn't stepped foot in Pavieau in more than thirty years.

"Have you been in contact with the Royal Family of Pavieau since the state funeral?"

My breath checks, and Père's mouth sets. "I have not had that honor."

Mama interjects, "The floral tribute sent to His Majesty King Gilles included tiger lilies, a native flower of Pavieau and favorite of the old king."

Is she saving Père from awkward questions? Or saving herself?

Mama nods, concluding the topic, and the reporter moves on. "Princess Alma, the press would like to know when Sondmark will be hosting your wedding celebrations?"

It's strange that the date has not been set. Generally, these things are hammered out long before the public even knows they are to be anticipated. But Alma has always held her cards close to the chest.

She tips her head consideringly and tells him that a bride has so many arrangements to make that the date completely slipped her mind. It's meant to be a joke as well as a non-answer, and the bevy of press laughs approvingly. I remind myself to get to the bottom of it the next time we're raiding the palace kitchens for down-market chocolate.

Noah is asked a question or two about his derelict buildings scheme and then whether he likes being a bachelor—a back-door way of asking if he is seeing anyone seriously—and he tells the reporter it suits him at present. Ella is asked about rabbit show jumping ("I didn't expect it to come at me as it did. I would have dressed for it if I'd have known.") and Freja fields an inquiry about the exhibition. ("It will open around Christmas. A gift for us all, I think.")

Then the old man, hunched over in a perpetual half-bow, turns to me. "Princess Clara, the country has been charmed to watch you join your siblings as a full-time working royal," he says, presuming to speak on behalf of all 5.8 million citizens. "Are there specific projects you hope to champion?"

An answer is ready on my tongue until my eye catches my mother's for the briefest moment. I smile—as we have all been doing—and shake my head. "I hope to serve the Crown and the people of Sondmark in whatever capacity I am able."

As we turn to go, the cameras clicking and whirring, I wonder if any of us have spoken the truth.

By afternoon, the storm has broken into a sheeting rain, and I find myself driving past St Leofdag's Hospital like a jilted ex-lover, slowing to circle the parking lot. It's the third or fourth time I've made this trip, and I slot my Fiio into a space, taking out a notebook and jotting down observations. The hospital grounds, laid out in the reign of Queen Magda, are austere. There are wide, sweeping lawns no one would dare wander across, and I know from online aerial photos (and a reconnaissance mission) that there is an inner courtyard covered in concrete. I imagine a fundraiser to give residents more fresh air and an enclosed, safe place to linger where it is beautiful and green. The grounds are a modest fix, but I have to start somewhere.

I flip on the headlights and the windshield wipers, shooting out onto the busy street. I'm halfway to Max's cottage before I even realize I missed the turnoff for the palace a kilometer back. Palace security will follow where

I lead, and instead of turning, I glance at my watch. Late afternoon. Max might be home if he worked early.

Fifteen minutes more and I am pulling up outside his crisp white cottage, the tiny waves on the lake rimmed in white. My arm is flung over my head, and I race to the door, rapping several times and brushing off droplets.

It swings open and I don't think. I don't even pause. I grip his forearms and lean up, kissing him on the mouth. I freeze but he responds, the sharp stubble of his chin scraping mine. Shock catches up to me, and I jerk back.

"Hello," I say, ducking under his arm. But he catches me, pausing us in the tiny hall. I wipe the rain from my face.

"Hello?" His eyes dance. "I see how it is. Royals having the run of the country, pillaging kisses from peasants—"

"I forgot it was you," I laugh. His brows lower. "You know, like when you call your tutor 'Mama'. It was reflexive."

He lets my arm go but plants his hands, palms flat against the battered wood, on either side of me. I could escape if I wanted to. Do I want to? The answer is immediate. No. My heartbeat is racing too fast for sense to keep pace.

The distance between us shrinks and his voice drops to a coaxing growl. "We need a fair and equitable exchange of privileges..."

I roll my eyes, trying to keep things light, hoping that I fail. "We're friends, Max."

He nods and I smile, forfeiting to his logic by lifting my chin and closing my eyes when he dips his head.

It's only fair, I think. And then I don't think.

It's good. My head shifts, moving easily between the hard wall and his soft lips. Friends? Still that. But these weeks coming here, texting him before I go to sleep or after work, the way he slips into my thoughts when I'm distracted or heedless...this is something else.

My hand lifts, suspended like a bird in a current of air for a long, satisfying while, before I place my fingertips lightly against his chest. Even now I want him to misinterpret the gesture, to think I'm holding on instead of looking for space, but he reads my gesture at once, lifting his head only to shift it, resting it on the cool paneling next to me as we get our breaths back.

"Are we still friends?" I ask, taking a long drag of air into my lungs. A mistake. The scent of him fills my nose.

"Still friends," he responds, his voice tight. He takes another few moments before he lifts his head and pulls me into the cottage.

The day is drizzly and he's got a Dragons game on while he eats his meal. I inspect his plate resting on the coffee table. Roast chicken and a handful of raspberries.

I look at him hopefully as I slip onto my side of the couch.

"It's only leftovers. Do you—"

"I accept."

He goes to the kitchen and throws a dish together for me, bringing out a cloth to lay across my lap. The meal is nothing special. The game is hardly engrossing—Mallok is injured, and the ref is practically breathing with his whistle. I eat with my hands, wiping my mouth and setting the plate on the table. I curl up next to Max, happy to make the same exclamations as he does, and hold the flat of my hand out in protest at the overzealous rule enforcement. Kepler drives towards the goal when a defender slips between his feet and punts the ball out of bounds. For a fraction of a second, the players freeze and then Kepler does what all footballers do. His face twists in agony and he falls to the ground, clutches his shin guard, and screams.

"Foul, foul," the ref's whistle seems to shout, his arms signaling.

Max shakes his head, amused. "That's embarrassing."

"You think? It's a good performance. Look, he's even allowing the team doctor to inspect him."

"A dive is not manly."

But by this time, Kepler has taken his shirt off, spinning it above his head in acknowledgment of the crowd as a couple of teammates help him limp from the field. "It's a little manly," I laugh, inspecting the tattoo of a dragon writhing sinuously over his chest.

Max scoops up the plates and walks them into the kitchen, depositing them into the sink with a clatter. A giggle escapes me. "Are you jealous?" I call.

My words choke off. *Vede.* He's not a boyfriend I'm teasing. I have to remember that.

Max strides back, positioning himself behind the couch, crouching down to my level and resting his forearms—at least as firm as Sondmark's premier left winger's are—along the back. He's not laughing at my joke.

"People should be honest, above-board. Clara—" And I know in an instant that this isn't about a footballer's dive. This is about him and me. This is about what we are, hiding in plain sight. And I'm not ready for this conversation.

I scramble off the couch and stand awkwardly, the coffee table against the back of my legs. He straightens too. Though we are several paces apart, my heart is racing and I'm anxious to fill the silence before he can.

"I'm leaving this week," I announce.

"I know." At my look, he explains. "Your family goes away every August for the holidays. I'd have to be living under a rock not to know."

The Ermitage Hunting Lodge is up in the mountains and going there is a traditional throwback to the times when there was no air conditioning, the summer heat stifling. It used to take days for the court to remove themselves, but now I can get there in two hours along well-paved roads.

Usually, I love the holiday. Family comes in from every corner of Europe, we eat out of doors, play ridiculous party games, and go on long rambles in disreputable tweeds, the green copper roof of the late-Baroque building glinting in the distance. But Max won't be there, and the thought is like a blight of midges.

"You'll have time off for a summer holiday?"

He nods, his eyes still intent, not wholly committed to a conversation about vacation plans. "The family will come out to the cottage. Hals is teaching Ava to swim." The next sentence spills from the first like water over a rock. "Clara, we need to talk."

Despite my best efforts to put it off, to exist in this shadowy area for a while longer, the choice is out of my hands. "I know."

The air is heavy, and I can't get a good breath. My fingers tangle together, and I wonder with a mad panic what one of those blasted body language experts would make of this fidget.

"This friendship of ours...You know there's something more here," he says, his hand touching the space between us.

The television crowd erupts in a cheer and the announcer shouts, "Goooooooaaaaaaaallllll." Then comes the dull roar of a Sondmark drinking song as the crowd celebrates. *Live a long life. Kiss all the girls you can...*- Max picks up the remote and clicks it off, the sound extinguished.

Everything is about to change. I feel my toes tingle and knees soften, as though I'm standing on the edge of a cliff. What if I fall?

"I know."

He rakes a hand through his hair. "Then why are we pretending there isn't?"

My mind goes to the limping footballer. His team picked up a free kick, maybe even scored a goal, because he had enough sense to fake it for a little while. It might not be honorable, but it is strategic.

"Because nothing's changed. I still can't afford a string of relationships; can't have my personal life overshadow every other part of my public identity. My mother—" I'm shaking my head but his gaze doesn't waver. I wonder how he can be so still in the middle of what feels like a storm. Doesn't he remember that a relationship with me could hurt him? "Max, you want a command someday and this..." The word is like stepping into a rabbit hole. "This is trouble."

"Clara, we both knew the risks." He leans forward, hands braced on the back of the sofa, eyes bright. "But you didn't run away."

My voice is hardly a whisper. "I should have. *You* should have."

"You could still."

It's true. He's not holding me here, not even lightly as he did in the hall, hands pressed against the paneling. I could leave the cottage, battle a rainstorm all the way back to the Summer Palace, and keep the secret of us forever. The thought lodges in my throat.

"The promotion board wants a trustworthy, sober officer, not one whose girlfriend keeps dragging him into the press. This," I repeat, my palm traveling a path between us, "could ruin your career." My voice raises, almost wailing. Why won't he think of himself? "I don't want to do that."

"And I don't want to damage your standing with the queen for nothing."

I turn to the window, putting a few paces between us. "So you agree," I say thickly, swallowing away the threat of tears, "there's too much at stake to play around."

I'm glad I've convinced him. This attraction is too dangerous—it always has been. It simmers between us even when there's no orchestra or ball gown to help it along. We can be digging dirt or sunning on a dock and the warmth of our connection is like a pilot light, sending flames licking along my veins at a moment's notice. A friendship was supposed to put it out, smothering those hot feelings. Instead, it added fuel to the fire.

"I agree," he answers, turning the screw. I hear the creak of the old wooden floorboards and feel his calloused hand touch my arm, brushing down its length until his fingers clasp mine. "I don't play around."

He tugs me and I turn, tilting my head back. He keeps hold of my hand, fingers brushing slowly over mine. It's meant to be soothing but I feel sparks at each touch. His eyes are unwavering.

He lifts his free hand to my face, brushing my jaw. "I love you."

My heart tightens. The words haven't been dressed up or disguised. They are as bare as a stone and my nerves ignite.

For a brief second, I fight it. It's the wrong time to be serious about someone Mama won't approve of. I search his face, looking for hidden meanings or an asterisk to add to his declaration. There aren't any.

"I'm scared," I admit.

"Of me?"

I give a watery laugh. "Of me."

I love him. The words stick in my throat, but they fill every part of me, the realization cutting through thoughts about Mama's patronages or St Leofdag's sweeping lawns—cutting through a mind churning with worries.

Like water flowing down a hill, I begin hunting for a path forward. Maybe I can tell my father and he will help me sway Mama. Maybe we'll let this thing grow a while longer protected by the secrecy these stone walls have afforded us. Maybe we can make it work.

A smile curves my mouth as I remember. Max doesn't play around.

"I'm not scared," he says, sensing my shift. A roguish grin lights his face. Whereas a bow is deferential, the way he hauls me into his arms is proprietary. "Admit you like me a little," he growls.

"I like you a little," I say, going up on my toes to kiss him under his ear. My fingers brush his neck. "I like you very much." The stubble along his jaw rasps my lips as I move along it, trailing light kisses.

He tires of my game and claims my mouth. In that moment, I make a deliberate choice not to think about all the ways things could go wrong. Instead, I focus on how Max's hand winds through my hair as he kisses me.

26

— · —

STRATEGIC IMPORTANCE

MAX

We have the rest of the day to ourselves. The summer storm passes, and we go down to the lake in the setting sun, swimming until the light fades.

"You should bring a suit next time," I say, pulling her out of the water, the summer dress clinging to her everywhere. We lay on the warm dock, lake water seeping into a kind of halo.

I expected her to be more tentative, but Clara props herself over me, laughing as I squint up at her. Then she draws near and blots out the sun. She's not laughing when she kisses me, not rushing away. Now she lingers and we take our time.

Still, we haven't said everything we need to.

"Come on," I say, standing. "I want to have a fire."

Later, after she's stolen more of my clothes, the fire is made, and on an old wicker loveseat dragged near the flames, she leans up against my chest, fingers brushing along my forearms.

"I thought I'd come over for dinner that first time," she murmurs, "and find out you wouldn't be able to talk about anything but the tides and currents, and that would be the end of that."

"Did you know," I say, lazily kissing the top of her head, "that the same gravitational pull that causes tides affects dry land, too? The solid Earth changes shape ever so slightly."

She turns, laughing, and I find her lips.

When she can breathe again, she groans. "I don't want to be gone for two weeks. It's too much time."

I'm silent so long that she leans away. "What is it?"

"It'll be more than two weeks. I'm deploying at the end of August."

She sits on her heels, and I watch her reaction. I haven't had the best track record finding a girl willing to put up with long, inconvenient absences, and I tense. It's never mattered as much as it does now.

"Is it dangerous? Should I worry about you?"

The pleasure of being worried over is a first. "Much of it's going to be routine. Nothing too hair-raising."

"How long?"

"A month."

She drags in a deep breath and scoots away, sitting on the edge of the old loveseat like she's listening to one of her mother's speeches. "I understand," she declares, giving me a princess smile.

I reach for her, but she gets to her feet. "I have to pack tonight."

I stand. "Clara. You're upset."

"I'm not upset."

She's upset.

I catch her gently by the wrist.

She takes a deep, cleansing breath, and I see her look inward, coming to terms with what this will mean. "I am going to worry. Just resign yourself to that. But six weeks apart, Max. I knew it would happen, but so soon—" She exhales and chews her lip. "Whenever my parents would go off on a tour, it was easier if I made a clean break. But I miss you already."

"I'll miss someone stealing my clothes, eating my food..." She chokes on a laugh and walks into my arms. "I'll be back before you know it. You can tell me about how you've been such a rockstar princess that your mom overturned the succession and insists on making you the heir."

That earns another laugh, but she reaches the salient point.

"We can't text or email?"

"Radio silence this time."

I stroke her back and feel the rise and fall of another large breath.

Finally, she nods. "You're going to tell me that you've been lieutenant commander-ing so well that the captain gave you the ship."

A smile tucks my cheek. "That's exactly how it works."

We stand holding each other for a long while, listening to the crackle of the fire and the gentle sound of the lake.

"Max, I'm not ready to tell anyone about us. Let me establish more of a track record. I'll get past the next few engagements and hope my mother will be pleased enough to accept the idea of me dating you. Then when you get back, we can figure out how to break the news to our families and your commanding officer."

I nudge her chin up and close the distance. "Fair enough."

The next morning, I'm on duty. A corner of my computer screen displays a breakfast news show. The smiling hosts comment on a kilometer-long manifesto painted on a coastline cliff by a Vorburgian ecological protest group. The activists, standing too near the edge, have let off flares and smoke bombs simultaneously, the wind whipping banners and flags. It looks like something out of an 80s music video.

"I know it tied up traffic on the A76, but the visuals are stunning," a host laughs, pivoting to another camera. "Now in royal news..."

They run a short clip of the royal photocall, speculating on Crown Prince Noah's love life in a giggling, morning mimosas way, before announcing that the summer holidays have begun for the royal family and that there'll be no important news from that quarter for weeks.

I nurse a cup of coffee, filling out reports, when there's a rap on the door. Moller enters at my call, and he makes his reports in a crisp, direct manner. I put him at ease and indicate a chair.

He hands over the mechanical report, annotated with his own notes. He only missed one or two points, and when I call his attention to the lapse, he supplies the information off the top of his head.

I nod, satisfied.

"Good job. Now go back and include all of this into the report. It's tedious but we need the records."

While we're talking, the captain barges into the tiny space. "On your feet, Moller." Moller springs up, tipping the report into my hands. I stand as well. "If you're finished here, get your *riv* back to work."

"Aye aye, captain."

The door closes and Captain Dusstock rounds on me. "Do you not like your lieutenant commander bars?"

I stand at attention, fists clenched at my side. Treating those below my rank with decency is one area where the captain and I will never see eye to eye. If he doesn't like me being friendly with my subs, he's going to hit the roof when he finds out I'm dating Clara.

"Permission to speak, sir."

"Hell no, you don't have it. Enough of these hippie drum circles, Andersen. They give their reports, and they get out. There is top brass," he shouts, pointing at his collar, "and there's everyone else. Know the difference."

He storms out again, and I unclench my hands.

After work, I take a long run, jogging around the nature reserve, the water dotted with a few boats. I get in late and pick up my phone, checking my messages from my secret girlfriend. A slow grin lifts my mouth.

Cousin Helmut is already trying to set me up with his son.

I tap back.

Age? Financial position? Title? Look out for your interests, Clara.

Three dots bounce and I reach into the fridge for a drink.

22. Loaded. In line for a duchy. Also, BURIED THE LEDE, he's my cousin's son. Ew.

So we're just going to pretend that King Malthe II never married his aunt?

Your store of historical knowledge is unhelpful. Also, for legal purposes, Rome declared them unrelated.

Okay, liefje. The endearment comes easily but this distance is killing me.

At the end of the week, I get a text.

Are you up for a drive?

If it means seeing Clara? Hell yes, I am. I look at the clock. Two hours to the hunting lodge, two hours back. I grab my keys before another text stops me. It's a map, tagged in a location along a rural route located approximately halfway between the lodge and my cottage. An hour there. An hour back. Lots of time in between.

I make it in record time, pulling into a wide spot on the road that serves as a trailhead for the eastern forest footpaths. I get out and lean against the hood of the car, waiting. There are a couple of hours of daylight left, and the air is soft and full of the sounds of the forest. A few minutes later, a car passes. A green Ciprio. Ever since spotting one tailing me into base all those weeks ago, I see them everywhere. But there must be thousands of them in Sondmark.

Clara's Fiio pulls in and she hops out, squealing a little as she flings herself into my arms. We're standing where any passersby can see us, but there's hardly any traffic on this road. I let myself go and kiss her up against the car.

"It's only been a week," I gasp.

"A long week, full of familial matchmaking."

I laugh. "If I'd known you were going to miss me so much, I would have made myself scarce before."

She pulls me towards the forest, and I see now that she has some old hiking boots on.

"A kilometer up and there's a waterfall," she says.

My heart feels like it sprinted a marathon. I wonder if we'll make it that far. The path narrows in places, giving me an opportunity to lift her over obstacles; to thread our fingers together.

"How's your family?"

"I don't want to talk about my family." I tug her hand and she clarifies. "It's a little tense. The House of Wolffe could teach a masterclass on having things to say and not saying them."

"Is something going on?"

She pauses.

"I don't know if it's because I have you that I'm seeing things through a different lens. It just feels like things are changing for us even if I can't put my finger on how."

I grunt, recalling the captain bawling out his subordinates, throwing his weight around the ship. It puts me on edge, forcing me to brace myself against a storm only I can see.

"Change doesn't make an appointment."

She nods, threading her arm through mine, leaning her head against my shoulder for the briefest moment. "How's work?"

I laugh, the sound rumbling through my chest. It's been a week of having the captain throw his weight around, scaring new recruits senseless. "I don't want to talk about work."

A breath of amusement leaves her lungs.

"So we'll talk about the matchmaking. That should be a laugh. I've spent this week turning down a number of my mother's romantic suggestions."

"Your mother makes suggestions about your love life, too?"

She jabs me with her elbow. "It's a dance. Mama lays out a list of potential partners—cross-referenced for strategic importance—and we get to say which ones we would like to meet."

"Does that actually work?"

"It's how Alma met her hairy grand duke."

I halt and our hands stretch between us before she turns around to look at me.

"That's a bloodless way to go about it."

"Mama was matched that way and Alma seems—"

"Content?"

Clara looks troubled. "Resigned."

"Is a hairy grand duke in your future?" I'm tense but try to make the question as easy as I can. We're dating, but I wonder if we're defining it differently.

"Oh no." The momentary relief I feel disappears at her next words. "By the time I get to choose, the grand dukes will be taken," she laughs, pulling me up the trail. "Like everything else in the family, the older sisters will get their pick, and I'll take whatever's left. I'll have to make do with lesser counts and barons, a distant cousin. Unless..."

"Unless?" I repeat, and I know I sound forbidding. It's hard to keep my voice calm when I'm right in the middle of planning how to lay waste to my rivals. I've halted again, feet planted, arms crossed.

She darts back and leans up on her tiptoes, brushing my lips with her own.

"Unless I ignore Mama's list entirely."

27

BATTERED TIARAS

CLARA

My morning begins with the day's agenda helpfully slipped under my door by Caroline. Breakfast, horseback riding, an hour of repose (commanded in a suitably impressive typeface so I know Mama means business), luncheon, and an afternoon audience with the queen.

I ought to be wondering what it's all about. I ought to be hoping that Mama has begun to take my subtle hints that I am diligently studying up on geriatric memory loss. Instead, I stretch, unable to hide my grin. I drove two hours in the car yesterday, the longest trip since returning from the States. The dashboard on my poor Fiio doesn't know what to do with such long distances except suggest a restorative cup of coffee and a rest with gentle but increasingly desperate *pings*.

I flop dreamily into a chair before my mirror. Seeing Max leaned up against his car yesterday, ankles crossed, his relaxed shirt hugging broad shoulders...it's a miracle I didn't steer into a ditch.

I begin to comb out my hair when a feather of doubt creeps in. I haven't told Max I love him. Maybe it's because I'm worried that the more he sees of royal life—the more he sees of the demands it makes—the more he'll wish he had settled for something less complicated. The man has to have as many chances as possible to decide what he wants before shouldering the weight of my feelings too.

I've worked out my reasons for delaying sensibly, but then I remember him helping me to the top of a massive boulder yesterday, the rock likely deposited thousands of years ago when the Weichselian glaciers rolled up and retreated to Scandinavia. I never worried for a second that he'd drop me. Max is strong, dependable. I couldn't be in safer hands.

Max can't make his choice to get serious about us before he has all the information. So that's it. Before he leaves on his deployment, I have to tell him how I feel.

A smile plays on my lips as I tie my hair back in an Hermès scarf and rush down to breakfast.

The morning flies by. I'm not an accomplished rider, but the activity keeps Cousin Helmut from singing his son's charms. Père mans the grill over lunch, and I swoop behind him, stealing a sausage before he can swat me on the backside. He curses me in Pavian ("May your face grow a duckbill.") and hauls me close, his other hand busy with the tongs.

"It's nice seeing you so happy, *Clarita*," he says, sunglasses obscuring his eyes. "Sometime you'll tell me what makes you smile, hm?"

Distant cousins have driven over from Schwascle, and their children are rolling down the lawn, giving the picnic lunch a festive air. There is no one from Pavieau. My father's family is never represented here or anywhere. Though I hope to confide to him about Max, the sheer number of sacrifices he's made for the Crown are laid before me.

"Your cooking makes me smile," I say, hugging him quickly. Running off to round up some of the children for a game of tag, I return with a sharp appetite.

My good mood lingers as I change for my meeting with Mama, digging my court shoes and hose from the back of my closet.

"I'm punctual," I tell Caroline who glances up from her makeshift office outside the library, a furrow on her brow. It's too much to expect her to laugh but is that pity in her expression? It couldn't be. "What is it?"

Caroline shakes her head and pastes on a fake smile. She is picking up all our worst habits, and I recognize a surprising impulse to touch her hand and ask her what's wrong.

The moment passes, and she ushers me into Mama's presence. A tingle of worry dances up my spine, and I paste one of those smiles on my face, giving her a curtsey. She bids me take a seat—not across a desk but in a cozy arrangement of chairs near the tea service. She pours out, the ritual of tea taking a few minutes while I try to guess what is in the thick folder on the seat next to her. A patronage assignment? I can't help it when an excited smile touches my mouth. Mama is finally going to give me a real responsibility.

"Have you enjoyed your holiday?" she asks.

"Yes, the weather has been good."

"None better than yesterday. We played five-pins on the lawn, and you were nowhere to be found. Your little cousins were sad to miss you."

I take a sip of tea, on my best manners, almost enjoying the novelty of having small talk with my mother. She loathes chit-chat and is usually in a position to hustle people along to weightier topics. "They're growing so tall."

"Yes. Though I've found that being tall and being grown-up have almost nothing in common." She sets down her cup and hefts the folder onto her lap.

"Do you know what this is?" she asks in a tight, polite tone.

I shake my head. The cover flips back and I see a letter headed with the insignia of NewsNook—the morning show program. Not a patronage. Disappointment ripples through me. A patronage would mean trust and trust might mean I could tell her about Max sooner.

"It seems that you are to be featured in the news, Clara," she says and my stomach drops into my court shoes. I feel like a tiny boat bobbing on the ocean while a leviathan opens its jaws below. This is not good.

"And look how much material they have to cover." She begins taking out photos and more printed paper, labeling each as she stacks them in a pile. "You've done a lot of things this summer. Meeting a certain lieutenant commander." Slap. "Planting his garden." Slap. "Painting his cottage." Slap. "Swimming. Kissing all over a nature preserve." Slap. Slap. "Running off for a secret rendezvous only yesterday."

My mouth drops open at each photo, some mercifully blurry, but some of them are as clear as day. The hike to the waterfall is rendered in near-perfect detail, and once again, Max looks like he adores me. I should feel butterflies seeing the way we look in these pictures—like two people very much in love. Instead, I feel like I've just swallowed an anchor and the weight of it makes me sick.

More pictures follow of my exploits in college—some of them captured by the press, some taken off social media pages of my sorority sisters and some of them are too private to have come from anyone but the person who snapped them. Friends and old boyfriends sold their photos to the press.

"Not only do we have a bevy of quotes from former palace staff, but there's also an interview with the best friend of the lieutenant commander's ex-girlfriend—a woman, take note, who is doing important work for the scientific community of Sondmark. She isn't merely giving speeches about solar panels. She's engineering them."

My chin tightens, but I touch the tip of my tongue to the roof of my mouth. I blink rapidly. No tears. I won't let them come.

"This friend suggests that your relationship with the lieutenant commander has been going on for a year. That you're the reason they broke up. That the stuck heel was some kind of prank you both pulled on the entire country during one of the nation's most important ceremonies. NewsNook," she enunciates it like the most popular television program in her country is a foreign word, "has asked the palace to comment about...what is it?" She reaches for the cover letter again. "'The Party Princess and her Scorching Summer Fling' before it airs on Monday."

Mama takes her glasses off and sets her hands in her lap, tipping her head slightly. I am shaking with fury—at the photographer, at the news coverage, at those gross words ('scorching summer fling') that seem to reduce Max to a toy and me to a child.

"I thought I told you to end this."

I blink, my focus snapping back to her. "Max and I are friends. There is nothing to end."

The words are reflexive, but they aren't even half true. We passed friendship so long ago that I can't even remember feeling the bare, uncomplicated pleasantness of it anymore.

Mama's smile ratchets tighter. "Well, you've managed to convince me," she answers, holding up a picture of us wrapped around one another, his hands on my waist, mine banding the back of his neck. It's going to be some of the best TV Sondmark has ever seen.

"I have friends of my own. Why does it matter who I spend time with?" I push back the slightest bit and she scents blood.

When Mama is angry, she doesn't yell. Her voice gets deadly calm, just as I'm hearing it now. "Do you know what it was that ignited the revolution in Pavieau, Clara?"

We don't talk about Pavieau and the shift confuses me. I blink. "The economic—"

"It was a few pictures of a young princess, one of your great aunts, biting into a piece of fruit and tossing it away. Maybe it was unripe. Maybe it was bruised. Maybe she was ill. None of her explanations mattered when they dragged her and her family through the press—called her decadent and wasteful. We aren't people to them, Clara. We're symbols, and there are narratives attached to these pictures that you have no hope of anticipating. That is why I care about who you consort with."

"I haven't done anything wrong." I'm choking with anger and bewilderment, but Mama's voice never falters.

"That must be why you told everyone in the family you were visiting him regularly. That must be why you wouldn't dream of skulking off yesterday." She clamps her lips together. "You knew what you were doing."

My emotions are under a microscope, shriveling in the bright light of my mother's inspection. "Is it so bad?"

"On its face?" She lifts an elegant shoulder. "But this royal family is one poll away from obscurity. One parliamentary movement away from having an 800-year-old tradition wrested from our hands—of having to show up to royal weddings like the Bourbons with their battered tiaras. Maybe we'll be reduced to shilling mass-produced mustard in television commercials. It's hard for the people to remember why they need us—to cool their partisanship, to be a healthy outlet for national pride, to ensure that some things don't change even if the prime minister does. It's easy to toss us aside while our foundations are..." She wets her lip, searching for a word. "Unsteady."

My spine straightens. "That is no fault of mine. Max and I—"

Her brow lifts the smallest fraction. Max and I. She will not hear it.

"You want to know why I care that your little secret is going to give the press weeks of headlines? Because this story will become my story. Not the tariff deal or the alliances I've crafted. The prime minister is going to have questions about the Violet Presentation, and I wouldn't rule out an official investigation. The lieutenant commander might face professional penalties. This is serious, Clara."

My mouth is set, the tea cooling in its cup. I set it aside carefully, breathing in and out, composing myself piece by piece. The enormity of the mess is becoming clear, and a rock the size of the one we scaled feels lodged in my chest.

"I thought you were finally getting serious about a patronage," she murmurs, suddenly sounding tired.

"I am. I've done weeks of research—"

She cuts me off with a gesture and looks around the library. at the warm wood and rich furnishings. "This was where I made my first address to the nation after my father died—at the desk over there. Twenty-four years old and scared I would botch the whole thing. My grandmother curtsied to me, you know, and I wanted to burst into tears." Mama's voice is distant, reflective. "I promised my subjects to serve them my whole life, and I have done," she continues, shaking her head and brushing her cheeks.

For the narrowest moment, I see her vulnerability. She blinks. It soon passes.

"If you're serious about your role, Clara, you'd better be prepared to make sacrifices."

She rests her hand atop a picture of Max and me, taken only yesterday. Queen Helena holds my gaze for a long moment, but when she nods, I am dismissed.

28

QUEEN'S **S**TANDARD

MAX

It's late, but the sun is only now dipping past the horizon. Mom and Dad have rented a small travel caravan and parked it on the drive in front of the cottage. Susi is sleeping with them, on a table that turns into a bed. I've given my room to Hals and Rita, and I hear the exasperated sing-song carrying on the night air as they take turns trying to persuade Ava that my house is an appropriate place to close her eyes. My two-man tent is pitched in the yard, but I'm sitting in one of the mismatched chairs in front of the fire, clutching a berrybeer and wondering how next year will be different. There's just enough room for everyone. Where will we put Clara?

I'm getting ahead of myself, I grin, tipping the bottle back, and remind myself that it's a two-man tent. Mom pads over the gravel drive in her nightdress and robe, her slippers kicking up the tiny rocks, and she drops into the chair next to mine with a sigh. The lake has turned a deep russet gold and the mosquitos are avoiding the smoke

A shout comes from the caravan and Mom scowls. "Dad doesn't think we're level."

"Are you level?"

She gives me a glower and I laugh, taking another swallow.

"How are you?" she asks.

"I'm level too."

She shakes her head, just as she did when I was ten, bringing her buckets of snakes to admire.

"Do we get to meet her?"

I laugh. "To find out if she's good enough for me?"

But her answer is serious. "Of course. I want to know if she's good enough. Princess Clara is as cute as a thimble, but you're my boy and I'd prefer not to give you to anyone I don't like."

"You like everyone. You liked Liva."

"I did not like Liva," she says, surprising me. I knew things were cool between them, but my mom has a marshmallow heart. "You think I couldn't tell she thought I was stupid? A plain, little *huisvrouw* with nothing in her head but the price of carrots?"

All true. We used to leave my parents' house and Liva would start in on how much they represented Little Sondmark.

"No, I did *not* like Liva," she declares.

The sound of the forest bedding down for the night enfolds us both, the crackle of the fire snapping in the cool night air.

"Why didn't you say anything?"

"What am I supposed to tell a grown man? 'I'm sorry Max, but you have to break up with your girlfriend because she wrinkles her nose every time Ava cruises past her on the sofa'?"

"It would have saved me some time."

"It would have made you mad at your mother. Will I like the princess?"

"Clara," I say. She's Clara.

I close my eyes and think of her popping a raspberry into her mouth, cleaning a fish on a rock outside my kitchen door, treading water in the lake. The images are so strong that I'm finding it difficult to remember the massive tiara I once associated her with.

It's hard not to imagine her here next year.

"Max?"

"You'll love her."

"As much as you love her?"

I smile into the fire. "No chance."

Rita and Hals come out, setting the baby monitor next to the wicker sofa. Dad parks and re-parks the caravan with Susi acting as his disinterested guide, glancing down at her phone and waving a hand now and then. We separate when the moon rises, and I duck into the little tent, spreading my sleeping bag on the hard ground. My phone lights up with a text.

We have to talk.

More matchmaking, I guess, getting comfortable, propping myself up on one elbow. "I'm here," I type, sending her a picture of my cramped quarters—the tent flap opening on the star-filled sky.

NewsNook is about to run a series on us. Pictures and everything. Most of them were taken from a boat out on the lake, we think. And there's been someone following us.

"Damn," I murmur. It's got to be the green Ciprio. I remember my initial suspicions, how I talked myself out of them because the idea of anyone following Max Andersen seemed ridiculous. Damn. Clara has been scared of this, and my captain is going to hang my guts from the mast. Still, there's another part of me that welcomes the end of us being a secret.

On the upside, I can take you out to dinner.

I expect her to send me a GIF of a laughing dog or vomiting penguin.

When she makes no reply I ask, "How bad is it for you?" There's a long pause.

Bad enough. There have been high-level talks. The Palace is crafting a reply. My mother is allowing me to use the grounds of Outingen Huis. I have to talk to you. Tomorrow? Noon?

She sends directions to the queen's rural seaside estate. It's not much more than a half-an-hour drive. I listen to the sound of my father's low murmur coming from the caravan. My family is not so tied to my presence that I can't take a few hours off.

Tomorrow, liefje.

I head out early, plugging the info into my phone, and arrive at the gates of the sprawling royal residence in good time. Though the circumstances of this meet-up aren't ideal, it can only be a good thing that she's invited me here to work through it together. I'm not a secret anymore; we're not hiding away at the cottage. Ready or not, Clara is ready to take us public.

That I'm not on my own ground any longer is hammered home by the royal crest affixed to the gold-painted gates. In the distance, the royal standard flutters on the rooftop of the main house, which means Queen Helena is here, I think. I glance down at my sharp-pressed shirt and wonder if Clara means to let her look me over. Should I have come in uniform? Then I think of Mom wanting to look Clara over, and the tension eases a little. It's not any different from that. The queen is a mother.

The guard at the gatehouse glances down at his computer monitor. "Take a left at the fork to the parking area and follow the path through the garden. It'll take you up the rise. Your party is at the summer house. Can't miss it," he says before pressing a button and waving me through.

I park the car and jog up the winding trail, which is long enough to make me wonder if I've taken a wrong turn. Finally, I catch sight of Clara sitting alone in front of an ornate summerhouse, the air carrying the scent of honeysuckle and the sea.

I register the strangeness of Clara looking more formal than usual in a silky dress and carefully smoothed hair. Of course, she looks formal. This is a royal residence, not a cottage in the back of beyond. She doesn't have to paint anything or wash up after.

I stop at the end of the veranda, and she must hear the scrape of my shoes on the gravel because she turns, her face wooden and eyes red-rimmed.

My chest tightens and I groan, lifting my arms, expecting her to launch herself into them, crying her eyes out all over my pressed shirt if she needs to. The queen will have to take me as she finds me.

But when Clara stands, clasping and unclasping her hands, I drop my arms to my sides. I'm not sure what she needs. The silence stretches on, and unease spreads through my stomach. We've never been at a loss for words.

"Our meetings have gone highbrow," I say in an attempt to lighten the mood. I glance over the formal gardens, imagining her in layers of petticoats and me in an elaborate waistcoat.

She doesn't laugh—doesn't even smile. I pace closer and I'm only an arm's length away when she halts me.

"We have to stop this," she nods. Her breath catches oddly, and the skin of her neck and face are washed in uneven red. My brows lower. Whatever is going on, I know she'd feel better—hell, I'd feel better—if only I could hold her and we could get to the bottom of it. Her mother must have put her through a nightmare yesterday.

"Stop the TV program? I don't think that's possible," I smile. "We still live in a constitutional monarchy."

Her tongue darts along her lower lip before she lifts her chin and says in well-enunciated Sondish, "I brought you here to tell you that it's time to conclude our relationship. We can't keep seeing each other."

Her words are a sucker punch, stealing my breath, knocking me on my heels before I've had time to raise my fists. But she spoke so clearly, and when I hear her words, really hear them, understanding rushes in on me. *Vede*. She wasn't ready. I moved too fast. I botched everything.

Too fast? A bitter breath leaves me. I knew after twenty seconds that Clara was it for me. I knew it on the terrace of the ambassador's house. I knew it standing next to her car under a summer sky making a ridiculous bargain. I knew it last year when my mouth dried up at the sound of her voice and I realized I couldn't carry on with a tepid, half-hearted relationship.

This can't be the end of us.

I lean against a balustrade, the sun at my back. I shove my hands into my pockets, careless of creases. "I get it. It's a bad time. We'll go back to friendly dinners," I suggest. Maybe if I'm relaxed, give her time to think, she can clarify what she means.

"No, that's a bad idea," she says, clarifying me right off a cliff. "It always was."

"Dinner was a bad idea? Come on, Clara."

"Come on, Max," she echoes, her tone exhausted, half-pleading, as though I know the script and won't stick to it. In that fraction of a second, she is herself again, emotions breaking past the manners, but my relief is short-lived. "It hasn't been just dinner for a long time, not for either of us. There's enough footage and photos to keep the press busy for months."

The press. The mere mention of them makes me want to launch a cruise missile at every green Ciprio in Sondmark.

"They should have to explain why they made it their business to sit out on a lake day after day with a long lens, spying on a young woman's social life. It's disgusting. They should apologize."

She tilts her head. "That's not how it works. That's not how it ever works." She swallows and takes a shaky breath. "We don't get to ask for fairness when they lay us out on a metal table, dissecting every part."

"Then let's beat them at their own game because breaking up isn't going to stop this. We can get out in front of it, scoop the reporters, and put out our own story about malicious stalking." It's a plan. Not a great one, but it's something.

But Clara takes a hard swallow and closes her eyes. "You don't understand, Max. Most hits we just have to absorb—the internet site with a countdown clock to my 18th birthday, rumors about Alma's engagement, vile claims about my father's background. That the Palace is crafting a response should tell you how big this mess is. They think we faked the Violet Presentation."

"*Stultes es.* That's asinine."

"It isn't when the prime minister is facing a credible challenge from the opposition party and needs to drum up popular support. By this time next week, half the country will be talking about how useless and spoiled I am, wondering why we don't dethrone my mother."

A breath breaks from my lungs. The queen. "Your mother married a man with links to a fascist state. She navigated her own life when it mattered. Why can't you?"

Clara gasps but lifts her chin. "Don't bring my father into this. I'm the one at fault. I had no business getting into a relationship with you when I knew things would take me in another direction."

"Things? Is that a euphemism for your cousin's son?" My control is slipping but I feel like a tree petrifying in the forest, turning to stone. My mouth is dry and my hands long to touch her, to close the distance between us and persuade her to forget who she is. It's worked before.

But her mouth forms a line. "I'm not dropping this so that I can be with anyone else."

"Not even your mother?" I shoot back, bitterness in every word.

She flinches, turning her face to the sun. "Until I'm established, my duties to the Crown are paramount. I'd forgotten that."

"I made you so cross-eyed with lust that you took your eye off the ball? Try another one, Clara. You've had your wits about you. I haven't kept you from your duties." I should take her explanations and go. I should make this easy for her. But I can't.

I reach for her hand and take a drag of air, "Clara, I need you to be brave for us. Fight. I'll fight with you."

For a moment, there is perfect stillness. Even the ocean seems to hold her breath. We balance there so long that I begin to hope. Then she slowly pulls her fingers from mine, crossing her arms over her stomach.

"I have responsibilities you don't understand," she says. She's tired, almost shaking with the effort to say what she's come to say. Her mouth tightens and pulls. "I'm not the queen. I'm not the important person in all this, but I've been the means of dragging my whole family through the tabloids more times than I can count. I have to do what I can to minimize it, and right now, that means setting aside my personal life. We're finished, Max." Her tongue runs along her lip. "I'm sorry if you think that makes me a coward."

Watching her, I slam the door on thoughts about the disaster this is for me; how I'll never get over her and how she could fight for us if she wanted to. Stupidly, my mind returns to last night; to the memory of my father parking and reparking the rented caravan, his shouts to my sister ringing over the lake, how the plastic chairs and battered wicker loveseat were arranged around the fire. It was nothing like this garden; nothing like the queen's standard waving over the mansion.

An ordinary Naval officer was always a longshot, and it's gotten too complicated. What remains simple is that I love her. If she wants to be free of me, I have to give her that much.

I nod and she swallows thickly. I can't detect relief or heartache on her face, only tense fatigue. I always thought I was good in a crisis. If warning bells are ringing or a vessel is taking on water, I always have the answer. Not now.

I lean close, pitching my voice low enough that the security camera near the ornamental hedge won't pick anything up.

"You want to know what I think of you?" The next time we meet will be behind a fortress of royal protocol. Her glance touches mine and darts away. My breath stirs the hair at her temple. "The girl underneath this royal shell isn't disappointing or spoiled. She has gifts, even if her mother has no use for them. She's fun, charismatic, and kind. She deserves to have a patronage because she's good at what she does, not because anyone has to do her any favors. She's enough, exactly as she is."

29

RELATIONSHIP WRECKER

CLARA

He steps back and bows slightly. An ocean breeze blows between us, unfurling the royal standard atop the house—the rampart dragon of Sondmark and the harp seal of the Sonderlands. The standard, I think, desperate to focus on anything but how Max is leaving me right now.

No one has seen a harp seal near Sondmark for almost a hundred years, and our claim to the Sonderlands relies on plate tectonics and a few Viking raids. Still, an enterprising ancestor stitched the harp seal into our flag and the moment someone discovers a natural resource we can exploit, there we are.

It looks like the dragon is about to devour the seal. The poor, sacrificial seal.

Emotion drags at my throat. I'm not enough. I have never been enough. Isn't that Mama's whole point? That I need to fit myself into this royal vessel and it doesn't matter how much I bend or break, there is no gainsaying the shape I must take in the end. Even now, I feel the walls closing in.

"I'll see myself out," he says.

Before I can respond, he's gone. I stare at the maze of greenery that swallows him up, and though I drag air deep into my lungs, I am unable to get enough. I don't deserve to cry. I don't deserve the release. Not for putting that look on Max's face.

I don't go down to the sitting room either, to report to my mother—as Caroline sits in the next room—that the thing is finished. Instead, I turn to the ocean, stumbling through the winding path with the sharp seagrass. I slip my sandals from my feet and jog down to the beach, setting off cascades of sand that wreck the smoothness of the surface. My security detail struggles in his loafers and suit, but he keeps a respectful distance as the wind buffets my face, pulling the tears from my eyes before they've had a chance to fall. I walk and walk and walk.

When we return to the lodge, Mama is tactful, her silence cloaking even her need to manage the world while Caroline sits in the front seat with the chauffeur and buries her nose in a paperback with an unexpectedly lurid cover. Mama doesn't even flip open a notebook and make a list to go over later. She keeps herself from saying the words I can almost hear pressing from her throat. *It was for the best.*

When we arrive, I race up the steps and Mama doesn't call me back. Like a good diplomat, she doesn't insist I come down for dinner when the family returns from a long ride, covered in mud and the smell of horses.

Alma finds me later, sliding onto the end of my bed and pretending not to notice that my eyes are puffy and bloodshot. She doesn't ask what's wrong but tells me about how a lizard scuttled across the path and how she almost fell off her animal.

"I'll be imagining beady black eyes all night," she insists, giving me a gentle, cajoling smile.

"Don't you ever feel like screaming?" I ask, hugging my pillow tightly, the question only superficially about the reptile.

She knows it too. Her smile checks and firms up. "I try to remember it will pass quickly enough if I don't lose control." She leans over and kisses me, curving her arm around my shoulder and staying there for a heartbeat or two. I look at my phone for hours, willing it to ping a notification and wondering what I will do if it does. I'm not brave enough to block his number.

At first light, I rise, pulling on a pair of tweed slacks. I pass Caroline in the hall, coming out of the garden smelling of fresh air and sunshine. I am startled at her appearance, momentarily shocked by the tangle of mousy hair down her back and the flattering simplicity of the wrap dress patterned in tiny blue flowers. Understanding catches up to me. It's her day off. I wonder if she dashed outside before everyone was awake so no one would catch her looking like a fallible human being.

She dips into a curtsey as though she were still clad in sober business attire. I should have known that, day off or not, she doesn't really get a rest from Mama's service when she's up here.

"Good morning, Your Royal Highness. Her Majesty wishes me to inform you that you're slated for a number of engagements when we return to the Summer Palace and asks that you supply yourself with a suitable wardrobe." Her stilted tone makes me wonder if Caroline is part cyborg. Perhaps she'll spend the balance of her day plugged into her charging station in the corner of Mama's office. "Your stipend will reflect your needs, and I'll forward the list to you this afternoon. She doesn't mean you to begin on your selections until we return to Handsel."

I feel battered by the events of yesterday, fragile even, but Caroline's words sound like a crisp schedule slipped under my door.

I take a fortifying breath. More engagements are what I wanted. They are what I've given Max up to achieve. More responsibility. More trust. I wait for the swell of satisfaction to begin to fill the void inside, but instead, there is a persistent voice. *She's enough, exactly as she is.*

"Will the Palace be making an official comment about the TV program?"

Caroline shifts slightly, and I notice for the first time how young she is. Maybe not even thirty. Teeth briefly worry at her lower lip. "It was decided—"

In a committee, I think, roiling with mortification. Aides and worthy advisors sat around a conference table passing judgment on this latest escapade.

"It was decided that the Palace will issue a reminder to the press to respect the privacy of the royal family while they are not actively on the job."

I give a short nod and she moves on. The official statement will not kill the stories, but I am thankful for even that much shelter as I prepare to navigate a difficult week.

We return to the Summer Palace, and by Monday morning, I'm sick to my stomach. I get up and try to act as though my day will go on as normal, but finally, I drag my laptop onto the bed and watch as jaw-tinglingly sweet morning news anchors sit on a semi-circular sofa dropping coy hints about bombshell news from the Party Princess and a certain uniformed officer.

When the segment airs, a series of photos play in a montage. Oh wow. They dug into the archives, unearthing every family photocall and Christmas card picture. The background music drops into a minor key and a menacing voiceover asks, "But who is she, really, our Princess Clara? Over-exuberant sorority sister? Or calculated relationship wrecker?"

Then a picture of Max—the one with his ex-girlfriend from his mother's Facebook page—digitally tears in half, leaving Liva off to the side like a fragment of a calving glacier.

My face is hot with embarrassment when Ella bangs into my suite, the door bouncing off the paneling. "What in the *flamen* hell is going on?" she roars. "I mean, what in the actual *flamen* hell? Did you see it? Have you seen it?"

I tilt my computer monitor at her, my face set, and she growls low in her throat. "Isn't there a law about this kind of trash?"

"We live in a free country, Ella. The prime minister—"

"The prime minister can eat his tie. This shouldn't be allowed."

The segment is wrapping up with a roundtable discussion as viewers are encouraged to vote in a live poll. Numbers fluctuate between 60-70% on the Relationship Wrecker side of the scale. So that's great.

The presenter gives a little laugh and tells viewers that new evidence will be presented tomorrow.

"Tune in!" Ella echos. Her voice is chirpy, and she's making an obscene gesture at the screen as it goes black. "Has the queen seen this? She'll go through the roof."

"She knows."

"Hold up," Ella says, lapsing into English. I know I'm about to hear some get-a-grip-girlfriend talk. "You knew this was going to drop and you just...didn't tell your closest sister?"

I blow out a breath and nod, wide eyes unfocused. "Yep."

"You told Max?"

Same nodding thousand-yard stare. "Yep."

"Mama ripped into you."

"Yep."

She sits down heavily on the bed. "What are you going to do?"

I look at the clock. "The Palace drops a statement within the hour, I go on with my increased duties and ignore this if I can."

"Poor Max," she sighs, saying aloud the words that have been cascading through my head all morning. "He must be going crazy. Do you have a game plan? You should introduce yourselves to the slavering public by having a few dates. Maybe a night at the ax-throwing gallery? The public would like to see his biceps. After that, they'll understand everything..." She trails off when she sees my face. "What?"

"Max and I aren't seeing each other anymore." My fingers twist together.

Ella looks to the ceiling and begins to growl. "What in the *flamen* hell? What in the actual *flamen* hell?"

I shake my head and pull up a tab on my computer. It's a website for Gina Dialli. The clothes have simple lines, bold colors, and precision tailoring. Mama likes that when she wears Dialli clothes, she can stand anywhere in a crowded football stadium and be seen and identified instantly by 50,000 subjects.

"I'll be too busy for a relationship," I say. "I've got the Leukemia Society dinner in a few weeks, an unveiling of a new branch line of the S-Train, as well as several charity events for some blue-collar organizations."

"Hence the soul-sucking clothes." Ella's tone is sour. "Did he break up with you or did Mama break up with him?"

I ignore that dig, feeling the tension in my shoulders tighten. "I told him it was time to bring things to a conclusion."

"You gave him up to be Mama's ambassador to the trade unions?"

"Trade unions are important," I shout. Instantly, I drop my voice to a furious whisper. "It's work that has to be done."

Ella's tone is scathing. "It can be done by any of us."

True, but there's something Ella doesn't know. I run a tongue along my lip. "Mama is talking about sending me on a royal tour. By myself."

This is big news, and even Ella is surprised. We've all been on royal tours but as pairs and trios. Only Noah and Alma have ever been by themselves.

"Where?"

"San Sabao, Tzeke, Kleingeshaft. I know they aren't large countries, but I have to begin somewhere, and I'll be expected to manage the engagements on my own." There is no detail too small to matter on a royal tour. I'll be expected to reflect the will and strength of the monarchy in my mode of dress, my choice of jewels, my selection of activities. The preparation will absorb my time for months.

I expect Ella to be interested, but she is rubbing the bridge of her nose. There is a sustained silence, and she flops backward on the bed, crossing her hands over her stomach and narrowing her eyes.

"Have you done any research yet?"

Though she sounds unexcited, I take the question as an olive branch.

"Some. San Sabao is known for its olive groves, and I thought that a visit to—"

"San Sabao is ruled by the Mirabaldi family. Grand dukes. The current heir to the fabulously wealthy country is twenty-three and unattached."

I am thrown off my stride. "Oh? I'll include that in my notes." I grab a notepad and begin to scribble.

"Have you looked up Tzeke?"

I click another tab open on my computer. "Primary exports are aluminum and nuts—"

"A principality. The old prince is very, very old. But his son is thirty-five and looking around for a wife willing to ignore the paternity lawsuits that keep springing up like weeds. How about Kleingeshaft?"

"What's with this sudden fascination with geography?" I snap.

"Divorced but hot. The crown jewels are citrine though. Pity you're not a brunette."

In the old days, we would be wrestling on the floor, pulling each other's hair out by the root as soon as Nanny's back was turned. We held no grudges but settled things like sisters—by scratching and kicking, as God intended. Ella is supposed to be my ally, but I am so furious with her that I wouldn't stop at a few strands of hair. I'd render her entirely bald.

Ella gets to her feet, standing like a girl who has the same instincts and memories as I do; standing like someone prepared to take a running tackle. She points a finger at the Tzeke tourism board's landing page, blue skies and blue water banding a quaint white village.

"All that"—she twirls her finger, encompassing the ocean and the aluminum and the Dialli coat dresses I intend to buy—"is not going to get you what you want. Mama loves her children, but when it comes to our service to the Crown, she has no sentimentality. She's not sending you on this tour to add anything meaningful to her network. She's sending you to meet some eligible men. The best thing in the world for her would be if you formed an alliance and got off her hands." The accusation lands like a punch to the gut.

"That's it," I say, unclipping my earrings, slapping them on the nightstand. "That is it."

"Are we fighting now?" she asks, dancing on her toes like a boxer. Ella is heavier than I am, but I'm taller. I like my chances. "I'm not the one who thinks so little of you. I'm not the one who made you give up Max."

"Mama didn't make me give up Max," I say, waiting to make my move until Ella shifts away from the hand-painted Limoges vase.

Ella narrows her eyes at me. "Not Mama. You."

I lunge, catching her off guard. We tumble onto the bed, grappling for supremacy, and I enjoy a second of victory before she hooks my legs, flips me over, and sits on my stomach.

"Now that you are ready to listen," she says, huffing slightly, "I have some things to say. First, if you haven't learned yet, you're going to now. You will never get what you want from Mama by asking nicely. She didn't get where she is by conceding her ground. When she fights, you fight."

"You're so good at fighting," I say, the breath squeezed from my lungs. I buck under her, but she holds on. "You're still wearing heels and hose to girls' field hockey demonstrations."

She ignores my point. "You take her seriously as an adversary. She is not your mother when you face her across a conference table. She is your boss, and she will try to wring you for every *fennig* she can. Second—" I try again to wriggle out from under her but she's got me fast. "Second, does this matter more than heels and hose? Is he worth fighting for?"

I don't want to answer. It's too raw. I keep remembering his face when I told him it was the end of us. I keep remembering how hurting him felt like twisting a knife in my own stomach.

"Ella, you are seriously killing me," I say. I catch a reflection of us in a dressing mirror. I look defeated, broken.

"You're not dead yet."

My face crumples, and I feel a tear slide down my temple. Ella shifts from my chest and flops down at my side. I should be able to breathe but I can't. Ella's question is too big. It matters too much.

I fumble for the truth. "Yes."

"Good thing," Ella laughs, "because he's hot. I saw the TV segment. It's a wonder the whole forest didn't burn down."

I laugh because if I don't, I am going to howl.

"Third," she says, her gaze meeting mine across the bedspread, "would he have fought for you?"

Stultes es. Ella does not play fair. Max's words haunt me again. *Be brave for us. Fight. I'll fight with you.* My heart is twisting in its cavity, straining to find an anchor. *I'll fight with you.*

"Yes."

30

LIFE RAFT

MAX

When my parents drive Susi back to civilization and Rita and Hals have packed up every one of Ava's toys, I get drunk for the first time in a decade.

I sit on the dock with a six-pack of Kurtzburg and tell myself that it's fine. I'm fine. The whole damn country is fine. There have even been long stretches this weekend when I haven't felt anything. Sure, the numbness aches like a *tayve*, but even that's fine, I think, taking a long pull of beer.

Liquid trickles down my throat, and I give the bottle a betrayed look. Empty. I throw it into the sailboat and reach for another.

Only when my family asked about Clara outright did it feel like I'd taken a torpedo to the chest, the force of it tearing a hole through me. I knew they'd stop using her name if I told them we'd broken up, but the words lodged in my throat. Even the Kurtzburg can't knock them loose.

The next morning, I am bleary-eyed and full of regret. I begin on my deployment checklist, hoping to lose myself in the routine, and lay the caretaker's binder open on the kitchen counter, updating each phone number and utility for easy access. My pen makes careful marks, tracking my progress.

Clean out the sailboat. Check.

Laundry. Check.

Dusting and sweeping. Check.

Take out the trash. Check.

Water the garden.

My pen hovers over the list, and I look out the window, at the rock wall and the spindly wildflowers, tops heavy, tapping against the stones and ready to bloom.

Vede.

Before I can dam them up, I am flooded with angry questions. The numbness cracks painfully, and I fire the pen at the wall. It bounces against the backsplash, skitters across the countertop, and rolls to a rest where we slid the seed packet back and forth. That was a lifetime ago.

Taking a long, careful breath, I rub my face and the bristles of my chin and then brace my hands against the counter, staring hard at the list. It's just a chore, no different than checking the expiration dates on the perishables in the fridge. But walking into the yard, my grip tightens around the pig-shaped watering can. I fill it from the spigot in the garden before I can succumb to the wish to fling it into the lake. I resolve to chuck it in a donation box when I return. I'll find something sleek and Scandinavian, so minimalist it won't even have a spout. After giving the plants a good soak—they didn't break up with me, this isn't their fault—I return to the checklist and strike a dark line through the task.

"Finished," it seems to say. Clara and I are finished.

On Monday morning, I leave a message for the caretaker, turn the key, and give the cottage a final look. Clara is in every corner of my property, has touched every surface in the house, like a ghost I can't banish.

I heft my bag over my shoulder and begin to talk myself into believing that I'll feel better when I come back to no Clara. Time is my friend. It's going to help me exorcise her ghost. If not, I'll sell the cottage. I'll get an apartment closer to base, within walking distance of loud bars, loud people, and so much noise I won't have to think. I'll swipe right and keep on swiping until I return to a life that looks nothing like the one I had with her.

I toy with the idea for several kilometers.

Ping.

My heart kicks up, but then a soothing robotic voice reads out the text and it takes me a few beats before I recognize it's from Mom.

Have you seen the news?

I ate a breakfast of cold cereal, grimly determined to avoid the news. It can't be anything but a distraction while I'm on deployment.

They're tearing her to shreds. I'm going to write NewsNook a letter. The executive producer is going to get a piece of my mind.

"Don't do that," I say, using the voice-to-text feature. I imagine such a letter becoming tabloid fodder. "You have to ignore them."

You're right. I have to brush up on being the mother of the man who's dating the princess. "L-O-L," the robot voice spells out.

I haven't talked to anyone about Clara and feel the constant pressure of it sitting in my throat, forming a hard knot inside my chest. It's too late to find relief in telling my mother. "I'm headed into base," I say. "I knew this was going to broadcast and was expecting it. Can't talk now. I love you."

Be safe. Love you.

I turn down the street leading to the gatehouse and notice a commotion near the front of the line of cars. A news van with a satellite bolted to the top is parked on the grassy verge with a green Ciprio slotted behind it. Several other cars litter the other side of the road. *Vede.* I wasn't expecting this. Members of the press spot me, and I reach for some aviator sunglasses, staring straight ahead even though photographers and reporters swarm my vehicle, knocking against the glass and shouting questions. I nudge the car forward, recognizing a temptation to gun the engine and wipe out a clutch of tabloid journalists. My muscles tense and my hands grip the steering wheel as I travel the length of the street inch by inch. This strategy of ignoring them only takes me as far as the gate. I roll down the window, ready to flash my badge when a microphone is thrust between me and the guardsman.

"Lieutenant Commander Andersen," they all seem to shout, voices fighting like a pack of wolves over a single bone. But one man gets his question in, spitting it out in a rush. "Is it true that you staged the escapade at the Queen's Day ceremony?" My jaw hardens. Click, click, click, go the cameras. "What would you say to those who suggest you dishonored our national heritage and fallen servicemen by pulling such a stunt?"

Another yells, "Was Her Royal Highness in on it?"

Now the temptation is to leap through the window and blast the journalist with my ideas about honor and what I think of him following a young girl around for weeks on end. Boiling frustration rips through my veins. The man can choke on his mic. Then the thought of Clara touches me on the shoulder—the brush as light as her fingertips.

The entire country may listen to my next words. My family won't care what I say but this matters to Clara, and for the first time, I get a taste of the battle she fights to represent herself as she wants.

How would she do it? She would lift her chin, so I lift my chin. She would be calm, so I am calm. The picture everyone will see is me jerking away from a microphone. So, I throw the car into park, take the sunglasses off, and exit the vehicle. For a stunned second, the little weasel with the microphone backs up. Soon there are enough of them gathered around to form a half-circle, and when I am content that it looks less like an ambush and more like a press conference, I give the journalist my full attention.

"Serving in Her Majesty's Royal Navy is the greatest privilege of my life. I would never dishonor the men and women who have made the ultimate sacrifice while wearing the uniform of our nation. If you'll excuse me, I have to report for duty. Good day, ladies, gentlemen." Two brisk Navy nods follow.

I flash my badge and the guard gives a salute, lifting the gate. I slide behind the wheel and drive through, the mob calling after me. I've lost the right to worry about Clara but can't keep myself from wondering how bad this is going to get for her.

Captain Dusstock comes by my berth with coffee in his hand, standing in the doorway. "You screwed up, Andersen. I told you. I *tried* to tell you." I salute and he laughs, shaking his head like he can't believe anyone is as stupid as his lieutenant commander. "Maybe you thought you were going to be something—admiral of the whole damned fleet—but this'll get you busted down a peg." He gives a mocking salute. "Farewell to your career, sailor. The promotion board probably already has your file flagged for river patrols."

"Is there anything you want me to know before we sail, sir?" I ask, stowing my gear. This deployment is going to be bad enough, but I'm serving under a captain who thinks he's cornered the market on brains.

I keep busy for the rest of the day, organizing supplies and overseeing the sailors coming aboard. I greet the resiliency counselor carrying a box of handheld video game consoles, a few terabytes loaded with American blockbusters and 500 hours of Sondish TV. I have a brief meeting with the department heads in the wardroom.

"We leave everything on land. No friends. No family. No gossip from Handsel," I emphasize meaningfully. The shifting glances tell me they've seen the news or heard it secondhand. "Understood?"

An affirmative rumble answers me. "Sir, yes sir."

I collar Moller after the meeting breaks up. "The supply chief bears watching," I tell him. At his sharp look, I wave a hand. "He's new, that's all. I don't want to breathe down his neck, but let me know if you see anything I should know about."

Once we're free of the harbor and the tugboats, the bridge crew takes us out, navigating the ship into the sunset, amber light dancing off the waves. The colors are lowered to the sound of the national anthem playing over the tinny speakers and I stand at attention until the last note dies away, the rocking under my feet familiar and welcome. I ought to feel at home. I love this part of the Navy—tradition, order, and the strange beauty of the endless ocean—but as I watch the blazing lights of the Summer Palace slip over the horizon, the refuge of numbness drifts away like a life raft.

I get through the next hours, carrying the pain like a live mortar, and when I finally slip into my bunk, I reach into my locker. The pressure in my throat and chest is physical, but it's not a problem I can't fix. Fixing things is what I do.

I tug on a folder and a stack of newsprint splashes across the floor. Shuffling them into order, I tilt the images in the light, looking at Clara's face with eyes now familiar with every expression. I see now that though she was smiling, it wasn't for me. It was a smile for the cameras. A princess smile.

My fingernail picks at the tape, folded over just so. What did I expect would happen between us? It was there from the beginning—how much I wanted her and how little there was for her to give.

I shove the pictures back into the locker. When I pass a garbage chute on my way to breakfast, I'll drop them inside. Though my decision to move on is made, the pressure in my chest grows sharper.

I reach for my phone. There's no service out here. No data that can tell me if I made the news tonight. I couldn't send a text if I wanted to. I tap the camera icon and scroll through a series of images taken over the last months. I have to delete these too. I'm stupidly looking for signs that she might have struggled to tell me goodbye; signs that there was something real between us.

A blurry Clara as she hikes through the forest.

Swipe.

Clara wielding her paintbrush, attacking the cottage wall like it's a Vorburg raider.

Swipe.

A low-angled picture of Clara stirring a pot.

Swipe.

Clara at the end of the dock, wrinkling her nose. Smiling.

That smile was for me.

31

ENOUGH SCANDAL

CLARA

I'm in my private sitting room working on patronage homework when I hear Max's name on the television. My head jerks up. I check the time and the station logo in the corner of the screen. This isn't the entertainment press. This is a respectable news program with a proper newsreader wearing serious glasses and a resolute expression. The report comes after segments on tariff negotiations and drought conditions in the inland territories.

Neer Hjefdal reads his lines on the teleprompter in a restrained panic, as though he has to get through the sentence before he vomits. "The prime minister's office is calling for an inquiry into what the press has dubbed The Flower Affair between Princess Clara and Lieutenant Commander Max Andersen of Her Majesty's Royal Navy."

Then comes a clip of the prime minister's smarmy press secretary, a young woman in a bouncy blowout and horn-rimmed glasses. "The presentation of the violets to our servicemen and women is the rare public event that unites the people of Sondmark, no matter their faith, income, orientation, age, ability, marital status, occupation, class, or political beliefs. Though Princess Clara holds the position of the violet bearer by tradition, the government calls on the Palace to assure the people that this ceremony is in responsible hands."

The newsreader swivels to a panel of experts. The first recounts the mythology of the Dragonslayer and the Maiden, tying it to the roots of the royal tradition. "The tale never actually names what sort of flower the young princess used to bind up the soldier's wounds, only that she found it deep in the woods."

Another panelist speaks as a former officer who participated in such an event when Alma was the young princess doling out posies. "She was as meticulous as you could wish, even congratulated me on making rank the previous spring. So controlled, I had the impression she could pilot the ship if we ever needed a second captain."

The last brings up the constitutional implications of abolishing the monarchy and speaks at length on my fitness as a human being. "Her Majesty has no control over Princess Clara whatsoever, that much is clear. In America, unsavory family dramas are played out by reality stars and paid for by advertising revenue. If that's what we can expect from our royal family, why are we footing the bill?"

I rub my hands tiredly over my face.

"There is some question about whether or not her heel getting stuck was planned as a kind of lover's joke," *Neer* Hjefdal interjects. "The prime minister's office will have to content itself for the time being with this statement made by Lieutenant Commander Andersen on his way to his deployment this morning."

"Oh no," I gasp. If Max didn't hate me before being hounded by the paparazzi, he's sure to hate me after.

Then Max is on the screen, and I shove my papers and laptop aside, crouching before the television on my knees. It's the first time I've seen him in days, and my eyes hungrily sweep the screen. The camera has framed him along with the gatehouse, and in his uniform, he's all business. He doesn't look like a man who spent the weekend licking his wounds after a breakup.

I subside on my heels with a cold knot forming in my stomach. I shouldn't feel upset that he looks like he still has his life together, but I do.

His statement is brief, polite, and professional. Practically a masterclass of image management and leaving no room for alternative interpretations of the events.

I slowly exhale, wishing this pain and longing would leave me as easily. I have messed up, and I don't know how to fix it.

At the conclusion of the broadcast, Her Majesty sends out a message via Caroline calling for an emergency family meeting in the morning. Sleep eludes me, and I work long into the night.

When morning comes, I run off my nerves, circling the grounds, finally popping in on Lady Greta. An old-fashioned recording of a Lars Velmundson ballad comes through the open windows.

When you were mine,
I kissed you whenever.
You stood still for me
Holding your breath
Until I lent you my own.

I skid to a stop, bite my lip, and clutch my side like I've got a stitch from running. My heart keeps breaking even though I keep telling myself I'm past the worst of it. I'm not past anything if this feeling—sick and sad and furious at the same time—can be triggered off by an old love song.

I sniff loudly and straighten. I can see my godmother swaying around her sitting room in a garish housecoat, her slippers kicked off. I smile, even as I make a quick assessment. She is worse today. The godmother I have always known would be more careful of appearances. Still, her dementia, something I hate so fiercely, has moments that make her brave, paring her personality back to the most essential elements—brightness, exuberance, love of sentiment. Her illness takes and takes but this is a gift.

"Come in, come in, *elskede*," she gestures. She can't remember my name, but she remembers me as one of her darlings, and I am glad for that. "What are you doing today?"

"I'm in trouble," I say, kissing her papery cheek.

"Scandal," she grumbles, returning to her swaying dance. "Scandal. It does us all good to have a little scandal from time to time."

"I've had quite enough scandal."

"Does your papa still insist you throw over the handsome prince?"

She hands out questions like party favors, poorly matched to each recipient. Who is Papa? Who is the prince?

"Papa never changes," I say, playing along.

Greta snorts. "Old goat. Why does he object? You'll have the boy in the end, I wager." Her eyes bulge. "What on earth are you wearing?"

Only some leggings and a fitted tank top, but if Greta is trapped in the past, they must seem shocking.

"My exercise clothes," I say and she lifts a disapproving brow.

"Like a bathing costume?" she asks. "Won't catch a man without a bikini."

I laugh but swallow back a sudden thickness in my throat when I recall Max tossing me into the lake fully clothed. This has to get easier. It has to.

Ten o'clock comes too soon. I shower, change into the most conservative clothes I have, and grab my computer before I depart. Freja comes upon me as I leave my suite, silently tucking her arm through mine, her vintage *ter Brandt* wrap-dress somehow perfectly royal and personally distinctive. How does she manage to work within this system and still retain such a strong sense of self? I wonder if she intentionally waited for me in the hall, ready to lend her quiet, undemanding support.

We arrive at the conference room, and I find that, again, Noah is early. Is that intentional too? He and Caroline are not friends—they are hardly on speaking terms. Still, he arrives early and covertly follows her progress around the room. I wonder if he's here because of excellent time management or because it affords him the chance to see her alone. The wondering occupies my thoughts, pushing aside my worries for a brief time.

"Are you dyspeptic?" Freja asks him. "I only ask because of that ferocious scowl. Mama has some pills, I think. Caroline, doesn't Her Majesty have—"

"I don't have indigestion," he snaps.

"Too many late nights?" she asks, failing to read the room.

"Mind your own affairs, Freja."

Freja shrugs and makes her way to the refreshment table, a recent innovation, and chooses a bottle of sparkling water.

Caroline places an agenda in front of me, and I glance over it.

Item: Prime Minister Torbald's inquiry

My stomach drops into my toes and stays there until the meeting begins. At the top of the hour, Mama leans forward, tenting her fingers.

"You've had such a busy summer, Clara."

I had hoped to gain her trust and confidence when I broke things off with Max, but those seem to have evaporated from her voice. I am the Party Princess again, fielding angry trans-Atlantic phone calls from my mother about what I owe the House of Wolffe and how my actions have damaged my reputation forever.

"You need to give me a clear, honest answer. Was the shoe incident staged? Yes or no."

I suck in a breath, but I swallow away the hurt. "No. We'd hardly ever spoken before—and then only in an official capacity. It was sheer chance that my shoe became stuck."

"You went from official ceremonies to secret meetings?" Noah is in a foul mood today. He braces his arm against the table and lifts his brow. "It looks bad—to the press, to the prime minister, to us—that you were obviously keeping it secret. Do you have something to hide?"

How dare he.

"Not everyone wants every detail of their love life splashed on the front pages of the tabloid news. I suspect even you have secrets," I lash out. My gaze holds his steadily. Americans have a wonderful expression I am finding enormously apt. Mess with the bull, get the horns.

"What's to be done about it?" Alma cuts through the tension with a diplomatic gesture. "The prime minister has got his hair on fire—"

"As usual," mutters Ella, who detests his way of practicing politics.

"—but there is no easy way to tell the entire country that the report is false. It drags us down to the level of the gutter press."

"Perhaps Clara might withdraw from public life for a time?" asks Freja, whose only aim in life is more personal space. She means it for the best, but I won't have it.

"No," I say, rejecting the idea outright. "I haven't done anything wrong or disrespectful, and it'll look like I'm guilty if I slink off like a dog with its tail between its legs."

Père raps his knuckles on the table. Pavian for, "Bravo, bravo!"

"It will be the worst possible thing for Max," I say, bringing his name—his actual name—within these hallowed halls. Mama almost recoils from it.

"The young man is not our concern."

My voice rises in response. "He's my concern. If you knew him, you'd know that Max would never be party to such a thing. If we behave like I'm guilty, then it looks like he is too. I won't allow this speculation to affect his career."

"His career," Mama echos. "He's what rank, again?" she asks, leafing through her notes.

"Lieutenant commander, ma'am," Caroline murmurs from the corner. Every gaze in the room swings towards the unexpected interjection. "Graduated top of his class at Knutsen Naval Academy. His current post is modest, but his future is promising."

I blink, confused. Is this support? It is difficult to tell from the way she delivers the facts in an even, informative manner.

"Pity," Mama says, like his career is already ruined.

Has she already decided his worth and determined that it's too little to regret the loss of his career if it gets things sailing smoothly again? It's a cold-blooded approach, but shame and regret burn through me. I haven't been any better than Mama. Didn't I break things off with Max as soon as our relationship became an obstacle to fulfilling my role? It's a merciless assessment, but it brings hot, unblinking clarity. I've hurt him enough.

"Max didn't have to say what he did at the naval base yesterday. He could have caused a scene and made it much worse for this family, but his statement has the potential to quiet the prime minister's offices, at least in the short term. We owe him our thanks for that. For the long-term, I have a proposal," I say. The monarchy will take a hit over this, but we can absorb it. We're like an aircraft carrier with one rusted antenna snapped off while Max's vessel is smaller and liable to be swamped in our wake if we don't take care.

"The best way through this is to trust me with a patronage that has some heft to it. If I'm working hard and can be seen to be working hard, this reputation of mine will eventually slough off like so much dead skin."

Exfoliation metaphor for the win.

Mama sighs as though saying, "Patronages again?" She is not won over.

Alma lifts her hand. "No, no. It's not a bad idea. Clara's assignments have been ridiculously light. When I was her age—"

"When you were her age, you were a sober-minded graduate student and the Princess Royal. I knew I could rely on your committed, loyal presence then, just as I do now."

Alma takes a quick, bracing breath. A muscle jumps in her cheek but she doesn't abandon me. "Clara knows how to work a room better than anyone at this table."

"Royal duties require more than being charming," Noah protests.

A surprisingly wicked smile spreads across Alma's face. "Not something you'd know much about."

"Brat," he fires back, but it's indulgent. They are close, those two.

"I want a shot at St Leofdag's," I declare.

Mama tilts her head. "The hospital?"

I nod, opening my computer. "Caroline, will you help me access the projection screen?"

She crouches in a ladylike manner before a console and digs around for the switch which will lift away the middling landscape to reveal a huge television screen. I catch Noah watching her, and I give him a bland smile. He frowns and jerks his eyes to the ceiling.

"You came prepared with a multimedia presentation?" Ella laughs, tugging my attention. She gives me a look that's more Stanford game-day than Sondmark emergency. "Nice."

"I came prepared to have my competence and judgment questioned." I stand, reminding myself that this isn't treason. It's a plan. Max believed in me. I saw it every time he looked into my face. I borrow some of his certainty now.

I tap on the keys of my computer, and Caroline dims the lights.

"St Leofdag's Hospital is an established patronage currently under the direction of Alma." I give a short review of the history of the patronage and the general work of the hospital. "Primarily known for its care for the elderly. There are several wings devoted to the long-term care of memory patients."

The next slide pops up, listing the number of patronages each member of the family has. Freja and Ella, just two years older than I am, have more than a dozen apiece.

The next slide contains a list of Alma's involvement with the patronage since she took it over from Mama. "As you can see, she's done good work, raising 250,000 *maarke* at the annual gala. However, because of her heavy patronage load, Alma's involvement is limited."

I give a direct but gentle smile to my sister, and she gives an encouraging nod. That she knows this isn't a knife in the back gives me the support I need to continue.

"Which brings me to what I have to offer."

Now comes a slide with a picture of Lady Greta on it. "Has anyone visited her cottage lately?"

My siblings look from face to face.

"Mama, you have tea with her from time to time, yes?"

My mother's nod is stiff.

"I try to pop in a few times a week. Though we see each other often, she has called me Helena, Freja, and Alma in the last month alone. Sometimes she thinks I'm a secretary and at other times, the queen. For more than fifty years, she served the Crown, appearing neatly dressed and well-behaved." I give them a brief reminder of her life and service, the parts of her personality that seemed intrinsic to her last year. "She lives a good life today because she has good food, companionship, and freedom within the walls of the Summer Palace. I like being around older people," I say simply. My hand hovers over the keyboard as I look into the smiling face of my godmother. "Most of them have great stories and no time to pretend to be something other than who they are. It would be worthwhile to spend my time making sure that more of them get the care they need."

I've worried for so long about twisting myself into a particular shape for royal life, but as I speak these words, I feel myself slipping inside a vessel that feels tailor-made for me. I clear my throat of the sudden tightness and press a key on my computer.

The next slide is an aerial map of the hospital, and I move towards the screen, pointing out areas of interest. "Years ago, as part of Alma's patronage, she had the idea of asking for a wish list of long-term needs the hospital would like help with. Some of those have been addressed, but many have not. The first thing I would like to do is to make use of these extensive grounds. Currently, memory patients are confined to an interior courtyard. With a big fundraising push, we can provide a safe, secure environment, giving them a greater degree of freedom, fresh air, and opportunities for gardening."

"Fundraising push? Money doesn't come from trees, Clara,"

I give my mother a tight smile and pull up the next slide. Here I have included a list of potential engagements I could roll out immediately to build awareness.

"These would build a strong narrative of the importance of memory care. Being candid about longer-term needs would give more focus to fundraising." I list the annual gala but include a family fun run and marathon, as well as the idea of publishing a cookbook submitted by the families of current and former patients. "Too, there are corporate philanthropies we can involve. I got the idea at Noah's entrepreneur event. Many who attended spoke favorably about current tax loopholes which allow for government matching of funds, and I imagine the prime minister would be pleased to tout one of his successful initiatives."

I signal to Caroline to cover the screen again and glance across the table.

"I'm good at opening car parks. I know where to stand and how to shake hands and smile. But the people of Sondmark are right to think I'm a lightweight. They aren't getting their money's worth out of me—not when I'm capable of more."

Alma swivels to Mama. "I like this idea. Clara's right. St Leofdag's has been on my list forever, but I haven't devoted that much time to its development because there are always other things that need doing. If we assigned Clara, it might kill two birds with one stone. The hospital will get more attention, and Clara can establish herself outside of this silly scandal with her boyfriend."

I see a flicker of interest from Mama, but she blinks it away, aiming a look down the length of the table. "Boyfriend? You claimed you broke it off, Clara."

My mouth is dry. "I have." I was doing so well. Not screaming or shouting or bursting into tears. I bite the inside of my cheek, fighting to maintain my composure. "That was a mistake. In future, I intend to fight for the things—and people—that matter. You taught me how important it is to do that," I remind her. She shifts imperceptibly, her mouth set in a tight line. Père draws a sharp breath.

I continue, "The North Sea Confederation wouldn't exist without your determination to fight for it. Anyway, this isn't about Max. It's about having a voice in this family. I would *like* you to give me this opportunity because I've earned it—because you're fair-minded enough to know I didn't cause this mess and you trust me to treat the lives of these people as carefully as if they were my own godmother. But I'll *take* this opportunity even if it's just a way to solve your problems."

Silence blankets the room.

"That was a very pretty speech," Mama says and Père slices his hand through the air.

"No, Helena. It was not a speech. Clara is right. If you *are* fair-minded, you'll admit her idea is a good one."

Mama inhales sharply and looks right past Père.

"Noah?" she asks. The reputation of the monarchy will fall on his shoulders someday.

"It's ridiculous that we're not employing her. No wonder people think she's ornamental when we use her so little."

A queenly silence fills the room and then Her Majesty lifts her pen, checking the item off her list.

"Alma, you will begin training Clara to take over the patronage and introduce her to key figures. I hope to release a statement to the press at the end of the week." She quickly concludes the meeting and sweeps out.

I almost gasp in surprise. I've won. The first thought that hits me is Max. I have to tell Max. I almost reach for my phone when I'm pulled to my feet and into my father's embrace. My sisters offer their congratulations while I smile and say all the right things.

Ella waves it all off and says, "Group hug." She and Alma envelop me. "You too, Freja," Ella says, voice muffled in my shoulder. Freja's feather-light embrace is added to theirs. We are strong, I think, the four princesses of Sondmark, standing together.

When they leave me, I make my way into the garden, heading for a wide swing under a spreading oak tree.

I did it. I actually did it. I made my stand against Mama. Maybe it's too late to matter for Max and me, but I'm stronger for it. The press will continue to be beastly. I'm not so naive as to think insulting tabloid headlines and shouted questions about my personal life will dry up just because Max made a strong statement and the Palace reminded the press of my boundaries. But I feel like I've been swimming against a riptide for years and finally feel the first grains of sand under my feet.

I grip the thick ropes, my eyes trained on the ancient stone walls of the Summer Palace. All I want is to talk to Max.

32

Damage Control

MAX

I step out on the bridge wing in my cap and windbreaker, standing in the fury of an early autumn storm chasing us into port. The wind and rain are bracing, and I breathe in the smell of the ocean. The sun is setting, and my view is gray everywhere, but we're only a few hours from the lights of Handsel.

The deployment has been a busy one, getting recruits up to speed, training away their rough spots as we patrol the waters of the Sonderlands and into the Baltic Sea. We engage in military exercises with the navies of Motovia and Tallinne, pushing our tactical capabilities to the limit. We sail by a tiny, disputed rock between Vorburg and Sondmark, sending a contingent of sailors scrambling up the steep banks to replace the Vorburgian flag and berrybeer with the standard of Sondmark and a bottle of Kurtzburg.

The rhythms of life aboard a ship are comfortable, and I anchor myself in them. Mustering with the crew each morning. Meetings. Inspections. Quick meals in the wardroom. Fresh strawberries that don't last the first week. Fresh cabbage that does. Drills for fires and drills for running aground. Free weights in the engine room and working out until I can't think. A Lutheran service on Sunday. Bells every half-hour. A bugle recording at the close of the day.

I look at the swelling sea, concentrating on keeping my stance loose, my knees soft. The busyness and routine haven't been enough to keep me from thinking about Clara. The thought of her tugs at me when I'm staring at a bulkhead before drifting off to sleep. It tugs at me even when I'm knee-deep in reports. A month of missing her. I'm supposed to have begun feeling better by now. I'm supposed to forget the way she likes to grab my shirt collars when I'm kissing her. I'm supposed to want to look at other women.

A low curse forms in my throat, and I hear Moller behind me. "Sir?"

More to avoid the question than anything else, I lift my binoculars, tracing them along the gray horizon. I jerk them down, use my own eyes, and lift them again to be sure. "Small craft. Riding low." I point to ten o'clock.

He lifts his binoculars. "Any distress calls?"

"No," I answer, heading back to the bridge.

"Captain wants us to make port by 1900 hours."

I watch the craft for another moment. "That's not going to happen," I say, calling out orders to change the heading. "Alert the captain."

The bridge crew is quick to respond, and I feel the difference in the way the waves crash against the hull. The captain must as well because he charges up the ladder.

"What in the hell?"

"Sir, we have a ship," I report, pointing towards it and handing him the binoculars, "three kilometers out. I don't like the look of it."

"Don't like the look," he scoffs.

"I'd like to come alongside and get visual confirmation before we sail on."

"You've moved up from babysitting the crew to minding every vessel in the Sondmark Sea?" It's a jab, but he lifts the binoculars.

The sight of the vessel sobers him. Soon he begins issuing commands in a low, intent voice, and the nearer we get to the small craft, the more obvious it is that this isn't going to be a simple case of sailing on by. I gauge the waterline with foreboding. The ship is going down. It's only a matter of time. I lift the com, my voice coming through every loudspeaker around the ship, "Rescue stations, ready."

A flurry of activity breaks out below, and the captain barks to the helmsman, "Throttle back. We'll swamp her coming in at that speed."

I hold my breath. Navigating so near another vessel—particularly one that's going under—is tricky. One small mistake in these choppy seas will spell disaster.

"Permission to arrange a rescue crew, sir," I say.

Never taking his eyes from the scene before him, he nods.

Adrenaline courses through my veins as I shoot down the passageways, heading straight for the helicopter hanger. By the time I've arrived, the doors have been raised, and gusting rain pelts my face. I brace my arm against it and take stock. It's not dark yet but it will be soon. All this and nightfall, too. *Vede.*

"Moller," I shout. He's at my side before I can blink. "Ready the inflatable craft for deployment. Five boats. We'll set up a processing unit with medics. Be quick about it."

I begin to take command, but the decks are not as chaotic as I fear. I've drilled the crew unsparingly, but I've made sure they understand the purpose behind each task, too. At my order, sailors carry the boat ramp in place and slot it into position with a loud, reassuring clang.

Medical personnel have arrived, and I have them ready triage stations. The ocean is howling beyond the protective walls of the hanger bay, but the sailors are quiet, speaking only when necessary.

I feel the rudder shift, and the distressed boat comes swinging into view, less than a hundred yards out. I raise my binoculars and find the identification markers that tell me this is an ancient Vorburg merchant craft. Fifteen meters long with streaks of rust along the hull. The load lines are far underwater. We've got maybe an hour—less if the weather worsens.

I sweep my binoculars down the bulwark of the other vessel and perform a quick count of how many there are. Then I call the master chief and lieutenants who form up in a tight circle.

"Two rafts will come alongside at a time. Get a headcount from the first boat. These aren't experienced sailors, so you'll have to keep your life jackets tight and your lights on." I look around. "Be safe. Everyone comes home." I clap a lieutenant on the shoulder and the conference is over.

Moller and I watch as the rubber rescue boats shoot down a steep ramp into the ocean. I note the dwindling light. We've practiced for this, but no matter how fast we move, much of this operation will take place in darkness.

"I think I saw this group on the news," I say, wishing I were on those boats. "They're bringing awareness to coastline loss."

"A scientific mission?" Moller asks.

"More like a filthy music festival on the open sea. There's a lot of passion here, but not a lot of brains."

"Did the news say how many?"

"Dozens. Maybe more than a hundred. They seemed to take pride that it wasn't well provisioned. They wanted to 'listen to the ocean.'"

I grunt. He grunts.

"Find an ensign to run up to the galley and get them to start sending down hot meals. Get another on bedding. We've got a long night if they have to sleep here."

He nods and salutes.

The first craft, bucking against the waves, returns. Passengers spill out, thin linen pants pasted to their legs. One pulls a pan flute from his life vest and begins a soft tune while a sailor makes his report.

"There are ninety-eight people aboard the ship, sir. That one—" He points to a mangy young man with long hair and a shaken demeanor. "He says they've got a couple of goats, too."

"Goats?" *Stultes es.* Goats. "I would've bet they were vegan."

"Oh, they are. The goats are um…protesting the coastline loss too." The sailor spreads his hands. "That's what he says."

"Got it. We don't touch the goats until the humans are rescued."

We discover that there aren't enough life preservers for even a third of the passengers, and we send over dozens more. I spot the goats through my binoculars and see some idiot strap a couple of floatation devices around each animal before securing his own. Another is waving his arms, gesticulating wildly, while arguing with a sailor about bringing along a… my eyes narrow. I think it's a didgeridoo. He gets pitched into the raft without further fuss.

I'm proud of these sailors under my command. Many of them are untried, braving high seas in small boats, and transferring passengers from the decks to the rafts in the dark amidst heavy swells. They wouldn't have known how to do this six months ago.

I feel the rudder shift periodically, and I gauge the distance between us and the other ship. We're not drifting at the same rate. The sea wants to push us towards the other vessel, and the frigate needs constant attention to keep us from drifting into it. I would take nothing to sink it now. Though my crew is moving swiftly, there are scores of passengers still in danger. I remind myself that the captain is good at these kinds of maneuvers, but I can see waves washing thinly over the deck and I pray for time.

Moller returns with a hasty salute. "Problem in one of our cargo holds, sir."

I don't have time for cargo holds.

"The compartment's half-flooded."

"Which one?"

He delivers the details, and I shove a clipboard at him. "*Stultes es.* Alert Damage Control and take over command. I'll be back soon."

I sprint down the passageways, sliding quickly down the ladders, each breath taking me farther and farther from the hanger, doors open on a howling ocean and sinking ship. My mind floods with the electrical specs and engineering blueprints I pored over all summer. Before I've even reached the hold, I have a tentative diagnosis. The fire main is kept under constant pressure, and if a pipe burst or sprinkler head got knocked off, there would be nothing to stop the water from filling the room. Out at sea, a thousand things can go wrong all at once, and they have.

The door to the hold is a hatch, and I spot the department head leaning over it. He looks up, his face white. Damage Control hasn't arrived yet.

"I don't know why this happened. The drains should—"

"They're not," I clip off, already shucking my shoes. I look down the hatch, at the water pitching back and forth with the movement of the ship, and take a bracing breath. I am surprised to find myself thinking of Clara, the memory of our summer strong, almost tangible.

"You're not going in there, sir," he groans, panic twisting his voice. "Not until we cut the power."

"We can't cut the power," I answer, pulling off my shirt and levering my body over the hatch. I'm wasting too much time, but he has to understand. "It'll take out the hydraulic pumps working the rudder, which is the only thing keeping us from steering into the other ship."

Again, he tries to stop me. "You'll get yourself killed. The water's going to take out the panel anyway."

I shake my head. "Not if I can close the valve and clear the drains."

He looks like he's going to throw up. "I don't know where the valve is."

I give a brief nod. "You'll know next time."

I slide down the ladder before I give myself time to think about the high chance of electrocution, landing in water that comes up to my chest. It's frigid, and I want to absorb the shock but force myself to keep moving. Clara is with me somehow, holding me around the waist and telling me to be safe. I feel the strangeness of the motion beneath me, hear the menacing splash and slap of water against the bulkhead as it nears the electrical lines.

A net has broken and everything that was not secured is now bucking wildly on the surface. As I maneuver around an obstacle, a heavy crate clips me on the head, spinning away to smash against the bulkhead. I feel a sharp pain and lose my footing, plunging under the water and sliding across the room with the rocking of the ship. Debris follows behind, crashing against me as I find my feet. I fling a hand out and catch netting, carving a path to the back of the hold, clawing along the ropes to stay upright. With every wave I adjust my balance, taking blow after blow, shaking water out of my face.

Finally, I reach the spot I've been aiming for. I take a large breath, pulling myself under. I'm blind beneath the water but make rough sense of the shapes I touch. After a few moments, my hand knocks against a curve and follows it. This is it. I grip the wheel and twist. It resists me and I feel a burning in my lungs. I put my back into it, bracing bare feet against steel. The valve gives and I feel it settle into a closed position.

I resurface for a large lungful of air, hardly acknowledging the victory. The drains aren't working properly. I close my eyes and try to imagine the engineering plans—the grid-marked circle showing simple gravity drains leading to the bilge. Though cargo continues to crash on every side, I pull myself to the center of the room, feeling along the ground with my bare feet when I encounter a thin film of plastic—a length of cling wrap, likely discarded weeks ago. I shift it and feel the tug of water near my feet.

I waste no time returning to the ladder, hauling myself out of danger and giving the lieutenant orders to observe it closely. "Sir, you have to see a medic," he answers, touching his brow.

When I touch my own brow, my hand comes away covered in blood. I return to the hanger deck. It's a hive of activity, but I see order in it.

Moller is deploying the final raft and gives me a shocked look.

"What happened?"

"It's nothing," I say, collapsing into a chair, feeling the warm blood dripping down my face. The medics clean the wound, jab me with a pain killer, and start stitching me up. I tip my head up to see the captain looking down into the cavity of the hanger as the last rescue raft returns, goats leaping from the vessel.

The night is long. I change my uniform and get back to organizing the logistics of fitting ninety-eight extra people (engaged in a literal hippie drum circle with mess kits and pan flutes and a smuggled didgeridoo) and two goats (bleating, defecating, and most definitely protesting coastline loss) on a ship carrying a full capacity of one hundred and forty sailors. I check on the cargo hold. I deliver my report to a subdued captain and return to my bunk in the early hours of the morning.

I have a bandage over my right eyebrow, and I rest my phone on my chest. Clara is the only thing I could think of when I dropped into that hold and reckoned the cost of my life. It was Clara with me on every step of that terrifying journey. She's the only thing I can think of now.

I run my thumb along the rim of my phone, imagining the text I would send.

"Hey," I would begin. Very cool.

What's up? she would answer.

I push my thumb and scroll through the images of Clara I haven't been able to delete. I imagine my response.

"I can't lose you."

33

His Personal Space

CLARA

Alma spends the month drilling me on memory care, ensuring I won't shame the family when I take over her patronage. By the time we're finished, I feel acquainted with every brick and tile of St Leofdag's Hospital and know every employee, from the director to the receptionist. Mama and I have settled into wary professionalism, which I hate but am willing to weather. At our weekly meetings, she doesn't ask about Max or how I fill my hours, only wants to know if the patronage is running smoothly. Alma assures her that it has never been in better hands.

My portfolio of royal engagements grows. I still make visits to the usual animal shelters and kindergarten classrooms, but these events are blended in with meeting dementia specialists and taking tours of cutting-edge biotech companies. I spend hours preparing for my first solo tour.

For the first time, I have a sense of purpose and satisfaction in my royal role, but when I slow down even the smallest bit, I'm hit with a mixture of longing, regret, and self-reproach that feels like a tangible thing—an entire frigate—weighing on my mind. Instead of growing lighter, the burden seems to double each week.

I remind myself that I was the one who broke up with Max. That I should be happy. That I've gotten exactly what I wanted—a patronage and a voice in the family. But there's this weight I can't shift. I miss Max.

The prime minister's office is quiet, and I fear they're waiting for Max's return to begin an inquiry that will damage us both. Reporters shout questions as I come and go from each event, but NewsNook eventually wraps up their exhaustive series on my love life. A group of royalists attached to the Queen's Day parade committee starts a letter-writing campaign to censure the government-sponsored news show, and the network issues a tepid apology. I absorb the hits and learn to appreciate, better than ever, Mama's strategy of steadiness and silence.

One morning, Ella bursts through the doorway of my suite. I snap my fingers frantically to quiet her as I wrap up the phone call with one of my brother's friends who also happens to be the head of a tech company.

"Many of the residents once worked on the water as fishermen or messed about with boats on holiday. We've sourced an old ship—a Norwegian sloop with a wheelhouse and everything—and gotten a construction company to donate time and materials to cut it down and situate it on the grounds with a wheelchair ramp. Noah informed me your company is looking for opportunities to give back to the Handsel community. I'd like to set up a time to meet to discuss it. The old ship would be a wonder if we could get the front windows fitted with a VR screen showing ocean views, responsive to the touch of the wheel."

His answer is warm. "Yes, yes," I nod, jotting down details. "Thank you, Marc. I look forward to our meeting."

I hang up and give Ella a high five. "Yes!"

"Pleased?"

"Very. That boat is going to be the centerpiece of the new gardens. The hospital director has been yearning for something like this for years. The tech will be a surprise—an ocean view, sounds piped in over the speakers, a retro radio tuned to popular music from fifty years ago." I bask. After weeks of hard work—including hauling around an Emotional Frigate—I deserve a bask.

"What brings you to my lair?" I ask.

"You haven't seen the news?" Ella has a glint in her eye. "Oh, this will be fun."

She leans across and pulls up the tab for the midday news. The live video feed shows a huge ship navigating into port.

My breath catches, and a flush blooms up my neck. Max. Max is home. Before anything else—before the worry about how we left things and the stress about the prime minister's office—I feel elated. After a month of missing him and filling every second up with work, I am starved for the sight of him.

Before sense takes hold of me, I'm doing the math. A quick trip to the kitchens for ingredients, then twenty minutes to the cottage, an hour of cooking...

"Clara?" Ella's voice yanks me out of my daydream. I broke up with Max. Going to the cottage and preparing his dinner is impossible. Anxiety and frustration drop into my stomach like paratroopers.

"Why is this news?"

"Read the caption," she says, tapping the text banner at the bottom of the screen.

"Rescue at Sea Involving Princess Clara's Partner." Partner. Ick. The word is bloodless. Worse, it isn't even true anymore. Lower still, the crawling text reads, "Doomed Vorburg expedition owes all to brave efforts of the Sondmark Navy. Lieutenant Commander Andersen gets commendation following accident at sea."

"Accident?" I shout, finger spinning furiously on the mouse. "What accident?"

Ella's hand covers mine and guides it to a block of text in an article below the video.

"He got a head wound while wading through the cargo hold to save the ship's navigation system or something. It's not very clear. But he's fine, Clara. Max is fine."

I read the sparse sentences twenty times over, trying to wring more information from them. Finally, I pound my fists against the desk and sit back. He's fine. Max is fine. I don't care if he's been horribly disfigured and has to lurk in the sewers of Handsel as long as he's safe.

"They haven't even properly docked yet," I say, hoping Max will get some peace before the press comes after him. "How did the network news find out about this?"

Ella's brow arches, leaving me to connect the dots.

Who would know a ship was coming in? Top brass, obviously. But why would they want to leak a thing like this? Who else? I fumble for clues and then realization starts deep in my bones. Who gets regular updates from every branch of government including the military?

"Mama."

Ella nods. "Very few people could have access to the story already, but she's one of them."

"She isn't the sort of person to ring up the newspapers and tell them her business," I say, eyes narrowing. "But her henchman might."

"Caroline?" Ella laughs.

"Bingo," I say, pushing past her and out of the suite. Ella calls for me, but I'm too intent to stop. If Caroline knows what happened to Max, I have to ask.

I burst into her office and, though I am unannounced, Caroline doesn't have to scramble to smarten up her appearance. She is unspectacular but sits with her ankles together, the hem of her grey skirt skimming her knees, and glances up from her screen.

Our eyes meet and I wonder if this is an enemy or an ally. I don't know. She always seems to be standing in front of my mother like some bloody-minded angel, sword in hand, waiting to strike down all who trespass. But there have been moments when I felt something like sympathy between us. Adversary or friend? I don't have time to do a diplomatic dance.

"Max is home," I blurt out.

She is composed. "I know."

"We need to talk about it."

Caroline stands, dons her suit jacket, and slips a piece of paper into her pocket. She grips me firmly by the arm and marches me across the hall and into the garden. We walk for several minutes, beyond the crunching gravel paths, and onto the turf. Only when no one could possibly hear the sound of our voices does she say, "This conversation is off the record, Your Royal Highness."

I nod. "The news reports spoke of an accident. I know you know something."

She shakes her head. "Hardly more than what you read in the news. I wasn't privy to the original report, only tasked with passing on a portion of it. The wound was described as ten stitches, no concussion."

"You leaked the incident on behalf of my mother?"

She takes a breath, the only sign that this conversation must be deeply uncomfortable. "Yes."

"I don't understand what she gains? What possible reason—?"

She gives a tiny cough. "We're entering negotiations with the Vorburg trade ambassador, and now the television and newspapers will be full of reports about the Royal Navy of Sondmark rescuing almost a hundred Vorburgian citizens from certain death."

Of course. "Leaking the rescue to the press had nothing to do with Max?" I ask, crossing my arms. "He's just a pawn? *Vede*, after what I put him through, he's never going to speak to me again."

Caroline regards me quizzically. "I've seen the pictures. I know you and the lieutenant commander spent every minute you could together. Her Majesty had me catalog the entire NewsNook file and cross-catalog the security records at the gatehouse." At my look, she swallows. "I'm sorry about that."

Sorry for doing the bidding of the queen? We're all guilty of it, and only in the last weeks have I begun to carve out room for my own wants and needs. How much harder would it be if I were her employee, depending on a salary to pay my rent and put food on the table? I shake my hand, dismissing the necessity of an apology.

"I think the lieutenant commander will hear you out."

"You think?" It's a needy question but I am in a place.

Caroline's mouth softens. "I think."

I'm not so sure. I chew my lip absentmindedly, wondering if Max will want to see me at all. I can hope all I want, but I've been drifting off to sleep for a month, trying out different configurations of words that will get him to forgive me. I'm going mad and haven't struck gold yet.

I am poised to return to the palace, but Caroline's question stops me.

"You really gave him up because she asked you to?"

I inhale. "I know what it sounds like—that I was my mother's puppet. She has a lot of power compared to most European monarchs, and she's careful to preserve it. No one in our royal family just marries anyone they like." Caroline gazes across the park, the breeze stirring the hair at her temple. She doesn't contradict me.

Instead, she lifts her chin, eyes bright in the morning sun. "I'm going to do something I don't ever do, ma'am. I'm going to imagine what else was in Her Majesty's head when she told me to leak that information."

I recognize this as the sacrifice it is. Caroline's loyalty to my mother is unwavering.

She takes a deep breath. "I don't think it was only about the trade deal. We're going to get favorable terms if your mother has anything to say about it. But she saw the same pictures and footage I saw. I suspect she knows your lieutenant commander is inevitable. So she got ahead of the press and put out a story of how your..."

"NewsNook says 'partner'." I give a watery laugh.

She smiles. "Of how your partner is a naval hero."

"You think she approves?" Dim hope lights in my chest. My mother's approbation is difficult to earn, and I'm not past wishing for it.

"No." Caroline's answer is direct and honest, resisting the impulse to curry favor with me or complain about the unfairness of her employer. "Approval is far beyond my ability to imagine, ma'am. I don't know if Her Majesty is playing for time or what she thinks of Lieutenant Commander Andersen. I don't even know what the consequences of pursuing a relationship with him might be. Only you can say whether the sacrifice would be worth it."

A month ago, I thought it was clear. I had to give up Max to gain more trust and responsibility. My eyes close briefly. I've spent an entire month without Max, wanting to climb the walls, reaching for my phone to text him in the middle of the night, drumming my fingers against the steering wheel as I bypass the turn to his cottage. These feelings aren't going to go away.

My mother asked me to pay a price and I paid it before I understood that the price was far too high—before I knew that I was willing to fight.

"My mother is right about one thing. He is inevitable. I don't know if I've ruined his career or his life, but I'm going to try to get him back," I say, a surprised laugh breaking from my lips. This is the plan. Without knowing it, this has been my plan for weeks. I can't go on like this, no matter how much I like my job, if I don't have Max. My mother wants to be in control, but she's adapted to my new role in the family. She'll have to adapt a little further. "I wonder if he'll make me promise to just be friends."

"You'd agree?"

"To have Max in my life, I'd do a lot more than that." My brows gather as I think it out. "I mean, I'd say we were friends, but we have a terrible record of keeping that promise. If I can get him to host to a few movie nights, I'll start invading his personal space again...he's really susceptible to that." My glance strays to the horizon. "I wonder when he gets off duty."

Caroline laughs, and at that moment, she becomes another person—warm, her eyes lighting with unexpected mischief. She slips her hand in her pocket and draws out a folded scrap of paper. "I made a phone call this morning," she says, as though picking her way through a minefield of dangerous words, "and identified myself professionally."

I think for a moment. "Private secretary to Her Majesty the Queen?" It does sound impressive.

"Just so. I never said outright that I was calling on her behalf and would certainly deny it if asked. The Navy was helpful."

She thrusts the paper into my hands, and I unfold it. Lovely penmanship, I think. It's Max's name followed by a date and time. Tomorrow. Eleven hundred hours.

"He volunteered to be something called the Command Duty Officer, which means he's not so injured that he can't work. It also means he stays longer than any of the other officers. But," she adds, helpfully, "when he does leave the ship, there shouldn't be a crowd."

34

WELCOME HOME

MAX

My stitches itch like hell.

As we near port, I stand with the captain on the bridge, observing the activity of the tugboats, and listen to the distant sound of our activists in the hanger bay chanting us safely into position.

"Someone would have died," he grunts.

I say nothing.

"I can't be sure I would have made the call to stop without a distress signal," he continues. "My wife calls me pig-headed, but this—"

"When you saw them riding low, you acted quickly, sir."

Another rueful grunt. "Good of you to say, but I would have failed my crew without you yesterday. Some of the hippies," he says, without heat, "would have been lost to the sea."

"The crew did their duty."

He releases a short breath. "Then when the nav system almost went out..."

He shakes his head slowly, eyes fixed on the horizon. "I talked to Moller and the Cargo Officer—"

"Lieutenant Baas," I supply.

"—after you retired. I know what you did, how fast you acted, how bad it could have gone if you hadn't. I radioed in a report last night, and a longer account will be sent over next week. You're a pain in the *riv* know-it-all, Andersen, but that operation went as smooth as a whistle. The promotion board will have a nice, thick file."

I raise my brows and wince against the pain. I should feel nothing but pleasure at his words, but my mind races to Clara, to how I want to tell her about it. And then it races on to the realization that I can't.

"Thank you, sir."

He gives another grunt, but there's a laugh in it. "You seriously volunteered to be the Command Duty Officer? Your girlfriend is going to kill you, Andersen."

He grabs his coffee and wanders out to the bridge wing, watching scurrying sailors tie off the lines securing the frigate to the pier. Many of the crew are eligible to leave within the next hours, and I spend my time organizing departures and meeting with a Vorburgian delegation sent to process their citizens.

"You're that officer the youngest princess is in such trouble with," one of them observes with a stupid grin. More than a month away and the story hasn't been killed yet. I want to punch the smile off his face.

I shuffle through some paperwork. "I have a couple of goats you'll need to take off our hands right away," I answer. He sputters about his car and his good suit, but I spread my hands apologetically, suddenly blind to the fact that my sailors have fashioned a pen for the animals and they are content enough.

"Navy regulations," I say, by way of explanation.

I get on with the meetings and reports, taking extra time with Lieutenant Baas, going over the proper process of off-loading supplies. I spend the night sleeping aboard ship as we recover from the weeks at sea—the last days laden with filthy passengers.

Finally, it's time to hand over the command to Moller. He's lost the thirsty look, seen his fiancée, and doesn't mind returning to regular duty.

I heft my gear over my shoulder and hitch a ride up the pier on a cart. My mind has already lived through this sequence of events, but I'm numb now, walling up the plans I had when it was Clara I would be returning to.

I get out and the cart speeds away. Turning on my phone, it immediately starts pinging and vibrating with a seizure of missed messages. I'm not ready to see her face or hear her name, so I slip it in a pocket while I fumble for my keys. Then I hear a sharp whistle.

My head jerks up as I track the direction of the sound across a huge expanse of concrete. It's Clara, parked on the other side of the fence like any girlfriend. Everything in my body clenches—stomach, hands, jaw—as I take her in.

She's leaning against her blue Fiio, her hair tossed by the wind. She brushes it back and bumps away from the car, drawing closer to the chain link. It's too cool for one of her summer dresses, and she's wearing jeans. She looks so good.

I'm guessing she's not here for Captain Dusstock and I approach the fence, loosening my hold on the bag which drops with a thump.

I halt several, protective feet away. I've spent every second of the last month missing this girl but don't know what to think. Maybe she's here to warn me about another public relations calamity about to befall the royal family. I have nothing left to sacrifice.

"This isn't a private street," I warn her. "Anyone could see you."

35

CHAIN LINK

CLARA

After a month, Max looks like a different man—stern, cautious. His expression is easy to imagine on the face of an underwater detonation expert, approaching a bomb. The small hope I started with this morning is evaporating, and I am mad at myself all over again for wrecking us.

For something to do, I look up and down the road. There are no news vans, at least. "I watched YouTube videos of ships coming into port. I thought this was where everyone waited."

He exhales sharply. "The spouses and children have a designated reception room. This is for temporary relationships."

Temporary. My blood is hot and cold, and it sluices through my veins, mixing roughly. I feel it in my heart, clashing along the skin of my neck.

"This stretch of road isn't the most respectable in Handsel," he goes on. "It's where girlfriends wait, and you're not even that."

My eyes drop and I want to run as far and as fast as I can. He's already moved on. I knew he might have. I should resolve to leave him in peace. I should wish him the best of luck.

Then I remember my words to Caroline. I told her I'd do a great deal to keep this man in my life, and I would. I will. I step closer, curling my hand around the chain link.

"I heard about your injury. How's your head?"

"It hurts," he scowls.

He's got a row of butterfly bandages and stitches securing an angry cut along his brow, the skin surrounding it an impressive array of colors. I want to offer to drive him home and make him dinner. I want to tell him he should rest, hand him a glass of water and a Brufen. But my placating attitude isn't working, and it's obvious he wants to fight. He has ten stitches, and I wonder if it would hurt to fight. Will it help us escape the small talk? I'm not a gambler, but I take a risk now.

I say, off-hand, "It doesn't look that bad."

He tosses his head, shakes it. I've seen horses in my mother's stable make that move at the first sight of a saddle. It's a *you've got to be kidding me* look. Those horses like to kick.

"It's not. It was a sacrifice in the line of duty, Your Royal Highness," he says, as furious and cutting as it is possible to be. "You should know something about that kind of sacrifice. Mine was far smaller than yours."

I should be quaking in the blast of his anger, but I'm not. These are things that need to be said and knowing I can still command strong feelings from him is some comfort. People who don't care, don't feel angry.

My eyes trace the line of the sticking plaster. He's going to have a scar, and I want him to tell me how it happened. I don't have the right to ask, yet.

"Far smaller," I echo. My heart is racing as fast as a hummingbird, and my breath won't fill up my lungs. I have to tell him.

"Giving you up was too great a sacrifice." My nose stings with a prickle of tears. I'm looking everywhere but at him, and I wait until the jagged lump in my throat can be swallowed before I speak. "I don't expect you to forgive me, Max. I was so focused on what I thought everyone else needed that I was erasing myself, but you were right. I got the patronage, but—"

"You got it?" he asks. His eyes widen in surprise, and his tone suggests he might want to high-five me. Against his will, of course.

I smile. "Yeah." I lift my shoulder. "I did."

"Good for you," he answers. I detect no sarcasm in his tone.

"Getting some real responsibility was supposed to solve all my problems, but I've been miserable. I binge-watched the entire Aksel Kroner catalog. You might have a point about all that penguin vomit." I laugh. He doesn't. "I kept thinking that if I'd told my mother I wouldn't give you up, I could have won that battle too. You've always been on my side, and when she first came to me with those photos, I shouldn't have abandoned you." I speed up, as though I'm running out of time. "I'm so sorry, Max. If we could just be friends—"

"I don't want to be friends," he cuts me off, his voice a rough growl.

My breath catches, and I can't seem to take another one. He grips the chain link over my hand. It's the first touch I've had in weeks that I've wanted to lean into and savor. Group hugs with my sisters were not cutting it.

"I want to fight," he continues, voice low and intent. "I want to drag you back to the cottage and argue loud enough to make the walls shake. And then I want—I want—" His chest rises and falls like he's run a marathon. His eyes won't let go of my face.

Hope comes roaring back. "I want that too."

His breath stops and his eyes narrow. "Some photographer is probably standing in the bushes with a long lens."

"I know," I answer. In these last weeks, I've held my own against a tsunami of bad press. I'm not afraid of them. "I'm not going to live as a hostage to the tabloids."

His face is guarded, and he releases a disbelieving breath. "What happens when your mother decides it's time to move on from me?"

I can't imagine a universe where I ever want to move on from Max.

"I told her I intend to fight for the things that matter to me."

His hand grips mine and he takes a deep breath, nostrils flaring. "Do you know what it was like being out there without even the hope of coming home to you?"

I want to reach through the fence and touch his face but settle for grasping the fence with my other hand. I nod. "I kept trying to text you. I'd grab my phone and want to call—"

His hand covers mine. "We can't do this if—I lied when I told you it was only dinner and then I lied when I said we could be just friends. *Vede*, Clara, I had a month to get over you and never even got started. And here's the truth now. I love you, but I can't do this if your heart's not in it."

His hand has become entangled with mine.

"I'm not asking for a promise," he says. "We could crash and burn next week because you don't like my floss—"

I grin. "I love your floss."

"Or my taste in movies—"

"I already hate your taste in movies. I'll always hate it."

"Or you think my career is too inconvenient—"

"If anyone's is inconvenient, Max, it's mine."

"You have to let me say this," he scolds, fighting for air, "because when I'm done, I'm going to kiss until you go blind."

Yes, please. "I'm listening."

"I can't do this unless there's a chance for something that lasts. I can't do it if you're already planning to toss me over for some hollow-chested, in-bred constitutional monarch in the end. I won't be a fling."

"Oh, good," I say, lifting my face. My voice is clear and firm. "I don't play around."

At my words, a smile tucks his mouth. Lines radiate from the corners of his eyes.

Braver than I've ever been, I say, "I love you."

The smile fades, and I wonder if I've shocked him. Maybe he wants to go slower than this. Then he looks up, and I follow his gaze, my brow wrinkling. All I see are three meters of chain link topped with vicious-looking razor wire coils.

I gasp. "Don't you dare. You'd be cut to ribbons."

He gives a dissatisfied, thwarted grunt. "Do you have to get back to the palace?"

"I blocked out the rest of the day," I say, tracing a square of chain link. "You know, just in case."

He backs away and slides on his aviators. Coupled with his uniform, this is inexpressibly hot. "I'll see you at the cottage."

Using all the talent of a big-city driver, I beat him by thirty seconds, enough time to find his spare key and slide it into the lock. We were going to fight until the walls shook, but Max throws the car in park and charges up the path, past the last of our wildflowers nodding against the rock wall. He slides me back into the hall, pulling me into his arms. His foot kicks the door shut with a loud bang.

Our breath mingles, and I know there are words we will say in the coming days and weeks. There is a divide between us that will have to be filled with enough words that we can walk across it and meet in the middle. But now is not the time for talking.

The narrow hall is three times wider than it needs to be and he slides his fingers into my hair. My hands trace the muscles of his back.

Welcome home, sailor.

36

EPILOGUE

CLARA, ONE YEAR LATER

The press spends the week before Queen's Day speculating on how I will upset conventions for the Violet Presentation. Upset conventions. I smile at the words. The tone of my coverage has shifted since significant improvements at St Leofdag's have begun to roll out. Headlines are mostly good-natured, even if the odd tabloid columnist wonders idly if I will wear a miniskirt and flash the brass band. (Not today.) Chat boards are running polls about whether Lieutenant Commander Andersen will get down on one knee and propose on national TV.

I don't let the amusement at that thought show on my face either as I step off the dais in a knee-length skirt and fitted jacket. My mother sent out orders for the surface to be gone over with a fine-toothed comb, checking for looseness and gaps. I am pleased to note that my shoes—block heels in a dashing leopard print——keep me sure-footed.

I lock all thoughts of Max away while I chat briefly with other officers, giving each one my undivided attention.

Well, not quite undivided. The cameras are clicking, hungry for more photos. Reporters have had almost nothing of us since last autumn. They face stiff fines for breaching privacy in the nature preserve and using telephoto lenses to invade private property. Maybe they thought a princess would be above pressing civil charges, but I wasn't, even if it almost lit Mama's hair on fire. I would never have won these suits in America, with their first amendment protections, but this is Sondmark, and we do things differently.

Max and I took to conducting our courtship inside the cottage and in other secure locations, not only the grounds of the Summer Palace. A smile flashes briefly over my features as I remember my frequent visits to the Andersen garden allotment and the way the families in each of the nearby garden plots combined to thwart the nosiest paparazzi this spring. Many of them developed amnesia about the Andersen family when asked for directions. The Maagensens proved especially inventive, blocking the paths that lead to our spot with moveable gates woven with surplus grapevine. The tactic kept spitting frustrated photographers back into the parking area.

Lieutenant Commander Andersen (who is so good-looking in his uniform that I want to whistle) steps forward, and I hear the sudden uptick of camera shutters. This is Max as I first knew him, an impossible crush. His face is a rigid mask of control, and I know that my own is. Neither of us wants to give that *flamen* body language expert an extra second of airtime.

I pass him the posy, and Max pushes the violets into his hatband on the first try. We are acing the fine motor skills portion of this test. Nicely done, Team Us. Now for the chat.

"I can't believe you still won't tell me what's in the pork roast recipe."

He tugs his gloves into order. "Rules are rules, Clara. If you're not an Andersen, I can't divulge our secrets."

I flick a glance at the dais where my family sits. What a year it's been for each of us. When it all comes out in the papers, the prime minister is going to start complaining about the cost of royal weddings.

"It's a foolish rule, Max. We've been engaged for fifteen whole hours." Delight takes hold of me. The news belongs to us, and I want to savor it before the press finds out. "We are practically one."

Bringing up his proposal is a mistake. I want to savor the memory of that, too. The sound of the lake frogs. The sofa that makes a deflating sound if I flop onto it too quickly. His pulse racing under my hand. Fingers touching my hair when he tells me he went to Père and Mama weeks ago. I hardly let him finish.

He's remembering too, and a light leaps in his eyes, crinkling the edges. It's a fraction of a movement, but that damned body language expert is going to get booked for days.

"If you want to elope with me, Clara, just say so."

I bite my lip, resisting the impulse to laugh.

"The second elopement in a year? I don't think my family could handle it."

ALSO BY KEIRA DOMINGUEZ

Her Caprice

The Telling Touch

The Sweet Rowan

ACKNOWLEDGMENTS

The Impossible Princess, a miracle book, began as a fun side project while I was editing the last novel in my magical Regency series. I'd seen Catherine, duchess of Cambridge's shoe get stuck in a grate while she was handing out shamrocks to the Irish Guards on St Patrick's Day years ago and thought it was a rom-com waiting to be born. Little did I know the novel would turn into a first-person present-tense POV or that I would spend the summer uploading chapters to the new Amazon episodic fiction platform, Kindle Vella. The only thing I had was a passionate reader, my sister Tia Hunsaker, who begged, cajoled and hectored me to give her more chapters. Without her being kind of the worst, *The Impossible Princess* would still be ten raggedy pages in a GoogleDocs folder.

Last year was the hardest of my life. In addition to pandemic worries, grumpy homeschooling, and quarantines, our kitchen developed a massive months-long leak that went undetected for so long that we had to gut almost our whole downstairs and do our dishes in the tub for a while. My mom was experiencing declining health and I was often away from my family to help my parents move. In the fall, as the last episode of *The Impossible Princess* was uploading, my dad passed away unexpectedly. Seven weeks later, my mom also passed away. They were the best of parents and loved each other very much. I was blessed to have them as long as I did. Neither of them were romance readers but they were both as supportive as can be.

While my house was undergoing reconstruction, I took my kids to my sister's house for a couple of weeks. My sister Debbie West is my most willing reader and re-reader and her daughter Stephanie McRae is married to Cory, who spent most of his career in the U.S. Navy. The McRaes were kind enough to be interviewed about the inner workings of military life and what it's like being on deployment. Without their willingness to let me ask all the questions, *The Impossible Princess* would be a much thinner book and contain no lost storage rooms used for unauthorized sexy times.

My beta readers and critique partners have been amazing. Christine Sandgren, Afton Nelson, and Kylene Grell did a great job telling me what I ought to improve. Special thanks goes to Bekah Beste who practically adopted my youngest during the pandemic and without whom my sanity would have been totally lost.

I thank my husband and five ducklings for adapting to their roles as Emotional Support Humans for the author in their life.

Finally, I need to thank Kdramas. All the Kdramas. As I worked to get *The Impossible Princess* prepared for more formal publication, I was wading through grief and the holidays. By chance I started my first Kdrama, *Crash Landing On You,* with my husband and it became a gentle nightly ritual to settle on the sofa for the exploits of Se-Ri and Captain Ri. I can't think of a better way to have spent this fallow time than by being nourished by first-rate storytelling.

What that show did for me is what I will always hope my books do for you.

ABOUT AUTHOR

Keira Dominguez grew up in Springfield, Oregon where she learned to refer to hazelnuts as filberts. She graduated from Brigham Young University with a B .A. in Kind of Random Historical Studies (okay, okay, Humanities) which would serve her well as a future novelist.

Though her personal style runs the gamut between "I'm kind of wearing eyeliner" and "I'm driving the speed limit so no one catches me wearing pajamas to the school drop-off", Keira enjoys having opinions about award show fashions, scandalous historical drama, and dishy royal trivia. The heart wants what the heart wants.

Keira lives in Portland, Oregon, finding a lot of romantic inspiration in the way her husband maximizes deductions when doing the taxes, brings her Advil when she's sick, and unloads the dishwasher.